A Message from the Author

Thanks for purchasing my debut novel; I'd love to know what you think of it. So, if you're interested, please visit my website below to reach out. You can also learn more about my journey, inspiration, and background.

www.authormatt.com

Our Beautiful Cage

Book One

Matthew R. Burton

Epigraph

"Our beauty blinds them to our strength."

CHAPTER ONE

Omens

My eyes snap open to the crack of a single gunshot; its echo ripples through my mind before dissolving into silence. With moonlight spilling into my cramped apartment, casting illusory shadows that watch over me, I ask myself: *was that real?* The chilling scream of a woman is quick to answer my question, cutting through the silence as though she were in this room. I'm familiar with intrusions waking me up, and I'll usually pretend everything is fine before drifting off again, but tonight, some unwelcomed urge compels me to investigate.

Rubbing the sleep from my eyes as I approach the window, I catch shadowy figures lurking in the apartments opposite mine, peeking through the slits of their blinds so as not to reveal their curiosity—but unlike them, I have nothing to hide. Towering buildings dominate the London skyline, leaving a small passage for the full moon to cast its glow on the narrow, cobbled street below, offering me a clear view of the scene. Two men hoist a burly corpse into the back of a black van. At first glance, they could pass off as friends who're helping an injured mate—but I know better. They're reapers, those who track and capture. Preying on your vulnerability when you least expect it, they lurk in plain sight and camouflage themselves in the mundane.

Ten steps behind them, a woman kneels on the unforgiving ground, her hands bound behind her back, and a stifling gag is freshly silencing her cries for help. A slender, fragile man wraps her in a seemingly gentle embrace—as if offering comfort in her distress—wearing a three-piece suit that clings to his skeletal frame. His outstretched finger points to a colossal figure lurking in the shadows. Muscles bulge from every limb of the darkened giant, with broad shoulders poised to consume its disproportionately small head and a curved spine yearning to break free from the skin imprisoning it. Undeniably, this is a creation born from some twisted experiment. You'd think you'd get used to their depraved methods to instil fear in us, but you don't.

Ensnared in its claw-like fingers, a small girl twists and writhes—desperate to break free—with long hair concealing her face. Taking deliberate steps, the monstrous figure advances towards the van and waves the child over the bound woman as if it's playing with an aircraft, presenting some twisted and playful nature. Wrenching the van's door open, it performs a cruel underthrow, and the girl vanishes from sight, swallowed by the vehicle. It breaks my heart to imagine the trauma she'll endure—confined in that space with the body of what I assume is her dad.

Hot blood rushes to my head, and I'm gripped by an overwhelming urge to scream out the window, to create a diversion of any kind, yet a deep-rooted instinct restrains me. I know too well it's pointless—I'm powerless to help them. In this moment of hopelessness, I ache for the comfort of my bed—for the blissful ignorance it once provided—but I'll confront this harsh reality. After all, the truth keeps me on my toes.

Reapers hoist the woman up, guiding her to the van. A deep longing to reunite with her now fractured family is evident with every step. She vanishes from sight, entering the confines of the vehicle, and the ghastly man slams the door. A fleeting pause ensues, only for him to twist his emaciated neck and look directly at me. Illuminated by the moonlight, each contour of his sunken features cast haunting shadows, with hollow eye sockets like portals into an abyss of misery and despair. I'm paralysed in fear. Slowly, the man's lips part, forming a wide, open smile that reveals two menacing rows of sharpened teeth, and with a frail, gangly arm, he waves, inviting the chills to race up my spine.

***

I hate mornings because they're the first thing to remind me I still exist. The jarring shrill of my alarm infiltrates my ears, drawing me from my hazy state and demanding I face life. Disorientated, I unravel myself from the protective cocoon I've formed, with my knees squeezed against my chest. Sunlight streams into my room, flooding the space with its gentle warmth, and a longing for sleep tugs at my weary body. However, my restless mind refuses to grant respite, replaying the haunting events of last night and hogging my every thought. I stretch and drag myself from bed, steeling my nerves because today decides my fate—prove unwavering loyalty or face execution. It's just another test in this life of servitude, and it becomes more challenging to succeed the wiser I get.

Taking deep breaths, I recite my usual gratitude affirmations, trying not to acknowledge the walls that cage me. "I have shelter, warmth, food, and drink. I'm forever grateful." Finally, with a forced smile, I'm ready to confront the day ahead.

Activating the HoloCast, a peppy news reader materialises in my room. His appearance may blend in with my dreary décor, but his personality should be somewhere more colourful. Though his hollow presence offers me company as I get ready, he's reporting on the development of a new energy deal with the United States, which is a topic I'm not interested in. I avoid dwelling on the immeasurable power held by the emperor as it makes me feel uneasy. Almost one hundred and fifty years have passed since the discovery of regonium—the mineral that grants us limitless green energy and far too much global influence. King James III unearthed it on Crown land in England, and the royal family's chokehold over the precious resource led to the True Ascension—granting them absolute power and the successive expansion of the Anglo Empire.

A photo of my sister—Fay—sits on my dresser, and she's judging me while I spend too much time contemplating which dress will make me look as cute and innocent as possible. You wouldn't know she has a mischievous nature because she looks positively saint-like in this photo, but only because I took it during our blossoming ceremony five years ago. We're twins, so we shared the same blossoming. Some call it a ceremony, whilst I call it a procedure, and every eighteen-year-old girl in the empire will endure it to freeze their youthful looks. Though Fay appears joyous in that captured moment, behind the scenes, we were riddled with sorrow. It was a celebration of us becoming trapped in the same face and body until we die, and my childlike appearance is a daily reminder that I'll always be the same frightened girl who does as she's told to fulfil the wishes of powerful men.

I'll take inspiration from Fay's blossoming look to transform myself into the most devoted subject anyone has ever encountered. Using minimal makeup will help preserve my rounded features (which society considers a beauty ideal), but I need to soften my dark eyes because they look far too commanding. I want people to believe I've been gifted with effortless style, so with great effort, I'll instruct my bronze hair to fall in deceitfully natural curls.

In this city, I'm desired like prey is to a predator. Hungry eyes bore into every inch of my body as I go about my day, and unwanted groping always forces me to fake a smile and bear the burden. I want more for me than this—I want to do something unique, but I'm insignificant. All I can try to achieve are small things, but with great dedication and love.

The news reader's excitement intensifies, catching my interest. "The people of Canada long for the empire!" he announces eagerly. "The nation's leaders have revealed their true guise of *corruption* by unveiling *malevolent* schemes that threaten to *ravage* our precious Earth. This week, their insidious agenda emerged as they proclaimed their intention to exploit and desecrate vast stretches of land in search of new oil reserves.

In response, the noble citizens of Canada rise with admirable fortitude, demonstrating staunch integrity as they voice their opposition to this announcement. Behold these captivating images ... the passion of their dissent as they surge the streets, dismantling symbols of devious democracy and proudly hoisting emblems of loyalty to our revered king and emperor: Emperor Magnus Hanover the Second!"

Peering over, I watch waves of holographic people swarm the streets of the miniature city and listen to the cries, screams and chants: "Save our home, give us regonium!" Taking a closer look, the scenes may be admirable and courageous to some, but to me, this is a society saturated with rage and violence. People burn down apartment buildings, and explosions appear on every street while large groups swarm smaller ones, leaving trails of lifeless bodies in their wake. Others carry banners that read, '*WE DEMAND THE EMPIRE*' and '*WE ANSWER TO THE EMPEROR*', to name a few.

The newsreader continues, "Desperate times are clear. With their toxic pride, the spiteful Canadian officials refuse England's gracious and selfless offer of clean energy despite knowing it will be their saviour. Since joining the empire, our newest kingdom—Egypt—has seen its once filthy air become eighty percent cleaner, in addition to receiving free and advanced healthcare. It no longer fears blackouts and The Crown offers a home to every subject.

Canada's attempts to locate new energy follow a breakdown in its infrastructure. After years of *neglect* and *incompetence*, they find their geothermal power plants crumbling. Our imperial sovereign will send the Duke of Crimsonford and Head of Imperial Defence, Sebastian Sinclair, to start early discussions around a solution to their current energy crisis. May our emperor's wisdom and light guide them through their dark times."

Another country to add to his collection.

Returning to my routine, I apply the finishing touches, slipping into a contemporary white dress that hugs my upper body and flows down to just above the knee. Bending to pick up some sensible white shoes, an untouched pair of bold, scarlet heels grabs my attention. They're dangerous, crying for me to wear them—*but why am I so tempted?* I'll stand out like a sore thumb, and today isn't about taking risks. I glance over at the photograph of Fay; her once sweet expression is replaced with mischief, and I submit to the urge—I *want* to do something different today.

✱✱✱

Emerging from my apartment building, I step onto the narrow, cobbled side street. The remnants of last night's events have disappeared as if a cosmic refresh button allows us to resume our idyllic existence. I trace the sun's path as it peeks through the slender gap between two structures; it casts a tender warmth on my face, arms, and legs. With a deep inhale, London's clean air fills my lungs, carrying the subtle scent of freshly mown grass floating in the breeze from a park nearby. The bustling main road awaits me, and I watch the regimented march flowing like a river. People's synchronised steps form a tenacious current, sweeping through the city with a fierce determination to serve.

"Clara!"

The familiar and friendly voice calls out from behind me, instantly delivering a smile to my face. I turn, and there she is—Celest. Everyone has something or someone they need to feel joy; for some, it's proving their loyalty, and for others, it's simply chocolate—but for me, it's Celest. With an energetic stride, she approaches, her lively blonde hair bouncing from side to side. I'm almost blinded by her pure, white summer dress that reflects the sunlight and accentuates her angelic aura.

Celest's wide eyes dart to the ground, and her contagious gaiety disappears, replaced with shock. "Your heels!"

"I know, don't ask," I respond with a cheeky grin. "What's new?"

"Going to the underground?" she asks, totally ignoring my question, linking my arm, and dragging me along the path towards the busy main street.

I go along with it and chuckle. "Do I have a choice?"

In silence, we merge into the stream of marching Londoners, engulfed by the dull-toned current of shades—from black to white and anything in between. This is a test of endurance; I consider myself a pro at walking in heels (considering how many lessons I had as a child)—but it's an entirely different challenge matching their regimented pace while maintaining poise.

I stare at Celest with apprehension, but she doesn't bite. "*So?*" I plead. "What's new?"

"Nothing!" She giggles. "Just … the same old stuff."

Despite her best attempts to conceal it, I know she's lying. I may feel insignificant, but my gift—or curse—constantly reminds me that I'm different. It's something that's baffled the empire's best scientists and doctors—I possess an innate ability to know when someone's being dishonest, outperforming even the most sophisticated technology. This proves to be useful in my line of work.

"Come on, Cee," I sigh. "You know I see straight through it. What's up?"

"*Not here*," she stresses through gritted teeth whilst maintaining a jolly smile.

We slip into the quiet haven of a secluded side street. It's our secret shortcut—well, it's not a secret, but Londoners dislike drawing attention to themselves, hence their reluctance to deviate from the march. Two marshals suddenly invade our sanctuary, appearing from behind a building ahead. Knee-length boots striking the pavement mark their imposing presence; each pounding step dominates the alley and cuts through the busy street's hum behind us. Despite their small stature and slender frames, they radiate aggression and latent violence. Enhancing their otherwise plain, tailored grey jackets is a fancy gold design that climbs the sleeves, lending them the confidence of a yapping dog. Their hats set them apart from the regular enforcers who also patrol these delightfully supervised streets. Crafted from polished grey leather, they provide tactical data through an iridescent visor. Marshals are a common sight, but they're usually placed in high-risk areas for criminal activity.

Celest's arm tightens around mine, her movements become rigid and forced, and her eyes reveal a deep terror despite wearing a radiant smile.

"I've been thinking about Fay," I announce, hoping to distract her. "We've only seen each other a couple of times since my blossoming."

Celest shivers; it's probably not the best topic of conversation right now. She didn't enjoy her ceremony either—in fact, I don't know anyone who did. It's traumatising—a physically and emotionally painful day for every teenage girl.

"She was recently relocated to Amberleigh," I continue. "A pretty town in Wiltshire. No housewarming invitation, though. I'm plucking up the courage to send her an arsey message."

With the marshals drawing nearer, Celest's grip on my arm cuts the blood flow to my hand, and I'm suffocating in her fear. Determined to stay strong, I take a deep breath and will myself to regain composure. "Blessed by his reign, gentlemen!" I beam as they pass.

One of them responds, with his visor adjusted to reveal a pair of downturned eyes, and now they've passed us; I peer over my shoulder to catch him stealing a glance at my rear. I can't refrain from rolling my eyes—they may appear robotic, but they're still slaves to their natural instincts. Celest's grip loosens, and she sighs with relief.

We proceed in silence, weaving through the current created by everyone's intuitive ability to act in harmony. Drawing nearer to the station, its massive mahogany doors, thrown wide open, extend a warm invitation. If you look closely, you'll see carvings that decorate their surface, depicting floral patterns and ancient scrolls. However, Londoners don't notice such intricacies; instead, we take them for granted (considering every building is just as pompous as the other).

The not-so-subtle message, '*MAY OUR SOVEREIGN SUPREME GUIDE YOU*', is fashioned from pure gold and displayed above the passage. "*May our sovereign supreme kiss my arse*," I mutter under my breath—barely moving my lips. I don't know what's come over me this morning, but whatever it is, I need to get a grip and be on my best behaviour. If I don't, it'll be my dead and naked body hanging from the nearby lamppost instead of the man with '*THIEF*' etched on his forehead.

The station hall resonates with the gentle drone of voices and rhythmic clacking of heels. Natural light floods every corner from four magnificent stained-glass windows, two on either side of the entrance. I feel them behind me, doing their job and lightening my mood, urging me ahead to seize the day. As the endless stream of people enters, they glide left and right around the golden statue of an ancient monarch standing in the centre. His cold gaze follows every passerby, a symbol of authority and control. Like his predecessors and successors—with their statues also scattered throughout the empire—he stands as a guardian overseeing us commoners.

With our arms still linked, Celest guides me towards him, and side by side, we stand directly before the old king, reading the placard's inscription:

'Bask in the glory of King George III (1760-1820), a powerful and revered monarch of the Georgian era. With a keen sense of duty, he upheld the honourable principles of monarchy and actively governed the expanding British Empire. His mighty reign left an indelible mark on the monarchy and society, ushering in a golden age in architecture, science, industry, and the arts. We celebrate his legacy; may we remember our joy and prosperity before democracy poisoned us.'

"They took Rebecca and Max last night, and Aria— their daughter," Celest utters nervously, still looking positively merry.

Though you couldn't tell, the news is a physical blow to my chest. I'm grasping the possibility—no, the certainty that I witnessed them being reaped last night. They're Celest's friends, and though I've never met them before, I know we're neighbours. Celest would often stop by mine after visiting them.

"I've spoken to Rebecca's sister," she continues. "Marshals pulled her into questioning around the same time. She popped over this morning—in *hysterics*. You should've seen her, but it's weird—I mean—ah, I don't know …"

"What is it?" I ask, unsure if I want to know the answer.

"I just—I can't stop thinking about something Rebecca asked me a couple of weeks ago ..."

"What was it?"

"I was looking after Aria when she visited family up north with Max—someone was ill, I think. Anyway, Rebecca was acting weird when they got back—a bit crazy even—and she asked if I could have Aria for a couple of months"— Celest's breathing quickens—"I didn't think much of it at the time, but now I'm like—*are they caught up in something?*"

Gently gripping her arm, I pull Celest to face me, softening my smile to something more natural. "Rebecca and Max are squeaky clean," I urge. "What could they possibly be caught up in? They're loyal!"

Now isn't the time to share what I know—I don't want to lie to Celest, but there are too many people here, and I don't want her worrying all day.

"Hmm"—her eyes widen as if she's had some revelation—"Hold on!" she gasps. "Don't you have your test of fealty today?"

"Yeah, in a couple of hours." I shrug.

"I'm so sorry, Clara," Celest chokes. "I shouldn't have burdened you with this! No doubt you—"

"Ah!" I blurt out quietly. I know what she's about to say. This information will throw me off during my test—or they may even turn it into an interrogation—but that isn't Celest's fault. "Don't worry, Cee," I say calmly. "C'mon, we should go. Fancy a drink later?"

"Sure," she responds with sorrowful eyes. "I'll meet you at Gold's around six. My treat for lumbering this on you."

"Don't be silly. I'm always here for you."

We stare at each other for a second, force the biggest smile and perform a deceptively gleeful laugh before separating in opposite directions towards our respective tube lines.

It takes too long to reach the platform, and it's the same routine every day, queuing and descending into the depths of the London Underground for what feels like an eternity, all to resurface and suffer an endless day's work. Ignoring the disgruntled huffs of commuters, I disregard my etiquette lessons and audaciously weave through the organised queues awaiting the train's arrival, fixed on a free spot at the far side of the platform (miraculously, my bum has only been pinched twice).

Now settled, I focus on the flicker of the turquoise energy screen that prevents subjects from escaping The Crown's grip—which many find tempting despite it being the same hand that generously feeds, clothes, and houses us. Concern grips me as I allow my thoughts to wander—I'm worried about Celest. If Rebecca and Max find themselves in trouble, Celest will undoubtedly become a person of interest—and I expect they'll want to snoop into my affairs as well.

The gentle whirring interrupts my brooding, and a cool breeze fills the platform, signalling the train's arrival. It slithers like a steel serpent from the tunnel, gliding into the station. The energy screen dissolves, granting us passage to board, and I accept its invitation, resisting an urge to escape the impending sense of danger.

The train propels us forward, and my mind remains plagued by anxiety the more I comprehend what Celest has told me. It's not unheard of for a person to become the subject of a full-scale investigation just because they're cousins with someone, who knows of someone else, who has a colleague with a friend who's suspected of being a traitor. I should prepare for an interrogation today.

The cylindrical carriage features rows of seats on either side, with an additional row running down the middle, forcing passengers to face each other. Still, they constantly lower their heads to avoid any intimate eye contact. With each bend in the track, the shuttle's far end remains obscured from view, and the rhythmic swaying motions comfort me slightly. That's until I catch a woman breaking from the crowd, lifting her head to peer at me before swiftly lowering it again. I recognise her. *Is she following me?* This is useless. I need air and open space. I feel trapped.

∗∗∗

Having exited the station earlier than usual, I'm forced to rejoin the march, eager to find something—*anything*—that'll distract me. I'm surrounded by the youthful faces of women, with their cloudy expressions and heads inside dreams, whilst the aged faces of men remain stern, their watchful eyes scanning the streets for potential threats—or opportunities.

One man stands out; he offers me a warm smile that feels surprisingly comforting; it's different to the usual cocky smirk I receive, but I'd be daft to think it makes him a suitable partner. The Crown will force me to marry some stranger if I don't find someone within the next two years. I've never connected romantically with a man—not because I always know when they're lying—but because my values are hard to come by. I'd marry Celest if I could, but that would result in us meeting the gallows. My mum used to tell me that if you spend too much time judging people, you'll find no time to love them, and she was right—but the way people behave in this city makes it impossible for me not to judge.

A girl, no older than fourteen, reminds me I could have it worse as she skips past, hand in hand with her husband—a greasy-looking man in his forties. Though she looks blissful in her dream-like state, her life fills me with deep sadness. I should be grateful for the path The Crown has chosen for me. As a child of the empire—when you turn eleven—you receive your calling. It's an assessment to decide what role you'll fulfil for the rest of your life, and once held, you're placed into work and specialist education until you turn fifteen—then you're ready to serve. Thankfully, my calling was not to be a wife—pumped full of drugs so you're always pretty, quiet, and obedient—a life inflicted on that poor girl, who must be coming to the end of her 'training'. Instead, The Crown chose me to be one of its many eyes and ears, placed in the 'prestigious' Imperial Intelligence Agency. I'm at the bottom of the barrel (and that's how I like it), but they'll sometimes use my unique ability when interrogating tricky suspects.

Rows of white stone skyscrapers flank me, each crafted with a unique blend of classic eighteenth-century elegance, modern grandeur, and a dash of conceit. Boasting grand symmetrical faces, tempting visitors to pass through two exaggerated pillars. Some are carved with showy patterns, whilst others are silky smooth. Some accessorise with a portico, whilst others want you to get wet from the rain. Ascending upwards, eccentric mouldings decorate rows of large windows, and as if that isn't enough, the higher levels tease you with wrought iron railing balconies draped with lush greenery (but forget about enjoying the view up there because it's exclusive to people better than us).

Towering above them all and dominating the sky stands the Grand Shard, rising like a colossal blade and stabbing a cluster of clouds. Its glass edge glints, capable of slicing through the Earth. Of course, The Crown's architects didn't waste an opportunity and designed the base to look like a sword's hilt—crafted from limestone and engraved with curves and teardrop shapes. Armed weapons float around the entire length of the intimidating structure, never following the same pattern of movement and always ready for the empire's enemies to attack (as if they would even try). Subjects praise this building as the great protector of London—rebuilt four times the size of its predecessor after the Civil War.

The streets are clean, and the air is fresh. I listen to the low buzz of vehicles passing by as they deliver goods or escort nobility. Ignoring my bitterness, I appreciate the city's beauty, but nestling amongst all its splendour, those with the audacity to desire radical change will occasionally rear their ugly heads.

Stepping into what should be a charming courtyard with vine leaves cascading from the terraced buildings' rooftops, I'm greeted by the striking presence of an immense black crown suspended mid-air. It carries an aura of hopelessness and despair. Dull, jagged fragments detach themselves and drift aimlessly throughout the open space before bursting into an explosion of colours, vibrant and bright, springing to life at their newfound freedom. Simultaneously, a sunny scent of hope overwhelms me. The gentle breeze carries notes of jasmine and rose that induce a sense of renewal and endless possibilities. Uplifting citrus undertones infuse a zesty energy, promising brighter days. The combination of colours and smells leaves me spellbound.

"P—please!" a woman frantically begs, snapping me back to reality. "It was *not* me! I—I'm devoted to the emperor—oh gosh! Please!"

Though her youthful appearance makes it difficult to gauge her age, she wears her hair in a tight bun, which tells me she's over sixty (women use hairstyles to indicate their number of lived years). Two enforcers—clad in plain, dark grey uniforms—drag the woman from a building, and the floating crown instantly vanishes. They toss her to the ground, where she crawls towards the crowd, which shows her no remorse, just looks of disgust.

"Julia!" she cries. "We—we are childhood friends. *Please.* Tell them I would never do this!"

Julia steps back, her arms folded, and with a tilted head, she peers down an upturned nose—her face filled with scorn and contempt. You don't need my ability to know this woman is innocent, and I want to step in, but that would result in me sharing her fate, so I remain passive (as I always do).

Rebels often plant projection devices displaying their group's symbol in loyalist properties, and she's fallen victim to their methods. The guards bind and drag her through the passage of hissing and sneering observers.

New smells of damp earth and fallen leaves suddenly flood my senses, invoking desolation and reflection. Hints of smoky incense and charred wood intertwine—causing me to think of a once vivacious flame that's now reduced to ashes. The hissing quietens, and the onlookers' expressions transform to pity, all sharing in this same experience.

Scent control. A smart play by rebels, it makes a change from their usual attempts to challenge the emperor's authority, like starting small fires in stores or defacing propaganda—they're becoming more creative. This is the second unsettling event I've witnessed today, and I've been uncomfortably close to both. Something is stirring.

CHAPTER TWO

A Test of Fealty

The remainder of my journey to work is uneventful. With nerves growing, I climb the stairs to the Imperial Intelligence Agency. Its sleek and minimalist design takes on the shape of a pyramid, with floors stacked one upon the other in a clear display of hierarchy. The uppermost level hosts a plethora of secrets—a clandestine world accessible exclusively to the esteemed and influential.

Two familiar-faced guards stand on either side of the entrance; one is a sentinel, whilst the other is a curious meerkat. Both are sporting sleek uniforms of midnight blue, with clean lines and a simple design to avoid unwanted attention. Though visible weapons are absent, their sleeves conceal lethal mechanical creatures—otherwise known as swarmers—poised to defend their masters in a flash. I consider myself lucky not to have witnessed them in action. These deadly creatures overcome their hapless victims in unstoppable swarms, moving swiftly and striking with precision, sometimes leaving just a pile of bones.

Quinlan is the meerkat, a short, lean young man who shuffles with exhilaration as I approach. His hair is intentionally dishevelled, and the sunlight reflecting off the white stone steps illuminates his wide eyes. My fondness for Quinlan extends beyond the fact he regards me with the admiration of a psyched-up pup. It's his inherent innocence that I'm really in awe of, a quality somehow preserved amid our cruel existence. I can't help but feel bad for the inevitable fate awaiting him. With just one misstep, the malice of our world will dampen his zeal and inflict wounds on his spirit.

Next to him, the sentinel Isaac stands—radiating pride and demanding respect, with a body exhibiting years of discipline and rigorous training. His meticulously groomed hair frames a stern, angular face, and one look can penetrate your soul, uncovering any weakness—even in the most self-assured. The contrasting qualities between the two amuse me, yet their positioning holds a strategic purpose—Quinlan's swiftness complements Isaac's strength, creating a dynamic duo ready to face any challenge.

"May his glory shine upon you, Clara!" Quinlan exclaims.

"And on you, Quinlan. United in devotion," I respond, throwing him a warm, comforting smile, which I know he appreciates from the way his pupils dilate and—more noticeably—how he quivers with excitable energy. Isaac remains silent and firm; he doesn't acknowledge me, though I still smile in his direction, hoping he feels its warmth. His behaviour isn't unusual; Isaac is renowned for his cold demeanour, taking his role of protecting the empire's secrets exceptionally seriously. In fact, he regularly keeps Quinlan's enthusiasm in check—and that's how I know Isaac feels responsible for his safety.

Crossing the threshold, I enter the expansive entrance hall. The air is thick and heavy, caused by sensors diligently scanning every inch of my body to determine whether I'm a friend or foe. Today, an unusually high number of guards protect the agency—their intense presence casts tension— it's as if they anticipate trouble, but what? The eerie silence amplifies the clack, clack, clack of my heels as their echoes beat against the walls. I regret my risky choice of footwear because I have no right to be making so much noise and asking for this much attention. The guards' watchful eyes are fixed on me from all directions, and I'm visibly anxious because the agency will question my integrity today (and I've already had a tumultuous morning), but I need to compose myself.

The energy barrier grants me access, and as I step into the lift, a plump man trails behind and joins—it's Ambrose, my boss. He greets me with a cautious smile and dissuades another person from entering with us.

"United in devotion, Clara." His voice shakes almost as much as his hands—I mustn't let his nerves feed mine.

"With hearts aligned, Ambrose," I respond sweetly. "I've received information this morning, which I want to share. Will we have time before my test?"

It's in my best interest to control the narrative, as it'll add value to my view of Celest's innocence.

"We won't, I'm afraid," he moans. "I have a meeting with—"

The doors slide open, revealing the agency's Head of Operations—Lavinia Radford—and she's clearly waiting for us. Rigid and tall, her black hair is cut into a sleek bob, parted in the middle with a glossy texture. Unlike most other women in the empire with their rounded features, hers are sharp and pointed, protruding from her slim, elongated face. Despite her frozen youth (made to look older using heavy makeup), she exudes a cold and harsh nature, always wearing a slim, black dress and drowning in gold jewellery.

She's threatening, and I'm fortunate to have had few interactions with Radford. As talented as I am at reading people, her unpredictable character puzzles me. Against all odds—in a country dominated by men—Radford has defied societal norms to secure a position of authority. Her career soared after playing a pivotal role in capturing a climate terrorist cell operating in Birmingham. This group acquired a small sample of regonium—intending to create a weapon of mass destruction. Radford became renowned for her strategic prowess and resourcefulness after she built a vast network of civilian spies—named her ravens—whose loyalty she guards closely. Each raven provided her with a breadcrumb that led to the capture and execution of these terrorists.

Radford is known for her innovative and deceptive methods that ensure the empire's protection. Whilst shrouded in mystery, one thing is transparent—her insatiable thirst to ascend the ladder and gain validation from the emperor's inner circle. She'll do anything to achieve her ambition, and this unwavering determination makes her dangerous.

"Ambrose," she says with a smoky voice (another tell-tale sign of a woman's age). "We shall start early. Your office will do." She pays me no heed.

"Of—of course, ma'am," Ambrose stutters, caught off guard by the ambush. "Clara, I'll collect you in an hour for your test—of fealty, that is."

"Thank you, Ambrose," I respond with a syrupy tone and turn to face Radford. "May the emperor's glory shine upon you, ma'am."

Her cruel, dark eyes burrow into mine—it's incredible how her glare fills me with such self-doubt. She scans my body, slightly raising an eyebrow, before spinning around to march away, dragging Ambrose by an invisible leash. It's unlike Radford to be on the fourth floor; only something important will pull her from the upper levels, and I suspect that 'something' is me.

***

I stare mindlessly at a report, sitting at my desk amongst the endless rows of agency worker bees—my colleagues.

"United in devotion, Clara." Leo greets me. A beaming smile contradicts his worry-filled eyes—the weight of some disturbing news is consuming him.

"With hearts aligned, Leo," I respond.

Many find his optimism overwhelming—wielding an extravagant personality that invites scrutiny people would rather avoid—but I find his company thrilling. We've always had a good relationship, both sharing the same values, like the importance of protecting the innocent from the crossfire of intelligence gathering—which I fear Celest will fall victim to. Leo stands in silence, staring at me with the same expression—totally out of character.

I giggle nervously to break the awkward silence and ask, "Erm—any luck with your case?"

"None. Ambrose is getting twitchy," Leo sighs. "Says he's under pressure to give the reapers some hard leads, but I've hit a dead end. The rebels are getting smart; they know all the blind spots in London." Shaking his head, the thick mane of golden hair sways from side to side; I sense him contemplating his following words carefully. "I suppose I can't ask you for help," he muses. "You're too busy … right?"

Leo knows I'll always find time to help him, even if I am busy (which I'm not). This is his way of telling me I'm the hot topic on the fourth floor right now.

"Mega busy," I respond. "But I'll make some headway with my case and will be helping you out in no time".

Leo perches in the empty seat beside me. "You're the most valuable asset this place has," he says quietly. "I know you'll be giving me a hand soon. I'll catch you later, Clara. Never alone."

"Thanks, Leo. Blessed by his presence."

With a final, sturdy nod, he departs.

I know, deep down, I'll be fine—I'm just concerned for Celest. Leaning back in my seat, I admire a photo on my desk. It captures a cherished moment suspended in time, where my parents—brimming with love—stand protectively on either side of Fay and me as children. Their radiant smiles fill my head with nostalgia, allowing fond memories to flood back. Fay attracted a band of horses that day using grain she insisted on taking in case any animals were hungry. She was born just a few minutes before me but has always played the caring and protective older sister role.

Fay's a counsellor—a dangerous profession considering her exposure to potential criminals and the information they burden her with. A job many people look down on. It's borderline sacrilegious to counsel those struggling because a struggle in one's life is an admission of discontent under the emperor's rule, and many consider this selfish when he benevolently feeds and shelters us. However, it doesn't stop

Fay; I admire her caring nature and passion. I'd love to share her courage and help others—teetering on the edge of law and deviance—but I'm too afraid to seek the opportunities. Instead, I take what comfort I can knowing I strive to protect innocent people from falling deeper into The Crown's relentless grip.

It's just a short time until my test of fealty, and I need my thoughts to be my ally, not my enemy, so I shift my focus to a large portrait of the emperor. Women obsess over his mesmerising blue eyes, and today, I allow them to invade me and ignite arousal—a master of my psyche. I draw lines over his chiselled features with my finger, running it down his angular cheek to his slightly curved lip that carries a smugness—no, a hint of mystery and allure.

Immersing deeper, I imagine how soft his chestnut hair is to touch, running my hands through its thick and gentle waves. He speaks to me; his voice is an enchanting instrument, resonating with a deep and velvety tone that—in my imagination—is gentle, carrying words of compassion. I hear him praising me, commending my ability and devotion to seeking the truth and protecting the innocent. His control takes over—these fallacies and images are vital to pass my test.

A tap on the shoulder prompts me to sit up from my almost horizontal position, and I find Ambrose behind me. His dramatic change in appearance is a shock—he looks exhausted, as though cruel tormentors have tugged and pulled him for days without rest, causing guilt to niggle at me. Ambrose isn't a bad person—yes, he may have sent a family of four to the work camps just last month, but he didn't want to. He doesn't deserve to become a victim of my indirect association with Rebecca and Max.

"Are you ready, Clara?" he asks wearily.

"Yes." Though I respond with defiance, I'm confident he sees the remorse flickering in my eyes—my silent apology.

We walk side by side through the rows of desks, and I detect heads lifting from their screens at my presence, averting their gaze before I can confront their curiosity with my stare. *Vultures.* I know they'll be feeding off my discomfort. I'm not popular here—and I don't try to be. Whilst I attempt to strut and exude confidence—trying to kid myself I have nothing to worry about—my body is stiff, refusing to loosen up. We enter a long, dark hallway and approach the interview room. Ambrose hesitates before the door, takes a deep, controlled breath, and we enter.

A dull light bathes the square space, with two chairs occupying the centre and positioned to face each other. Ambrose gestures toward the chair farthest away, silently instructing me to take a seat. Obediently, I settle into it, but my unease intensifies upon catching a glimpse of Radford lurking in the dark corner. Her features remain partially obscured, and she emits an eerie mood throughout the room.

Ambrose joins me, positioning himself with his back to Radford, and his discomfort is palpable, surpassing even my own. The air grows heavy as if a weighted blanket descends on me from above, indicating the sensors are monitoring my every movement, heartbeat, temperature, and facial expression—ready to snitch if I tell a fib. Like that nosy neighbour who's always monitoring you because they get a kick out of alerting the authorities when they can't hear you singing the anthem of allegiance on a Sunday.

Ambrose's protruding eyes dart between his tablet's screen and me before he formally requests, "Please state your name and age."

"Clara Rosewood, twenty-three years old," I respond.

"And what day of the week is it?" he asks, allowing the sensors to baseline my responses.

"Wednesday."

"Thank you," he says, staring at the tablet that rests in his sausage-like fingers. "We will n—not be conducting your test of fealty today, Clara"—*no surprise there*—"Instead, I must ask you about some … troubling intelligence we have received surrounding an—er—an acquaintance of yours."

"I understand."

"How do you know Celest Pendleton?" he squeaks.

"Celest is a friend," I respond coolly. "We met when my calling assigned me to the agency. She'd been here for six months—helped me settle in."

Ambrose stares at his device before glancing up, remaining silent—he wants more.

I continue cautiously, "She—she comforted me through a tough time. I had awful homesickness when I joined the agency, but Celest—she made it feel like home. We've been close ever since."

Radford scoffs in the corner. I'm not angry; it's sad that any sign of sentiment has such an effect on her.

"Why is Celest no longer working at the agency?" Ambrose asks.

I was expecting this question.

"Two years ago, Celest's test of fealty produced inconclusive results," I respond. "The agency felt it wasn't appropriate for her to continue working here."

She's the one person I know who's had an inconclusive result—it's usually a pass or fail (live another year until your next test or be hanged). They transferred her to work for a catering company that provides food and services for the upper classes.

"You say you're close to Celest," Ambrose states. "Does she tell you everything?"

"I believe so, yes. Celest trusts me."

"Wh—what crimes has Celest committed?" he stutters.

The blood rises to my head. She's shared some opinions that the law considers criminal—but I can't reveal them—they would lock her away or execute her.

"Gosh," I sigh with a shaky voice. "I—I can't think of anything."

With concern etched on Ambrose's face, worry lines draw paths through his features. He finally utters, "I—er—"

"Why are you lying, Miss Rosewood?" Radford's cold voice cuts through the tense air like a knife.

"I'm—I'm sorry," I choke. "Let me think"—I have an idea; I just hope it works—"Celest told me a story once—from when she was a child. She spilt a drink over a statue of King Henry when she fell." I force a nervous giggle, hoping to smooth some of this friction. "She lost sleep for months over it and was too ashamed to tell anyone. I can't think of—"

Radford leaps from her chair and spits with a clenched jaw, *"That isn't funny."*

"I—I'm sorry, ma'am." I lower my head, praying for forgiveness. *I should've known better not to have laughed. I've been playing this game long enough.*

"Right." Radford glides over to Ambrose and stands behind him like a predator stalking its prey. "You are dismissed, Ambrose." She leans over his shoulder with her back hunched, extending her neck unnaturally like a vulture.

Ambrose turns slightly to see her menacing smile; he nods and scuttles out of the room. Radford takes a seat, and like a fog lifted by a gentle breeze, her features soften and morph into something playful—a cheerful light dances in her eyes.

"It's just us girls now," she whispers impishly, leaning into me. "I see much of myself in you"—*I don't*—"You're not like other girls who are weak and pitiful. You will be climbing the ranks in no time—I just know it. All you need to do is *grasp* those opportunities when they present themselves."

"Thank you, ma'am," I respond with a pleasant smile.

"Just remember," she declares, pointing her index finger to the air. "Success is not an accident waiting to happen. It's a controlled blaze, deliberately ignited by your passion and determination."

Why is she telling me this? I nod and smile.

"Right, my love!" she exclaims. "Let us make this quick. Is Celest a traitor?"

"I have no reason to believe so."

"Interesting," she says. "What sacrifices are you willing to make in the name of loyalty, Miss Rosewood?" Her smile turns into something more sinister—I think I know what she wants from me, *but why?*

"Though I may find it difficult, I'm willing to sacrifice what is required if it's in the name of loyalty, ma'am." I'm confident in my response because I'm telling the truth. Radford has slipped up by failing to specify the owner of my loyalty—allowing me to construct my own interpretation and fool the sensors. It may help the conviction of my response, but it won't stop her imminent request.

Her eyes flick between the tablet and me, and her menacing grin extends larger. "I want you to gather evidence against your friend, Celest," she demands coldly. "I want to know which terrorist group she aligns with and what she does for them." Now grasping both my hands, her expression and tone relax to something more consoling. "You have an opportunity to prove your loyalty in the best possible way, Miss Rosewood. I would *hate* to see your talents wasted in a filthy work camp because of your poor choice of friends. I look forward to your findings in a week. Any questions?"

"No questions, ma'am, but I cannot guarantee—"

"Ah, ah, ah! I *know* Celest is a criminal"—she's lying— "Do not doubt your abilities. You will succeed and make me proud."

I sense the desperation in her voice. *Why does she want this so much?*

"Thank you for this opportunity to serve, ma'am," I respond with what many would consider genuine gratitude.

"Never alone, Miss Rosewood."

"Blessed by his presence."

Radford struts from the room, leaving me to mull over her instruction. *What game is she playing?* Celest has Radford's target on her back, yet Radford isn't sure of Celest's guilt. *"I know you will succeed and make me proud."* She wants something more from me—not just proof of my loyalty—but what does she want?

Hopelessness and fear crush the anxiety I once felt; I only see myself losing in her twisted game.

CHAPTER THREE

Celest

Two men wander St James's Park with a husky dog—I've been observing this footage of them all day. Their identities remain a mystery to me, but I know they hold significance as people of interest. This task is tedious; it won't keep me occupied too much, which is good because I'll have the headspace to establish a plan for the unofficial case that Radford placed me on this morning—a case of betrayal. *How do I protect Celest?* I have the impossible task of gathering evidence against her, and perhaps I'm in shock because I don't know what to think, but I need to think fast as I'm meeting Celest after work, and cancelling will only worry her.

I notice minor signs of suspicious behaviour in the two men, and I dutifully instruct my device—using my mind—to make notes. Mind-typing requires practice, and I tread carefully, ensuring I record the relevant observations, guarding against stray thoughts that may intrude upon the process. For some time, interrogators used mind-typing technology to establish a suspect's beliefs during

interrogations—resulting in The Crown executing
thousands of innocent people. Somehow, a band of
psychologists and scientific experts successfully removed it
from practice. It's reassuring to know—amidst the cruelty
and disregard for true justice—there are still those who
uphold goodness and strive to improve things.

In the rare instances these men interact, I scrutinise
their gestures, noticing a perplexing inconsistency. They
point assertively at specific objects, mainly trees or beautiful
plants, but their motions are more subtle when directed at
buildings—notably, a platform positioned directly ahead of
Buckingham Palace. Their repeated actions suggest they're
diligently surveying the area—but why?

❄❄❄

Gazing out over the crystal-clear waters of the Thames on
Lambeth Bridge, I maintain a subtle vigilance of my
surroundings—alert for any signs of potential followers
accompanying me to see Celest. Radford will have her eyes
observing my every move until she gets what she wants. I
didn't notice anyone following me from the agency, but I'm
confident they're nearby.

An immense statue of King James III poses with
superiority atop the remnants and debris of the old Houses
of Parliament, towering at a height equivalent to a five-story
building. This monument reminds us of his triumph over
democracy, and the juxtaposition is striking—the dark
rubble of the once grand building contrasted with the
monarch's bright stone portrays good destroying evil.

They teach and regularly remind us about the dark days
of democracy, an age marred by lies and corruption that

plagued the halls of Parliament. Greed's insidious grip took hold, resulting in widespread poverty, ill health, and the irreversible destruction of our planet. However, King James emerged as a beacon of hope once he discovered regonium—the key to restoring our Earth's health. His bravery in challenging Parliament's authority resonated with the hearts and minds of the people, paving the way for the rise of an absolute monarchy in England.

However, alternative versions of history occasionally surface—conspiracy theories, of course—presenting contrasting narratives. Some stories speak of military regiments forsaking their commander-in-chief to stand with the English people, and others sing of proud and valiant Scots, riding from the north—fiercely pushing back against the newly oppressive regime.

A tale accepted as truth is that of the civil war in London, where epic alliances formed to dismantle the monarchy and build a republic—with support for their cause from select European countries and, more subtly, a broader array of nations. Of course, their efforts proved futile—the deployment of regonium ushered in rapid advancements in military capabilities and weaponry, granting King James and his supporters unrivalled supremacy over all opposition.

A man and woman who've paused to converse nearby casually lean against the bridge's railings. Both are wearing bland shades of grey to blend in with the crowd—but I know they're my shadow for the remainder of this evening. I discreetly note their faces, ensuring they imprint in my memory for future recognition, and stride across the remaining stretch of the bridge, stealing a glance to catch sight of their pursuit in my peripheral.

***

Arriving at Gold's café just in time, I find Celest seated at a table outside in the bustling square. My chosen coffee—a simple black Americano—awaits me. The warm weather has drawn out groups of people engaging in light-hearted conversations after a day of dutiful service, all maintaining an air of decorum. I'm saddened to see Celest's usual smile is noticeably absent, and as I approach, she musters a feeble attempt to show some happiness, but I see straight through it—I know her too well. Celest is selfless and won't be concerned for herself, just for Rebecca, Max, Aria, and me. Taking my seat, her gaze drifts towards her coffee—a subtle indication of her distracted state—so I use this opportunity to accidentally scan my surroundings, seeing the same man and woman from the bridge settling at a table near us. They'll be listening to our every word.

With Radford's assignment, I'm comfortable sharing a certain level of information with Celest, especially if I argue it's necessary to gain her trust and achieve my objectives. However, my foremost concern lies with her responses; I'm determined to protect her and remove any suspicion of guilt in our observers' minds. I hope she catches my signal that we're not alone.

"United in devotion," I express delightfully.

Celest lifts her head, with one eyebrow raised and mumbles, "With hearts aligned."

"I have been thinking about you all day, praying for his grace to lift your mood," I declare, squeezing her hands.

We never show signs of fealty when in each other's company, and my so-called prayers indicate we're not alone.

"Thank you," she responds pleasantly, catching on. "I've taken comfort in his generosity today, which has helped. How's your day been?"

"Mostly uneventful," I respond, taking a sip of coffee. "Of course, I was asked about Rebecca and Max during my test, but they were understanding. The rest was standard casework. Have you heard anything from Rebecca's sister?"

"No, she hasn't been in contact," she sighs. "When—when they questioned you … did—did they happen to shed some light on the situation?" Celest is cautiously inquisitive.

"Nothing!" I shrug and share a puzzled look. "I pray his light will reveal the truth, and they'll return soon." I hope I'm not overdoing this, but I'm expressing less adoration than most people.

"Yes … me too," she says. "They're a good family. I'll be stopping by the enforcement station on my way home to hand over a character statement—hopefully, it helps them"—I nudge her foot—"Oh! Of course, I'll—I'll also tell them about Rebecca asking me to look after Aria for a while. They might be interested."

"Yes, good idea," I respond with a nod; Celest must realise they've been watching her all day and would've been listening to our conversation in the station. There's no hope in her eyes—although she doesn't know Max is dead—she realises their fates are sealed.

We sit in silence, and usually, it wouldn't feel this unsettling, but the atmosphere is heavy with unspoken tension, and I can't shake the eerie sensation of someone else's eyes locked on me. Casually glancing around, I confirm the presence of our followers engaged in light-hearted conversation, and I continue to scan … finally locating him. A lone figure to my right with an untouched pastry and coffee. I'm gripped by his firm, dark stare that's shadowed by a strong brow. It's a stern expression betraying no hint of warmth or friendliness, and it's unusual—disturbing even—for someone to be so brazen.

Solid shoulders accentuate his powerful physique, with both elbows propped on the table and a slight hunch that suggests he's making an effort to remain inconspicuous. Despite his smart attire—carefully chosen to blend in with the crowd—his messy hair and scruffy beard give away his wild nature, making him seem somewhat dangerous. I find myself involuntarily drawn into the depths of his enigmatic allure. There are no signs of fondness or attraction towards me, but his stare is so forceful—which leads me to think he desires a connection of some sort. *What does he want?*

I break free from this man's invisible grip and return my attention to Celest—where it should be. I need time to consider how best to protect her. If I could prove her innocence this evening, Radford may realise her trail is cold and shift her scrutiny elsewhere—but until then, I can only try to cheer Celest up.

"We should get away for a while," I announce, wanting to give her something to look forward to. "We haven't been on an adventure in ages. How many travel credits do you have?"

You earn credits through good behaviour, like showing up to work on time or watching at least thirty minutes of news each day—hopefully, they haven't frozen Celest's account.

"Enough for a two-hundred-mile trip," she responds, finally lifting her head to smirk at me. "Do you remember the Lake District?"

"D'you know what," I reply. "I was thinking about it last week. I saw some kids—in the park—practising a new dance that's gone viral. It made me think of that ridiculous one you choreographed to scare off those blokes eyeing us up when we were sunbathing."

Celest snorts, almost spraying me with a mouthful of drink, and we both breakdown into laughter as she proceeds to imitate the same dance while seated—her upper body moving in a wild and uninhibited manner as her head twists in a circular motion—like a bird's bizarre mating ritual. We achieve a few disgruntled looks from our neighbouring tables—but I don't care. All that matters right now is Celest's company.

"We should plan something over a few *proper* drinks," I suggest. "What do you reckon?"

"Good idea," she agrees.

It's nice to see that sparkle of joy return to her eyes.

***

"We could go to the zoo!" Celest elates. "Or—will I feel bad about the animals? We should *definitely* visit the museum—maybe take a picnic—no!" She claps her hands. "I want to see the botanical gardens—"

"Slow down!" I chuckle. "I can't keep up."

With Celest's mood lifted, she's become increasingly erratic since leaving the bar, not requiring much to drink for it to affect her. A beautiful, warm pink glow wraps the cloudless sky as the sun sinks, bidding farewell to an unruly day and casting a magical hue over the city. We weren't ready to say goodbye after having a couple of drinks (our weekly allowance) at the bar, so now we're wandering through the quiet streets of London and allowing our chat to flow uninterrupted. The bustling chaos of the city has momentarily receded, leaving behind a peaceful ambience.

Thankfully, I hadn't seen the wild-looking man since the café; he would've distracted me from Celest's company and cast a shadow over our evening. Things are going well; I've protected Celest without raising suspicion—but I still need to prove her innocence.

"Oh my god—"

"Gosh, Celest, *gosh*," I respond abruptly.

I don't want them arresting her for being blasphemous. *Surely, she hasn't forgotten they're listening to us.*

"Oops!" She giggles. "*Oh my gosh*, do you remember that bloke you met in Camden? What was his name …"

"Oh go—sh," I stutter, almost blaspheming myself. "Peter."

"That's it! He would've had so much potential if he wasn't such a wimp," Celest responds bitterly.

"He wasn't a wimp, Cee," I respond. "I've scared other guys off before."

Like many men I've dated, Peter decided we weren't compatible, but only after discovering what I do for work. It's as if they'll fall victim to a woman's scorn at one misstep in our relationship. They think I'll report them as traitors to the empire if they leave dirty laundry on the floor or forget to put the toilet seat down.

"We should team up!" Celest declares. "Find two nice blokes, one for you and one for—"

She's interrupted by a mass of bustling city workers scurrying through Admiralty Arch and into The Mall. Despite appearing small in contrast with its dominant neighbouring buildings, the arch emits genuine opulence, with a glimpse of the distant Buckingham Palace peeking through the central archway. It's a commemorative wonder, reflecting the maritime heritage and naval dominance of the ancient British Empire.

Curiously following the city workers in silence, we pass under the arch, and I feel myself succumbing to its authority as it grants us passage into The Mall. They're working tirelessly to dress the grand, sweeping thoroughfare before us. Rows of trees abundant in green leaves invite us to step into a noble world that resonates with the echoes of history.

Huge imperial flags are freshly mounted and meticulously placed on each side of the extensive runway in perfect symmetry. Each one is the same; within their rich, olive-green backgrounds, a golden crown takes prominence in the centre, surrounded by a laurel wreath extending outwards in a circular pattern. It reminds me of the empire's perpetual pursuit of dominance—each leaf symbolising its determination to expand. Interwoven are a network of red chains—further exemplifying a compulsory bond of allegiance between the empire and its conquered lands. Finally, soaring above is the embroidered image of a red kite, with its wings majestically spread in a regal pose. Copper and russet shades capture its feathers' details—highlighting the bird's vibrant appearance. Its sharp, penetrating gaze warns us of the empire's watchfulness.

Progressing in silence, we observe other frills that dress The Mall. Tall banners in deep hues of rich burgundy flutter in the breeze, their fabric gilded with patterns illustrating bountiful fruits and vegetables. The occasional black flag—with similar intricate designs—infiltrates the display, but their fruits and vegetables are rotten, and it's a similar theme for the wreaths. Carefully placed—amongst the groups of wreaths that host beautiful and boldly coloured flowers—are those made from brittle and withered foliage. These symbols of death snuggled within the garnishes offer us insight into the upcoming festivities.

"*Harvest preparations,*" Celest sighs; her mood instantly dampens.

Cities and towns within kingdoms celebrate the Harvest Festival at the end of summer, and I dread it each year. Communities gather in a display of union and devotion to celebrate the execution of traitors to the empire. The Crown encourages subjects to snitch on their colleagues, friends, or even family members. The rules are simple: you want to pick someone who rubs you the wrong way. Then, you stalk them and snap a photo or record a video when they do something illegal. Once you've successfully played detective, package up your findings with a nice bow and offer them to the authorities as a 'submission of light'.

Submissions vary, from disgruntled neighbours casting light on the man next door for using too much water (branding him a climate killer) to someone reporting their colleague for stealing time from their employer. If you provide a worthy submission, you're titled a Light Bringer, and you're rewarded with a front-row seat watching the people you report get what they deserve—a meeting with the gallows.

If you're really lucky and provide an exceptional submission, you'll be titled the Bright Light—making you extremely important because there can only be one in the empire each year. But you must be a remarkably faithful subject and possess a story of true devotion that bolsters The Crown's authority, setting an example for all others. You'll be treated like a celebrity, people will love you, and you'll even attend the Harvest Ball as the emperor's guest of honour (making all your friends extremely jealous). The Harvest feeds hope and aspiration; it nurtures fear throughout the empire; it kills thousands each year.

As we continue our stroll, I become increasingly aware of Buckingham Palace's scale. With evening approaching, its white stone exterior is backlit by the sun's gentle glow, emphasising its vanity. With a smooth, polished surface like flawless skin and windows like watchful eyes, I instinctively adjust my posture as if the building will berate me for looking unladylike. We stand before the mighty, golden gates protecting it and stare at the ornate gallows that crave their next victim.

"D'you know what," Celest huffs. "I'd love to see the emperor's corpse dangling there one day."

My heart stops, and my stomach fills with burning anxiety. With a sharp inhale, I instinctively grab Celest's hand and turn my head to face her. It's impossible to lift my jaw from the ground and hide the fear that plagues my features. I'm overwhelmed by the same nauseating feeling from when I learned of my parents' deaths.

With the slightest hesitation, Celest loses all colour from the sudden realisation of what she's said— remembering we're not alone. It feels like time has slowed. She turns her head to face me, her once bright blue eyes, now dimmed, lock with mine, filled with pure terror. I watch a single tear glide down her cheek as muffled footsteps grow in intensity behind us. In a single breath, her head is thrust into a cloth bag, and our two tag-a-longs are dragging her away.

I'm quick to tighten my grip, but she's wrenched from me—imprisoned by her captors' obstinate determination. Disorientated, Celest is thrashing around—attempting to break free—her muffled screams emerge like fraught whispers trapped within the confines of a suffocating cocoon. My heart takes control, drowning out rational thought as I run towards her.

"Let her go!" I beg. "*Please.* She didn't mean it—she's been drinking!"

They pretend I don't exist, and as Celest continues struggling, an enforcer approaches—enticed by the commotion. "STOP RESISTING," he bellows at her.

She doesn't listen—but they never tell you twice—so he lifts his muscular leg and stamps his boot down into Celest's chest, totally demobilising her. I drop to the ground and wrap my arms around her waist, desperate to protect her from further harm—but it's useless. A firm grip clenches my hair, jerking my head upwards—almost removing it from my neck. A gun is pointed between my eyes, then … a green flash.

CHAPTER FOUR

The Stranger

"Find me! Clara!" Celest calls out playfully.

I catch a glimpse of her skipping behind a bush. The dense canopy of trees stretches above—their branches intermingle like an elaborate tapestry. Sunlight filters through the leafy ceiling, casting eery patterns on the forest floor.

"Gotcha!" I exclaim, lunging behind her hiding place, but she isn't there ....

"No, you don't!" She chuckles in the distance.

I race towards her, jumping over the exposed roots and fallen branches, heading towards movement from behind a tree. Now creeping to soften the crunch of dry leaves from each footstep, I'm determined to catch her by surprise.

"Found you!" I announce.

Celest is slumped against the tree, ensnared in a thick web. All I hear is the faint scuttling of spiders crawling along the threads, their beady eyes glinting in the dim light.

"Wait!" I cry, tearing the trap apart. "Leave her alone—Celest! I'll help you—"

***

A cold sweat is the first thing I notice, then my racing heartbeat, and finally, the dull throbbing behind my eyes. I dart upright in bed, and my room materialises before me.

"Go easy …" A deep growl drifts from the darkness.

I clamber off the bed in a disorientated attempt to create a barrier between the stranger and me.

"Get out!" I cry.

"You're safe," he says.

"What—who are you?" I ask, my voice trembling with fear despite him being truthful.

"I'm a friend of Celest's"—*he's lying*—"Well, I don't know her personally, but me and her—we're in the same group. My name's Silas."

"Lights on," I instruct my apartment, and it reveals the same rugged, dangerous-looking man from the café. *"Why the hell are you in my apartment?"* I demand heatedly.

"You were stunned. I arranged to get you home safely. A couple of enforcers owed me a favour."

Though his deep voice feels reassuring, and he's being truthful, I remain cautious.

"Ce—Celest … I was with her." I jump to my feet. *"Where is she?"*

Remaining seated, Silas leans closer with solemn eyes. "I'm sorry, Clara. The agency took Celest."

His words open the gates to flood my mind with memories. "There's been a misunderstanding. I nee—"

"*Stop*—Clara, please"—the desperation in his voice prompts me to pause—"Before you do anything, please—let's chat first."

"You're a stranger in my apartment," I snap. "Why should I trust you?"

"I'm in the same group as Celest, and I'm not here to harm you," he declares. "Am I lying?"

"No."

"That's all I can offer to gain your trust."

"You mentioned a group. What is it?

"The Folc—"

"Forget it—get out—"

"Wait—no one knows I'm here. I've—"

"*Out!*"

"They're not listening!" Silas stresses. "I've blocked your devices." He gestures to my wrist and waves around the room.

"How?" I should scream and alert my neighbours, but it's never a good idea to draw attention to yourself because that could give a wannabe Bright Light everything they need—besides, I'm slightly curious.

"This." He waves a small, wand-like device. "Press it against your SyncLink to block certain signals without alerting the agency. They've got no idea what you're saying or where you are."

SyncLinks are implanted in your wrist and act as a communicator, camera, and more. They project displays containing messages and maps, to name a few things. Naturally, they also provide a means for the intelligence agency to monitor conversations and activity, alerting them when you use certain words—which makes you always think twice before saying anything.

"So ... you're part of the Folcriht?" I ask tentatively.

"Yeah."

"And Celest?"

He nods.

"I need to hear you say it," I demand. It's the only way I know if he's telling the truth.

"And Celest," he confirms.

We've been friends for over ten years; *how did I not suspect anything?* Though I maintain composure, it feels like my world is crumbling apart. The Folcriht are a radical group responsible for the event I witnessed in the courtyard yesterday. Its members want a republic, for democracy to return and to wipe out the monarchy. I've never understood why anyone would want to hand power to a society that celebrates their friends and family being executed or one that sits idly by as children are snatched and forced into labour. I have no idea what to ask; my head is spinning.

"What do you want from me?" I ask plainly.

"Oh—Okay," Silas stutters, appearing taken aback as if he was expecting more of a challenge. "That Lavinia Radford woman wants you to gather evidence against Celest, right?"

"Yes …"

"We want you to give her what she wants."

"*What?* No. I won't betray—"

"*Celest* wants you to do this. It was her idea."

"Why?"

"I can't tell you."

"I won't sentence my friend to death."

"Clara …" Silas releases a heavy breath like a dam has broken, and he's restrained his following words for too long. "Celest didn't survive the beating from that enforcer when they arrested her"—a heavy shroud of disbelief hits me, and my heart sinks into the pit of my stomach—"I'm told she passed away … *I'm sorry.*"

The world blurs as I'm washed by grief—it overwhelms every part of me—and each breath becomes an effort. The weight of this news drags my body from its position—at the edge of my bed—to the floor, where I slouch and submit myself to the crushing heartache.

※※※

"What *exactly* do you want?" I demand.

I don't know how long I've been sitting here in silence, but the sky's a deep violet, indicating dawn's approach. An ache radiates through my body, my eyes are burning, and I feel exhausted from the endless rush of emotions—but I've come to accept this isn't going away. It's strange; I cried every waking hour, every day for five days when my parents died, but the waterworks have already stopped. Is grief easier to handle as you get older? Or should I feel guilty for the tears that refuse to escape me?

"How're you feeling?" Silas asks uncomfortably.

"I'll pull through"—*I don't know how*—"What do you want?"

"D'you … wanna chat about it?"

"Yes," I declare impatiently. "I wanna chat about *what you want from me.*"

"Sorry, of course," he acknowledges, taking a deep breath. I sense emotions aren't something he's used to handling. "We need you to provide evidence against Celest to regain the agency's trust."

"You told me this was her plan."

"It is."

"Had she survived her arrest, they would've executed her. Are you telling me she was willing to sacrifice herself?"

"Yeah."

"Why would she do that?"

"I can tell you once Lavinia has her evidence," Silas sighs.

"No. Tell me now," I press.

"I can't."

"You can. You're just choosing not to."

"Fine. I won't."

"What could you achieve from me betraying my friend?"

"I'm not going—"

"You think it'll grant me a place in the Harvest," I theorise. "Perhaps even the Bright Light title. Correct?"

Silas remains silent, staring at me for ages before nodding reluctantly.

"This is mad," I say. "It doesn't sound like something Celest would do."

"She thought if you gave Lavinia evidence against your *best friend*, you'd stand a good chance at becoming the Bright Light. Celest's cover was blown once Rebecca and Max were caught, and she knew there wasn't a chance for her."

"But the sacrifice is too big," I respond, shaking my head. "It doesn't make sense—I mean—*her life?* On a hunch that I'll become the Bright Light? *And for what?*"

"Listen," Silas orders gently. "There was nowhere for Celest to run. She'd be putting the Folcriht *and* you at risk. She wanted to do this."

"And what makes you think it'll be enough to grant me the title?" I ask.

"We know Lavinia is desperate for her next promotion," Silas says. "She would take a significant interest in this case because—"

"Because mentoring an underling that becomes the Bright Light will be her ticket to that promotion," I interject.

In her words, 'success is not an accident waiting to happen. It's a controlled blaze, deliberately ignited by your passion and determination.'

"Exactly."

"And why do you want me to become the Bright Light?" I ask. "Because it sounds like a horrible idea."

"I can't tell you anymore, Clara," he states, shaking his head. "Not until we can trust you."

"Until *you* can trust *me*?" I scoff.

"Don't get me wrong, I'm not proud of this," he urges. "We're asking you to risk everything with sod all information—it's not right—but the less you know, the better." He takes a deep breath and asks, "What can I do to help you trust me?"

"Will I be placed in danger?" I ask bluntly.

"Yeah, unfortunately."

"What evidence do you want me to provide?"

"You're on that case now—with two men, right?"

"And a dog, yes. But it's—"

"It's all there," he reveals.

"*What?*" I ask, shaking my head. "I need more than that—I've observed almost all the footage and found nothing."

"This *needs* to appear organic," Silas urges. "I can't tell you where it is. I'm told Lavinia is—not my words, but brilliant. You need a good, honest explanation of how you discovered it."

"Wait," I say curiously. "How did you know about the case I'm on?"

"There's so much to tell you," he responds. "Just not now."

What would happen if I refused? Celest's sacrifice would be for nothing. I'll remain untrustworthy in the agency's eyes (and likely sent to a work camp as punishment for failing Radford's task), especially after my erratic behaviour during her arrest. What if I agree to it? I could be thrown into the lion's den that's Buckingham Palace—and I have no idea what Silas wants me doing there. I'll be doing what Celest wanted, which is good, but something doesn't feel right. This is out of character for her; she wouldn't endanger me. Or would she? Did I know her as well as I thought? Or was she friends with me to keep a foot in the agency's door? *Stop.* I hate myself for even considering it. Everything this man has said may be truthful, but I know *nothing* about him. It's too risky.

"I'm sorry, Silas," I mumble. "I can't do it."

"I understand," he says acceptingly with a gentle nod and stands. "It's a lot to ask, and I'm just some strange bloke that's invaded your home. Listen … I really am sorry, Clara—for everything that's happened tonight—and for putting you in this position. I hope things—you know, get better." He winces. "*Jesus.* Sorry, I'm—I'm not good at this. Goodbye, Clara." He turns to leave and pauses, leaning his forehead against the door.

"Keep going," I instruct.

"I was asked to pass on a message."

"Sure, go ahead."

Silas turns around and clears his throat, and as if scripted, he says, "Stop dwelling on the world's problems. Discover your passion and chase it because the world needs passionate people."

My stomach flutters. Celest would say that to me when my actions at work result in people facing The Crown's wrath—like when I reported a man for insulting a duke and spent hours crying after discovering they executed him. She was always encouraging me to find ways of protecting people from cruel injustice.

"Your name," I respond. "Why did you tell me your real name if you can't trust me?"

"I—I don't know …"

"Is this really what Celest wanted?"

"This was *her* plan," he proclaims. "She genuinely believed in our cause … and you."

Has Celest offered me an opportunity to do something worthwhile? She knew I longed for a purpose, and I don't want to return to my old life—or worse, be sent to the camps. The scarlet heels glow a dangerous shade in the corner of my room, and the photo of Fay on my dresser is urging me to do the right thing, and I think this is it. I want a change—this isn't just for Celest.

"Fine," I blurt out. "I'll do it."

Silas appears shocked. "You will?"

"Wait. If Celest is—oh god"—I can't bring myself to say it—"If Celest is gone … they'll have no one to hang, no one to punish. They won't be interested in my submission for Bright Light."

"They'll use a hologram," Silas confirms. "It's been done before. The audience won't know any different, and that's all they care about."

I'll need to watch her die, even if it's just an image.

"And what happens after I hand Radford the information?" I ask.

"We wait for your invite," Silas responds, now picking his nails and shuffling his feet as if there's more to share.

"Spit it out!" I urge. "Why'd you look so nervous?"

"There's one more thing I want to ask from you," he says gingerly. "Only if you don't mind."

As if he isn't asking for too much already.

"What is it?" I ask.

Silas returns to his seat, pulls a cube-shaped device from his pocket, and plonks it on the table. "I need you to steal intel from the agency."

"*What?* You're mad," I stress, shaking my head. "*Massively* overestimating my abilities. That place is a stronghold. There's no way I'll—"

"We've made arrangements," he reveals. "You'll have a window of opportunity, and this device is untraceable. They'll never know."

"What arrangements?"

"As I said. The less you know, the better," he replies. "Just make sure you're in the women's loos, on the fourth floor, at two fifteen p.m. tomorrow." He strides towards me with a stern expression. "Even if you don't do this, be there."

"If I agree, what is it I need to do?" I ask, and his eyes light up.

Silas runs through the plan—it sounds simple. Once I hand Radford the evidence against Celest, a 'signal' will prompt me to complete my second task. All I need to do is plant a device in one of the server rooms on the twelfth floor. I'll have a clear path with no cameras monitoring my movements. I know the risks, but what other choice do I have? My old life has burned to the ground.

CHAPTER FIVE

No Turning Back

Anticipation grows once again as I ascend the agency's stairs, but it's not as bad as yesterday before my test of fealty—despite the dangerous task I'll soon be completing. I spent most of the early hours pacing my apartment, attempting to make sense of the turbulent events I experienced. I'm trying not to think about losing Celest; this life-changing—or life-ending opportunity will keep me occupied. There'll be time to continue grieving in the future (if I haven't finished already). Now, I must focus on my two tasks—prove Celest's deviance to gain Radford's trust and gather intel for the Folcriht.

Quinlan and Isaac are on duty at the entrance, and I offer them my typically warm greeting. The number of guards on patrol has reduced to normal levels, which is reassuring. What has Silas organised to grant me access to the server room? I can only imagine it being a false alarm, perhaps a small fire.

Entering the office, my colleagues are just as curious as yesterday, and their 'casual' glances in my direction hint that word of my recent experience has spread fast. For an organisation specialising in secrets, it still can't defeat the incessant rumour mill. I don't know how I'll justify my attempt to save Celest to Radford, but my upcoming findings will be enough to achieve her forgiveness and trust. It isn't a coincidence that I have the very case containing Celest's guilt, but the question of who's responsible for assigning it to me remains unanswered. I wouldn't bank on Silas telling me—his enigmatic nature is infuriating. I didn't scrutinise his behaviour until my walk to work this morning—how he dared to trespass on my personal space and ask me to place my life on the line. Nevertheless, he did save me from the enforcers, and in my eyes, he's merely a mouthpiece for Celest, as this is what she wanted. I owe her that much for bringing me happiness … *don't cry, Clara.*

✲✲✲

I feel different about work today. Dare I say, beneath my nerves, I might be enjoying it. Hours have passed of me watching the footage that'll fulfil Celest's dying wish and prove her guilt, but I've found nothing. Though my eyes sting from staring at the screen, and my mind is tired from typing (both accentuated by lack of sleep), I press on. Surprisingly, Radford hasn't visited or called me to her office above. I expected her to question me by now, but she must have bigger problems.

The two men are currently sitting outside a café, nursing a cold drink in a picturesque sculpture park, and as usual, they don't speak a word to each other. They're in a town just outside of London, and their husky is lying on the floor in the shade cast by a table. Small groups walk past, occasionally stopping to chat with someone they know. This is typical behaviour for those outside a city—town and village folk feel more at ease and will socialise without the overwhelming presence of enforcers and marshals.

After speeding up the recording, something catches my attention—it's the dog's behaviour. He'll regularly lift his head from the ground to sniff the air and stare in the same direction for extended periods, where a young man and a woman sit in the path of his gaze. They look like common town folk; he wears a light grey linen suit, and she's in a yellow summer dress, with fashionably styled hair containing braids across her crown. Enjoying each other's company, they hold hands and laugh, oblivious to the dog that's longing for their fuss. It's enough to pique my interest.

I instruct my device to read their lips and transcribe their conversation—allowing it to intrude into the life of what's probably an innocent couple. I often feel guilty for spying on people, and I find no moral justification for it to appease my conscience. In no time, the transcript becomes available:

MALE:

We could plant explosives beneath the stage using chemicals and a time trigger. We can't use a remote one.

FEMALE:

No ... Pen says he might not go on the stage. They change it up yearly to minimise threats.

MALE:

What about planting it in his throne? Triggered by the seat.

FEMALE:

Too risky ... they'll have someone testing it, or it could be triggered when it's moved. Besides, we would never get close to the throne.

MALE:
Pen wants a decent idea by the end of the day. We need time to make the arrangements.
FEMALE:
Mind manipulation. If I can get close to one of the stage workers … I mean really close … I can plant a NeuroLink on them each night for a month. That should be enough time to trigger them in the festival. They'll be close enough to the emperor to kill him, and Pen can plant the weapon.

'Pen' must be Celest—a shortened version of her surname. This is something, but it's not enough, and though we don't need much to establish guilt in the empire, I continue looking for more. The woman fumbles with a pendant around her neck, and zooming in, I instantly recognise it; Celest had lost the same one three weeks ago. This will be enough to appease Radford; no doubt she'll find a way to bolster what I've discovered.

"Claaara!" The melodic voice carries from the distance, and peering over the rows of desks, I find Radford waving in the doorway of a meeting room. Her use of my first name is unnerving.

"Come, darling!"—*'darling', that's even worse*—"We need to chat," she shouts.

Taking gentle steps, I approach. She's caused quite a stir amongst my colleagues, who chatter hushedly as I pass.

"*Get back to work*," Radford hisses at them, oblivious that she's responsible for disturbing the peace. "All of you!"

Entering the room, huge windows display a panoramic view of the Thames.

Radford skips to the table, pulls a chair and motions to it with dramatic effect. "Come! Take a seat."

I force a smile, grasping the tablet to my chest, hiding my trembling hands, and prepare for her behaviour to switch—to scold me for my poor performance last night.

Clearing my throat, I utter, "Th—thank you, ma'am. United in devotion."

"With hearts aligned!" Radford says. "I have been *so* worried. How are you feeling?"

What game is she playing?

"I'm fine," I respond. "Thank you for asking. I should—erm—explain what happened—"

"No explanation required!" she proclaims. "I am *furious* at the operators for interrupting your mission last night—totally out of your control. Believe me, I will punish them appropriately."

"Yes—yes"—*I can justify my actions*—"I was desperately trying to stop them—to make them realise that I didn't have the evidence I needed without—well—blowing my cover."

"That was clear!" Radford says. "But I must say." She leans towards me and whispers, "Using EthoVeraxin on Celest was quite the move"—*EthoVeraxin?*—"I am a huge fan of unconventional methods. I won't pressure you to reveal how you came about it." She attempts to wink in a struggle to instruct her muscles, but it looks more like she has something caught in her eye.

EthoVeraxin is the closest thing you can get to a truth serum—it inhibits specific cognitive processes that enable people to withhold information. I now understand why Celest was becoming increasingly wired after the bar—it wasn't the alcohol—someone planted it in her drink. *But who?*

Radford continues, "I was looking forward to hearing what else that little traitor would spill before those meddling idiots ruined everything"—I beat back the anger that's screaming to escape. She has no respect towards Celest or what's happened to her—"No matter, we can still get the information we need. All I want you to—"

"If I may, ma'am." My interruption startles Radford, but I can't listen to her for one more minute.

"Yes?" she asks curiously.

"I have something." I hand over my tablet displaying the transcript. "It will prove Celest's guilt. It's weak, but it's something."

"Excuse me?" She casts her dark eyes over the transcript suspiciously.

"I'm unsure which terrorist group Celest aligns with," I confirm. "But I'm confident the 'Pen' in this transcript is a shortened version of Celest's surname, and that necklace"—I point at it on the screen, which now displays the couple—"It was Celest's."

"But how did you—"

"I was placed on this case a few weeks ago, ma'am," I respond, shaking my head in phoney disbelief. "It's a—gosh, it's a miracle. I truly believe this was part of God's plan."

Radford is a pious woman, and I hope she sees past the staged coincidence. I tell her of my instructions to observe the two men and how my attention shifted to this couple—I'm pleased Silas didn't tell me what to look for because it's much easier to make this appear plausible.

"Good lord!" she exclaims. "This is—well, it's fantastic. I knew you would make me proud, Clara." Radford is elated, with a smile revealing her perfect set of teeth. "I shall take this and have someone dig further. You take a break"—she leans across the table and awkwardly grips my shoulder—"You have *earned* it."

***

"Clara … Clara?"

Lifting my head from my hands, I find Leo standing beside me in the lunch hall.

"Hey," I reply. "I didn't—sorry, united in devotion."

"With hearts aligned." He takes a seat. "How're you feeling?"

"Tired," I sigh. "I haven't slept. Other than a few hours gifted to me by a lovely enforcer and his stun gun."

"Yeah, I heard about what happened. I just wanted to say I'm sorry." He stares into my eyes, flooding me with empathy. "I'm sorry to hear your friend is a traitor."

I know he doesn't mean it, but being cautious of those listening is crucial.

"Thanks," I reply softly. "It's been—no—I'm delighted to have discovered it." The air around us is like a gloomy cloud, stifling any further words and feeding on our shared misery. "Tell me something that'll cheer me up, please, Leo."

He inhales sharply. "Well, there is something," he declares. "Remember I told you I had a date?"

"Yes!" I gasp. "Of course. How did it go?"

Hunching closer, he whispers, "It was bloody amazing. They were kind, genuine, good looking. We're going on a second date."

Leo continues telling me about his evening with the prospective partner, and he has me laughing at the story of him tripping in the Regal Heritage Museum, only for an ancient suit of armour to catch him. I'm mesmerised by the excitement and passion in his voice, but I feel sadness for Leo—I know his date was with a man. I wish he didn't have to hide his true self out of fear of the ultimate persecution.

✳✳✳

Ten more steps to the women's restroom … I'm almost
there. I reach to open the door, and Radford bounds out—
almost knocking me over.

"Clara!" she gasps. "Perfect timing, I was heading your
way."

"I'm just popping to the loo, ma'am," I respond. "Shall
I meet you there?"

I have one minute until my signal.

"This will only take a moment," she says, shaking her
head. "Anyway, I want to tell you now!" Radford quivers
with a feverish buzz. "So … I had Joseph review the
evidence and follow up on a few things—do you know
Joseph? Short lad with—"

"Yes, I know him."

"Ah, good," she says. "Well, he discovered that one of
the stage workers has recently become acquainted with—
wait—guess who!"

"The woman in the footage?"

"Yes! We're tracking her down. Isn't that fantastic?"

"It is!" I exclaim. "I'm pleased I could—sorry"—I try
shifting around Radford, but she side-steps to block me—
"I'm pleased I could help, ma'am."

"Oh, Clara," she beams. "That is not even the best bit! I
have taken your case and—"

A muffled growl from below us interrupts her. I feel
gentle vibrations beneath my feet, and we both glance down
in confusion. A rumble above us follows it—much louder
this time—and the walls and ceiling tremble violently,
causing Radford to grab my shoulder for balance. Screams
of terror erupt from the main office and penetrate our

surroundings, swiftly followed by the shrill of an alarm. Radford looks at me—her eyes resemble those of a deer caught in the path of a predator, widened, with pupils dilated as if foretelling the impending danger.

BOOM. The blast assaults my senses, and time seems to slow as I witness a shockwave surge down the hall—the force of an invisible bull charging towards us. Both helpless, we're caught in its path, and it hurls Radford into me, launching us through the air in a disorientating whirlwind.

I tumble on the carpeted floor—gasping for breath— with a severe shooting pain in my ears. One is wet with blood, confirmed by my fingers painted red, and it's a distressing sight that adds to my panic. Taking a moment to steady myself, I lie still, allowing my body to recover and regain composure. Radford lies motionless nearby, and with urgency, I crawl towards her and check her pulse, relieved to find signs of life. *So that was my signal.*

Rising to my feet with difficulty, I find balance in the chaos and navigate through the battered hallway—the debris-littered path remains passable. Determined, I stumble into the dimly lit stairwell, where faint lights are flickering, and despite my lingering injuries, I steadily ascend the stairs, occasionally using my hands to support me. Every step is a conscious effort, with intent fully focused on achieving my task. I encounter others fleeing in a frenzied state; the echoes of their hurried footsteps bounce from each wall and travel throughout this vertical tunnel, but I press on—knowing that time is of the essence.

Finally reaching the twelfth floor, my breath is laboured, and my body is weary. The door exiting the stairwell is open—a sign of disruption to the security systems caused by the explosions—just as Silas assured me.

As I enter the hallway, a wave of horror washes over me, forcing an involuntary gasp to escape my lips—the scene is one of utter devastation. Walls have been torn down, leaving jagged edges and exposed infrastructure. Cables hang precariously from the ceiling, swaying like tendrils that long to ensnare their prey, and roof sections are missing.

Drawing closer to the main office floor, my heart sinks. Lifeless bodies of men and women are strewn throughout the area—beneath and above the wreckage. It's a gruesome sight, and I tread with great caution, mindful not to disturb the fallen out of respect for their tragic fate. A metallic tang hangs in the air, blending charred wood and a sharp, chemical smell. Despite my careful steps, I stumble over an object, causing me to jolt forward and inadvertently land on top of a woman's corpse. A wave of guilt and shame washes over me, and I whisper an apology—acknowledging the intrusion. Taking a moment to steady myself, I turn back to see what had caused my stumble—a dismembered leg. The gruesome image sends my stomach into a frenzied revolt, and I struggle to suppress the urge to throw up.

Casting my eyes over the ruin once more with newfound clarity, I realise my subconscious has been shielding a truth from me. The Folcriht—without regard for human life—have detonated a bomb amidst innocent civilians, and the magnitude of this tragedy hits me like the shockwave downstairs. These were people like me, just trying to survive. They were mums, dads, sons, and daughters—their lives snuffed out instantly. Questions of morality linger—what misguided belief led the Folcriht to think such ruthless actions would earn them support? How could they justify the immense suffering they've inflicted on the innocent? I *must* control my thoughts to steel my resolve.

There's more to this mission, and I'm determined to uncover its true purpose—I can't let their deaths be in vain.

Navigating through the debris, I locate and enter the server room. Power to the agency is disrupted, but this space remains illuminated by its servers' glowing lights, casting an array of colours around me. As instructed, I find the singular purple server and attach the device. The colour shifts to green—just as Silas said it would.

Suddenly, shouts echo from outside—growing louder and more intense as they draw nearer to my location. I rush and close the door carefully to avoid alerting them to my presence. Listening to the heavy footsteps thundering past towards the emergency exit, I slide down in relief and slump on the floor, but it isn't long before a gentle push from behind unexpectedly nudges me forward. My body tenses, and I instinctively hold my position, hoping whoever's pushing it will eventually give up and move on—but they don't. A second, stronger push propels me forward, causing me to lose balance and land face down on the ground.

"*Clara?*" Quinlan stands over me in bewilderment.

His swarmers—the deadly mechanical creatures—encircle his body mid-air; their metallic forms are poised for any potential attack. The sight sends a chill of fear coursing through my veins, and I clamber backwards, desperate to distance myself from him.

"No, no!" he exclaims, holding his hands out. "Don't worry!" Quinlan's voice is filled with reassurance and concern, and the swarm gravitates towards him, streaming up his sleeves and disappearing from sight. "Sorry, I didn't mean to frighten you," he says ruefully, extending his hand to help me off the ground.

With a mix of caution and trust, I reach out—allowing him to pull me back to my feet.

"Thank his grace, you're here!" I exclaim. "Sorry—I—I'm just—*what's happening?*" I put on an award-winning act, hoping Quinlan wouldn't question me hiding in a room I'm not allowed to be in.

"Someone planted bombs in the agency," he responds, flustered. "I'm looking for survivors. You need to get out, Clara. We don't know if there are—"

He peers nosily over my shoulder, and I turn around to see the server is now flashing blue—indicating the download is complete. Without uttering a word, he passes me and approaches the anomaly, taking a moment to inspect it with scrutiny before finding and removing the compact device. The server shifts back to a steady purple glow.

Returning with the data-filled cube, Quinlan asks hesitantly, "Is this yours?"

He struggles to maintain eye contact, and I sense his deep disappointment. Quinlan may be naïve, but he's not stupid, and I have more chance at forgiveness and escape if I show him some respect.

"It is," I respond shamedly. "I'm—"

"And the bombs?" he snaps, turning red.

"No! I didn't—I had no idea they were—"

"What is it downloading?" he demands.

"I'm unsure, Quinlan—look … I'm sorry. If I—please could—"

I'm lost for words; my heart is racing, and sweat drips from my forehead, shortly accompanied by clenched fists as Quinlan's swarmers creep from his sleeves and take to the air, hovering around him. I stare into his rageful eyes, silently pleading for mercy.

Thud … thud … thud …. The heavy footsteps approach from behind—like dark omens—causing my legs to tremble.

A deep, cold voice pierces the air, sending a shiver up my spine. "Put your swarm away, Quinlan," Isaac commands.

In this moment, all hope of escape fades away, replaced by a daunting realisation that Isaac will never let me go. Quinlan complies, and the swarmers return to him, concealed from view once more. I gulp and turn around reluctantly to face my punisher.

I had a teacher—Mr Johnson—in the agency's academy (where I studied from the age of eleven), and his favourite method of punishment was 'the vacuum'. It was a tiny, pitch-black room where he removed the air randomly, starving you of oxygen and allowing you to brush death's imminent embrace. Rumours of children suffocating to death would often float throughout the academy, and it should've been enough to deter any misbehaviour. I was always fearful as a child but also reckless. Once, Mr Johnson caught me whispering to Celest during a hive psychology exam, and his penetrating glare gripped me with terror because I knew I was destined to meet the vacuum.

Isaac's stare reminds me of that moment, and I'm thrust into the mind of my fearful younger self. Lowering my head to face the ground, my legs are trembling, and my breathing is shallow—there's nothing I can do.

Isaac raises his hand and beckons me towards him. "Come here, Clara," he demands. "Now."

I inch forward, but swarmers burst from Isaac's sleeve before I can react, wrapping me in their dark embrace. In the prison of this storm, I clench my eyes shut, every muscle is tense, and my throat traps a scream—but I feel nothing, and it shouldn't take this long for them to tear me apart. *Am I dead?*

Colours dance behind my closed eyelids, and I hear a faint gasp and thump behind me, so I turn around to be confronted by Quinlan, who lies crumpled on the floor; an expression of horror mixed with confusion is carved onto his once warm and friendly face, and a gaping hole in his chest reveals the absence of his once-beating heart.

I whip around and face Isaac in disbelief. His expression remains stoic as he claims control over the swarm once more.

"Quin was a good lad," Isaac sighs. "He didn't deserve that."

"But … why did you—"

"No time," he says. "You were never here. I'll deliver the drive."

"Wh—what do I do now?" I stutter, battling my shock.

"*Get out.*"

CHAPTER SIX

An Unexpected Visit

Two days have passed since the agency bombings, and strict instructions confine me to my apartment, as they do for everyone else working there. Medics didn't take long to determine my wounds weren't severe, allowing me to return home. Many others suffered worse injuries, like broken bones, burns, and the loss of limbs—then there were those who died. Radford was nowhere to be found when I returned to the fourth floor, though I later discovered she was treated in hospital and has made a speedy recovery. I did, however, stumble across the disorientated Leo, who was doing his best to help others.

Someone detonated the bombs on three floors. Whilst the ground and fourth floor suffered their share of destruction, the final explosion remodelled the twelfth floor into a haunting gallery of death. The scene remains etched in my mind—a chilling display of bodies scattered like sculptures, frozen in eternal agony. Then there's Quinlan—I imagined this cruel world would simply dampen his zeal, but it killed him. Or was that me?

Something has been niggling at me since the event, and I'm not proud of it, but exhilaration lingers beneath my sorrow and guilt.

My SyncLink rings—it's Radford. We haven't spoken since the attack. I instruct it to answer, and her sharp face manifests in the corner of my room. Thanks to the wonders of our renowned Imperial Health Service, there are no signs of her recent injuries.

"United in devotion, ma'am," I say.

"With hearts aligned," she responds. "How are you feeling, Clara?"

"Blessed by his reign. Thank you for asking. How are—"

"It's fantastic." She shakes her head. "Only fifteen people dead. Still, I despise giving those fanatics even that satisfaction. They truly are neanderthals—planting bombs in locations that even a child would know are disused." She scoffs. "Except for the twelfth floor. It's strange; I would think—never mind—listen!" She becomes excitable. "I referred your case to the Harvest division …"

I stare blankly, suddenly realising she's keen for a reaction, so I shuffle eagerly to the edge of my seat. "What an honour! Thank you, ma'am!"

"Between you and me," she says with a smirk. "I think it's Bright Light worthy." Raising her chin, Radford looks like someone who's just won a prize.

"My gosh … that would be—I don't know what to say!" I cry out, throwing my hands in the air. "I couldn't have—well—I'm thankful for your mentorship."

"Take a week off. You should go on that trip you were planning with Celest." She snorts. "A lucky escape if you ask me. Imagine holidaying with a traitor!"

"Yeah …" I strain a chuckle, heat rushing my cheeks. "Imagine that. Never alone."

"Blessed by his presence."

***

Laying my clothes out neatly on the bed, I assess each item to ensure it'll suit the vibe of a small town. With Radford's permission to travel, I've decided to visit my sister, Fay. It's been too long since we last saw each other, and although our communication has dwindled over time, I ache for her company—especially since losing Celest. I want to surprise her—she won't expect my arrival, but I know she'll welcome me with open arms. It's in her nature.

I've had plenty of time to reflect over the last two days, and it's allowed me to recognise that I've distanced myself from her, cutting off our connection, and all because of the shame I feel for working in the agency. Oddly, my guilt for those who died in the bombings is lighter than my guilt for serving the empire, which makes me conflicted.

I pack an assortment of classic summer dresses, which I'm satisfied don't scream city girl. I appreciate their flowy design from the waist down, allowing free movement—but they're a hellish assortment of floral patterns and pastel colours.

***

An eery atmosphere hangs over the streets of London as I head towards the station. The pounding of marshal's boots will often disrupt the stillness—they're on high alert following the attack on the agency. Those brave enough to leave their apartments are tottering around with their heads bowed—each reminding me of a wilted flower, exhausted by the heavy strain of suppression and fear.

I, however, am feeling invincible. Each passerby receives a joyous greeting and warm smile—I don't know why I feel this way; perhaps it's the adrenaline following the events or a subconscious coping mechanism quelling my underlying grief and stress.

Unsurprisingly, there's a queue to enter the station, and everyone patiently waits for enforcers to interview and permit them to travel—well, almost everyone.

"YOU CAN'T CONTROL ME LIKE THIS," a woman screams, jabbing her finger in the enforcer's face who denied her the privilege to leave the city. "WHY'RE YOU TREATING ME LIKE A CRIMINAL?" As two enforcers drag the woman away, the queue stirs with discomfort at the unnerving scene. "THEY WANT—" She's promptly muzzled and thrown into a black van.

People in the front become increasingly twitchy and distinctly frustrated, and a muttering hum grows louder. It's contagious, riding down the queue towards me like a wave. Adults start shouting whilst small children look puzzled at the commotion—this sudden shift in their mood is startling, but it finally hits me. A pungent and acrid odour fills my nose, carrying the scent of burnt sulphur and smouldering embers, flashing the image of a destructive fire that consumes everything in its path. Quickly recognising what's happening, I promptly distance myself from the crowd and its growing tension—it's like an overly inflated balloon ready to pop.

The Folcriht are using scent control to invoke anger, and I watch the once orderly queue transform into a riot at a safe distance where the smells can't overrule my inhibitions.

The crowd has grouped, surging forward like an unyielding tide that crashes against the barricade of enforcers protecting the station's entrance. The occasional green flash batters the dense wave, indicating the enforcers' attempts to stun and weaken their collective strength—but it's futile as the potent scent captures more people in its influence. It's a chaotic yet admirable sight, different to when I watched the riots in Canada a few days ago—this fight is worthy.

Before long, reinforcements arrive. Marshals are marching in organised rows through the street—ploughing through anyone who stands in their way. Those leading the small army hold large energy shields, and the rows behind them carry massive guns. With hammering footsteps like a drumbeat, they chant: "SUBMIT OR SUFFER." The harmonious thunder would usually subdue the fiercest riot, but this group are beyond control.

With the marshals in position, the second row rests their guns on the shoulders of the shield bearers. The rioters' intentions shift from gaining entry to the station to the new arrivals that aim to stifle their dissent and establish obedience, and everything is tense as each side becomes a coiled spring. Suddenly, the rioters shatter the deathly silence, unleashing a mighty battle cry while charging towards the newly formed blockade. In response, the well-equipped marshals release bolts of red lightning that crackle through the air. The shots find their targets, ricocheting through the mass of people with chilling accuracy. Agonising screams engulf the area as bodies drop to the ground, writhing in pain. The once defiant group is instantly immobilised, their resistance quashed in a brutal and swift display of force.

As I witness the unfolding terror, a profound realisation hits me—joining forces with the Folcriht means subjecting myself to even more pain and suffering than I'm used to. I may even find myself responsible for inflicting it upon others, but I must confront and accept this harsh reality to continue this path, or it'll slowly eat away at me.

Taking a deep breath, I refuse to avert my attention from the horrifying scene. Men and women are thrashing around like a school of fish out of the water, and all I hear are their distressed screams and pleas for help. Hapless children—unaffected by scent control—observe their parents' suffering. Some cry, whilst others cover their ears and squeeze their eyes shut. I lift my head high, reminding myself of the end that *must* justify the means.

❋❋❋

I don't get out of the city enough, and it's not for lack of travel credits because I'm incredibly well-behaved—or used to be, at least. It's because the distress of returning to London always trumps the ounce of enjoyment I get from being away.

The train flies me through the picturesque English countryside to Amberleigh—where Fay lives. As the landscape unfolds alongside the tracks, dazzling wildflowers greet my eyes. Bursting with life, red poppies sway together in the gentle breeze, and lush forests stand defiant in the distance, offering a sanctuary to wildlife. The glimpse of a deer darting through the undergrowth or a fleeting bird soaring across the sky adds a touch of untamed beauty to the scene.

Before I can fully immerse myself in this idyllic daydream, the train plunges into darkness, entering a tunnel. Caution permeates the air as its pace slows, navigating the obscurity carefully. Emerging, I enter a realm of eerie darkness as thick trees twist and wind over the tracks—their branches block most of the sunlight, casting an ominous shadow that engulfs this new and mysterious realm I've entered. The train slows, allowing me to take in the haunting scenes that unfold before me.

An abandoned town comes into view—its once lively streets reduced to ruins. Dilapidated buildings are grim reminders of a bustling past, with shattered windows and walls plastered with messages of defiance. Deliberately placed throughout the town square are piles of human bones; they serve as a stark reminder of the lives lost to a doomed cause. Even the bones of children have a designated space on this grim display, illustrating the ultimate price they paid for the actions of their mums and dads.

Amidst the ruins, a gleaming marble statue of King James III stands defiant, its presence taking centre stage. Surrounding the figure are miniature sculptures depicting men, women, and children, all bowing with their heads lowered in submission. The train comes to a halt before the graphic display because it's more essential to strip its passengers of any foolish desire for change than get them to their destination five minutes earlier. I reluctantly read the accompanying message that seeks to reveal its significance:

'Here stands King James III, triumphant against the treasonous vermin of Briarford. Concealing themselves in the shadows, they sought to block his light and cast darkness over England.
May we remember the consequence of choosing a path of destruction.'

Instead of succumbing to fear—the sight feeds my fire. With renewed determination, I press onwards, leaving the shadowy forest behind.

✳✳✳

Amberleigh, a town constructed a mere decade ago, bears a striking resemblance to London (albeit on a much smaller scale). Also inspired by the eighteenth century, the white stone buildings are symmetrical, boasting a blend of proportion and elegance. The absence of enforcers and the scarcity of people create a peculiar mix of liberation and unease.

The station is perched on a hill, affording me a panoramic view of the town below as I walk towards my destination. An intimidating yet magnificent white church in the town centre is the first thing to demand my attention. Its sheer size, with a stately face and grand columns, demonstrates its authority over the town's people. The godly building balances a bell tower stretching towards the heavens.

Climbing down the church's polished stone steps, you would enter a spacious market square that's filled with food stalls and bordered by charming shops and restaurants. In its centre is a gilded statue of Emperor Magnus II, who's illuminated by a heavenly beam of light radiating from the church—as if it's bestowing him divine power to validate his reign. Rich vines crawl from the ground, wrapping the lower portion of his legs—as if to forge an inseparable bond between the emperor and nature itself. Though I can't see from this distance, I've no doubt he's wearing a sleazy-looking smirk with his hands behind his back.

As I navigate the labyrinthine streets, I rely on my SyncLink to guide me through the unfamiliar setting. This town, unlike any I've visited, has a weird vibe. People I encounter—usually friendly outside a city—cast perplexed looks and exchange hushed whispers as I pass. The town is a shrine devoted to worshipping the emperor, with imperial flags fluttering from almost every building and ornate metal sculptures proudly displaying symbols of loyalty and allegiance. The worst I've seen is an exhibit in someone's window of him kneeling on the ground and feeding a load of plump children from the palm of his hand—like you would feed a farm animal. I'd love to climb into these peoples' minds to understand the extent of their delusion.

A man stops abruptly and watches me from across the road, and he doesn't even try hiding his bafflement, with his mouth agape like I've got my skirt tucked into my knickers. He grabs a poor girl who was merrily skipping past and minding her own business to whisper in her ear. She nods and darts out of sight through an alley. I'm suddenly attuned to the palpable twitchiness lingering in these streets, causing my body to stiffen as I continue my journey, acutely aware of the heightened interests of those around me.

Fay's house nestles itself deep inside the stone maze; beautiful and ornate terraced buildings rise from either side of her street, each composed of several storeys with evenly spaced sash-framed windows. I stand at her door and wait as minutes pass without a stir from inside—either the house isn't informing her I've arrived, or she's not in, so I tap an old-fashioned door knock against the wood—just in case.

A figure approaches—growing more prominent through the frosted glass—and Fay's look of shock finally greets me. Silent as a mouse, the word "Surprise" escapes my lips, followed by a surge of emotions that rush into me and overflow into tears. Overcome by the weight I've been carrying, I take a step forward, only to crumble under the immense release, and just as I'm about to hit the ground, Fay swiftly catches me in her arms, offering a familiar and comforting embrace. We sit here for a moment, with her warmth and tenderness nurturing me.

"C'mon, I'll make you a cuppa," she says once I gain composure, her velvety voice wrapping around me. "Something tells me you need a chat."

With Fay's support, I rise from the ground and follow her into the kitchen. It's a beautiful open space, bathed in the warm glow of sunlight streaming through the windows. Sitting on a breakfast bar stool, I watch Fay prepare our drinks.

"Blonde suits you," I say. You couldn't tell the difference between us if it wasn't for our different hair colours.

"Thanks," she responds. "It's because—well, I just fancied a change."

Fay smiles and places a warm cup of tea before me, which I accept, but not without throwing her a perplexed look (which she ignores). I won't ask why she lied about the reason for dying her hair because it winds her up when I catch her out.

"When you're ready," she says, grasping my hands. "Start from the beginning."

Drawing a deep breath, I gather my thoughts and recount my story, starting from the killing of Max and the capture of Rachel and Aria. I tell her about my interrogation at work, the impossible task that Radford chucked at me, and my desperate attempts to buy time, ultimately leading to Celest's capture and her brutal demise. I finish with the attack on the agency. Still, I hold back on sharing further details, avoiding the dangerous territory that could place Fay at risk—like how I've been collaborating with the Folcriht and the evidence on Celest I handed to Radford. She doesn't even realise she could be in the company of this year's Bright Light.

Fay sits in silence—deep in contemplation—her grip tightens around my hand.

"Oh, Clara," she chokes, leaning closer. "I'm so, *so* sorry. Celest was a beautiful person. She didn't deserve—oh god." Fay is welling up, prompting me to do the same. She continues, "I always worry about you in that bloody city, but Celest, she—knowing she was with you put me at ease. I'm pleased you came."

"I was nervous about visiting," I admit.

"*Why?*" she asks, shaking her head.

"I'm a rubbish sister," I respond, lowering my gaze to the table. "And I don't make enough effort. I'm sorry."

"You have *nothing* to be sorry for. You're always welcome—you know that! Tell me how you're feeling after sharing it all."

"Oh god. You're not going all counsellor on me, are you?"

"I'm going all sister on you," she sighs. "I don't get to do it often!" Her expression shifts to something more earnest. "Listen, there's something you're not telling me … right?"

"What makes you think that?" I ask, lifting my head to meet her suspicious expression.

"Because I *know* you," she stresses. "I see it—in your eyes. You want to tell me more."

I do, but I can't place you in danger. "No. There's nothing else. Perhaps I—I don't know, I've just been dealing with a lot."

"This is a safe space, you know. *I don't even have a SyncLink.*"

"Listen … there's really nothing—"

"I tell you what," she declares, sitting upright. "Let's turn this into a proper session." Fay clears her throat and recites, "In my presence and *only* by his grace, you are free to share your honest thoughts without fear of condemnation—or punishment! You are a *respected subject*, and I am here to help you through *any* challenge so that you may return to a *happy* and *fulfilled* life."

I stare at her—dumbfounded. "Is that supposed to make me feel better?"

We both break down into a fit of laughter.

"Look, I do my best with what I'm given, alright?"

I won't burden her with this secret. I could never forgive myself if something happened to Fay. Besides, I'd be betraying the Folcriht.

***

"Tempted to move here yet?" Fay asks.

We're lying on the soft grass, with the gentle breeze caressing my skin and the vast expanse of the night sky displayed like a cosmic canvas. I'm mesmerised by the constellations that flicker across the indigo backdrop. Each twinkling star holds its own story, whispering from the depths of the universe.

"Do you think they'll notice if I don't return?" I respond, half serious.

Fay and I spent the afternoon and evening lost in each other's company. She took me on a tour of Amberleigh, highlighting its unique attractions. We visited the traditional-style sweet shop filled with tempting treats and the Farmers Market that offers fresh, local produce. We shared laughter and amusement as we explored the clothing stores, noting the stark contrast in fashion compared to the city. The women here float around like petals in the wind. They don delicate floral dresses, whilst the men sport three-piece suits, determined to prove their importance, even in the sweltering heat. As we explored the streets, I noticed a change in the townspeople's reaction to me being here—no longer did they cast perplexed looks my way. Fay knows everyone, and we paused frequently to engage in friendly small talk. We spent the remainder of the evening in this park nestled by a gentle river, feeding the ducks and basking in the warm embrace of the early evening sun.

"C'mon … we should head back," she yawns. "I'll make you a hot chocolate, and we'll get you tucked in."

❋❋❋

"Well, don't you look delicious!" Fay proclaims, beaming at me while she slices freshly baked bread.

"Sickly sweet," I respond miserably.

Taking Fay's advice, I wear a light-yellow dress with a pleated skirt, and I've styled my hair with half a ponytail so some of it can frame my face, which somehow makes me look five years younger—precisely what's expected of the women attending church.

"I know, it's crap," she acknowledges. "But God forbid we enter the church looking like old hags. We'd combust on the spot! Here, a coffee will cheer you up."

"Cheers," I respond, taking a sip. "I haven't been to a service in years,"

"Oh yeah … I forgot you city lot watch it in bed," Fay scoffs. "Do you still get travel credits for watching it?"

"Yup, and a beating if we miss it."

"That sounds fair," she responds sarcastically and downs her coffee. "Let's go."

We leave Fay's house and join the vibrant stream of churchgoers; their conversations create a lively atmosphere. Unlike the marches in London, here in Amberleigh, the people are chatty and less disciplined, which adds to the sense of liberation. As we make our way through the streets, the crowd swells in size, the sound of chatter growing louder as more individuals leave their homes to join the procession towards the church—it doesn't take us long to get there.

Stepping inside, a spacious and light-filled hall welcomes me. The high, arched ceiling soars above the aisle, and large windows cast a warm, inviting glow on the ornate woodwork and artfully crafted pews. The crowd's babble falls silent—a sign of respect for this sacred space, and we find our seats and settle in as more people enter. The grand doors close with an almighty thud, shutting off the outside world and signalling the priest who's hobbling up to the podium; each of his delayed and shaky steps is hitting the wood and bouncing off the walls in this cavernous space. I can't wait to hear what nonsense they feed you in this town.

"My strong rams! Lovely ewes! And sweet little lambs." His deep trombone-like voice doesn't match his paper-thin form. "*Welcome* to this gathering as we congregate on this blessed Sunday morning. We seek solace and strength within these hallowed walls today, for our neighbours in the Capital have fallen victim to the hate-fuelled and sinful actions of the radicals."

The assembly hiss, including Fay, causing me to involuntarily shudder—the hairs on my arms stand upright. Two rows ahead, one man sits with his arms crossed and is bobbing up and down as if amused. The priest is quick to notice and silently tells him off with scolding eyes; the man lowers his head in submission. These town folk certainly have it easier than us; he'd be whisked away and dangled upside from the church's tower if it were London.

The priest continues, "Though our spirits may be weary and our hearts burdened by such tragedies, we find *refuge* and *hope* in our almighty king and emperor. In this age of uncertainty, where the echoes of greed resonate through our land, we gather here not merely as individuals … but as a united body, bound by our shared devotion to the divine. Let us cast aside the worries that weigh upon us, pray for him to smite those who deserve it, and find solace in the sanctuary of this holy space.

We must remember that our faith remains unshaken *even* in the face of adversity. Our king-emperor watches over us with benevolent eyes. He offers guidance, nourishment, *and strength*. It is within the embrace of his love and grace that we find our purpose and resilience.

May our worship be a testament to our loyalty, may our collective faith serve as an unbreakable bond to our ideals, and may God's mercy and blessings be upon us all. Amen."

"Amen," the crowd echoes.

"Now," the priest says, clapping his hands. "Join me in singing our anthem of allegiance."

The organ's solemn chords fill the hall, and for what must be the thousandth time, I join the chorus:

> *"O hail, O hail, our almighty king,*
> *In whom our loyalty shall forever sing,*

In your name, our hearts are steeled,
To you, our king, our devotion sealed.

O by your grace, fuelled with love,
We admire you, standing above,
In unity, we mount, our loyalty proclaimed,
To our king, our hopes and dreams are named.
Your wisdom and justice, our guiding light,
For you, we march with honour and might.

O Anthem of Allegiance, solid and true,
Our voices join in praise to you,
With unwavering faith, we take our stand,
Defending the ideals of our honourable lands,
In this precious world, we hold fast,
To the vision of a future that shall outlast."

With the hall falling silent once again, the priest continues his service. In parts, he invites people to the front so they may offer a story of their devotion to the emperor or confess a sin they've committed for all to hear. One man speaks of his desire to own a classic car and the shame of knowing it would pollute the planet. He talks about the steps taken to avoid fulfilling his desire—taking comfort in knowing he has everything needed to survive, but only by the emperor's grace. Penance here is another example of the contrast between Amberleigh and London; instead of a prolonged lashing, a few members take turns to lightly slap his cheek. I'm not complaining; it's easier to endure, but what's the point?

***

I always despised attending church as a young girl. I had much better things to do, like getting stuck into my mum's collection of illegal history books or practising how best to style my hair.

Settling at a table in the bustling square, the breeze carries the buttery aroma of freshly baked goods. Fay suggested we indulge in pastries from the café, a reward for our pious behaviour this morning. Attending church in the city is reserved for the upper classes, but it's open to everyone in the towns and villages. As we enjoy breakfast, Fay and I recollect our childhood, when we would feign illness so our parents would let us stay in bed to avoid the Sunday service. Revisiting these memories of simpler times and the blissful ignorance of our youth brings a smile to my face.

A husky appears out of nowhere and perches next to Fay. With a wagging tail, the dog is eager for her cuddles. She attempts to casually shoo him away, but he remains firmly in place; his tongue sticks out, and his chest rises and falls rapidly with each excitable breath. Curious, I lean down to observe him more closely, and a familiarity creeps up on me. His markings and mannerisms resemble the very same dog in the footage that confirmed Celest's involvement with the Folcriht. I beckon him over to take a closer look (and because he's adorable), but he shows no interest in me—just in Fay.

"Fay?" I ask curiously, raising my eyebrows.

"Hmm?" she responds nervously. It's as if her features are poised on a tightrope, delicately balancing the weight of her unease whilst desperately trying to maintain a casual performance.

I scan the square and notice a handful of people directing concerned expressions towards us, just for them to look elsewhere once I catch them. I follow the direction of their newfound focus, and it leads me to an archway in the distance, where a man's formidable figure lurks in the shadow. He steps forward, revealing his messy hair, weathered face, and untamed beard—it's Silas.

A wave of revelation causes me to catch my breath, and I look at Fay, who now wears a shameful expression. As Silas approaches, his presence grows larger and larger until he pulls a chair beside us and takes a seat. The weight of this situation settles heavily upon me.

"He wasn't supposed to—" Fay stutters. "I—I was waiting for the right time to tell you, Clara." She throws Silas a cutting glance. "*Not* like this."

"It's Bruno's fault." Silas shrugs. "You know he's a free spirit." He turns to face me, and with a grin, he says, "Hello again."

CHAPTER SEVEN

Amberleigh

It's incredible how shock can bind you in place. Though I won't take long to process this news, right now, my thoughts are spiralling, struggling to rationalise the unfolding situation.

I flick between Silas and Fay before me, who both apprehensively await my backlash like a couple that have announced they're committing adultery. I grapple with conflicting emotions, doing my best to resolve the feeling of betrayal with the belief that Fay wouldn't act maliciously by withholding her involvement with the Folcriht—after all, I kept my involvement with them a secret from her. Silas adds a layer of complexity, and I'm questioning my role, almost feeling like a puppet in a larger show controlled by unseen puppeteers. I'd rehearsed my reunion with Silas, like all the questions to ask and how to share my dissatisfaction with his radical actions, but this unforeseen turn of events has thrown it all out of my mind.

"I was going to tell you, Clara. I promise," Fay urges, breaking the silence. "I wanted to tell you last night. That's why I was pressing you to share more." She faces Silas and says, "She kept it a secret. Didn't say a word." Then, she turns to me again. "Listen, I've been with the Folcriht for over two years. After The Crown executed my friend during a Harvest, I went looking for them. She had a dispute with her neighbour, who falsified evidence that she was smuggling petrol across county lines. I just"—Fay begins sobbing—"the look of terror—her lifeless body. I was desperate."

"It's—I'm confused," I respond, shaking my head. "First Celest, *now* you? I feel so stupid."

"Don't," Fay says. "I didn't know Celest was Folcriht either."

"She was a deep agent," Silas adds. "Only Cas and Lawrence know their identities."

"Cas and Lawrence?" I ask.

"You'll meet them soon," he says.

"So, you had nothing to do with Celest's plan?" I ask Fay.

"No!" she exclaims. "I found out a couple of days ago, and I wouldn't place you in danger—I mean, I'm sure Celest had a good reason."

"It's strange." I lean back and take a bite from my croissant. "I kinda wish you'd told me sooner. Don't get me wrong, I'm still getting over losing Celest, but these past two days—I've never felt so *alive*."

Fay appears both staggered and relieved at my sudden casual demeanour. "I—I know the feeling."

"Wait! I get it now!" I blurt out.

"What?" Fay asks.

"Your hair," I respond smugly. "You were lying when you said you fancied a change. You dyed it so people would know the difference between us in case I visited."

"Yep," she snickers. "I still like it though."

A second—but now dire—realisation hits me, causing me to lunge forward and whisper, *"We're talking too loud."*

Being blindsided by Silas has made me forget to be vigilant, and it's a skill I've spent years nurturing in the city—*how could I be so careless?*

Fay snorts, and Silas's chest rumbles in amusement.

With his voice raised, he announces, "Someone might hear that we're Folcriht!"

"Shhhhh—"

"Clara!" Fay's now in hysterics. "Surely you see that everyone here is Folcriht?"

What? How? I glance around at the people going about their everyday lives. A man at the table closest to us is snickering. He winks and waves.

"Everyone?" I ask.

"Bloody brilliant, right?" Silas responds proudly. "You don't even know the half of it. Fay, d'you mind if I borrow your sister?"

"Clara?" she asks, checking with me first.

This man is responsible for almost blowing me up just a few days ago—killing many of my colleagues—he owes me an explanation.

I nod. "I'm good. I'll meet you back at yours."

Fay stands and hugs me from behind, whispering a final apology in my ear and affectionate words before beckoning Bruno to join her—leaving Silas and me alone. I sit up straight, crossing my legs and folding my arms, locking my eyes directly on his. Silas shifts with discomfort under my scrutiny, and the silence hangs heavily between us—each moment stretching out as I wait for him to break it with an explanation or response.

"What do—why're you looking at me like that?" he asks nervously.

"You know exactly why!" I stress. *He can't be this clueless, surely.*

"Wha—it's not a huge deal … is it?"

"Not a huge deal?" How is he so comfortable with killing people?

"Fay would've told you—today, probably!" he responds boldly. "And I didn't realise you were in the square. I'm sorry."

Is this man for real? I throw the remainder of my croissant at him. "I'm talking about the bombings!" I hiss. "You killed fifteen people, Silas!"

"Ah shit," he sighs, looking flustered and genuinely remorseful. "Sorry, I—it's not right. I'm not proud of it. I forget sometimes—forget it's a big deal … ya know?"

"No. I don't know," I respond bluntly. "You almost killed me! *I was tripping over peoples' limbs.* You haven't even told me if you got the intel you wanted!"

"We got it," he says, picking out the croissant crumbs from his hair. "Thank you, Clara. Listen, those bombs they—there was an issue with the twelfth floor. We never wanted to kill anyone. They were supposed to knock out security and create a diversion, but our guy on the inside ran into problems. He—he had to hide the bomb under a bloody desk."

"By the guy on the inside, you mean Isaac, right?" I ask.

"Yeah."

"You're lucky I can handle surprises," I say casually. "But now's the time to tell me what else I'm missing. Surely you trust me—I mean, that's why you almost killed me when you could've just asked Isaac."

"Let me show you one more surprise, c'mon." He stands up.

I shoot him a disapproving look before reluctantly agreeing to follow.

Silas continues as we cross the square, "I didn't ask you to gather that intel to prove your trustworthiness. I already knew."

"Then why put me at risk?"

"Ah, it wasn't a risk. I knew Isaac would have your back. I needed to see if you were up to it." He sighs. "You know there'll be more of that—death and stuff."

"Mmm … I suspected as much. How many people live here?"

"Almost twenty thousand. We keep up appearances so tourists don't become suspicious, and the mayor is responsible for relocation admissions. That means we choose who lives here."

"And the enforcers?"

"They're all Folcriht." He gently grasps my arm, and we stop beside an ornate fountain—the running water is soothing. "Listen, I gotta say this. Fay never wanted to put you at risk. We've wanted to recruit you for ages, but she insisted against it—to keep you safe."

"But when they caught Rebecca and Max, I was placed in danger … finally giving you an excuse to recruit me."

"Exactly."

"You want me in the Harvest Ball," I respond, visibly perplexed. "I'm jumping from the frying pan and into the fire."

"Fair point," he says, with an acquiescent look.

"And why is it you want me at the ball?" I ask. "Wait—don't tell me … to assassinate the emperor."

"No," Silas responds. "As great as it sounds."

"*Then why?*"

"Cas thinks you're the key to sparking a coup."

"Oh yeah?" I mock. "I can't wait to meet him. How'd he figure that?"

"Do you know anyone else who can literally read people's minds?" he asks rhetorically.

"I don't know who you've been speaking to, but I'm not a mind reader. I can just tell when someone's lying."

"That's good enough," he says. "You're the only person that could find a weak link in his privy council. You'll have exclusive time with them—at the dinner and ball. Then, you can figure out who's *most* likely to turn. Imagine it! You could be responsible for tearing it down from the inside."

I don't mirror Silas's passion. "It sounds like a terrible plan." My blunt response kicks him in the gut, and I feel slightly bad. "But I'll humour this Cas bloke."

We enter the same traditional sweet shop that Fay showed me yesterday—the air is thick with the scent of sugar, caramel, and chocolate. Jars are filled with sweets and stacked on shelves from floor to ceiling. Silas nods at the shopkeeper and growls, "Morning Ben."

"Sir," the shopkeeper responds while filling a glass jar with liquorice.

"*Sir?*" I ask.

"Yeah," he responds. "I'm the Folcriht's commander-in-chief and Minister of Defence."

"Aren't you a bit too important to be recruiting me?"

"I hope you're worth it. No pressure." He winks and notices me eyeing a jar of chocolate buttons. "Take some!" he says. "We produce ammunition for the empire, which grants us some luxuries—along with a few random inspections courtesy of the Domestic Security Agency. But if we play our part, they never suspect a thing. They're too ignorant."

Silas pauses before a display shelf, his palm pressed against the side, and after a few seconds, a mechanism clicks, causing it to lower into the ground—unveiling a cramped space barely large enough to accommodate two people. He steps inside and turns to face me.

"Sorry, it's a bit cosy," he says, scrunching his face.

"Hold on. What—where …?" I'm too perplexed to string a sentence.

Silas holds his hand out. "Trust me."

Tentatively, I step inside, forced to face away from him to squeeze in—his massive frame dominates most of the space. As the shelf rises from the ground, it encloses us in this cramped compartment, bathed in the soft glow of blue light overhead.

The smooth descent continues for what feels like an eternity. Silas's warmth pressing against my body creates an unfamiliar sense of safety. His breath grazes the back of my neck, causing goosebumps to ripple up my arms, igniting an excitement within me. As he shuffles back to create more space—out of respect, I assume—his body brushes against mine, setting my heartbeat racing. *What's wrong with me?* For some inexplicable reason, I find myself exhilarated.

The lift eventually comes to a halt. I leap out, taking a deep breath to steady myself before fully comprehending my new surroundings. Unable to conceal my astonishment, I eagerly examine the sights. That tiny box has transported me into the belly of an immense dome. Lights reflect off its polished metal surface to create a bright and lively atmosphere, and the vastness of this space makes me feel miniature.

A towering spiral staircase ascends through its centre, bolstering platforms on multiple levels that branch out in various directions and encircle the colossal cavern. Hundreds—no, thousands of determined people dart around with purpose. Each level accommodates multiple rooms and entrances, forming a complex network of tunnels that burrow deeper underground. On some walls, images resembling windows project scenes from the outside world.

"The Folcriht's Fort," Silas declares, recovering from the cramped journey down with a stretch. "The old government built it over one hundred and fifty years ago, back when it was the United Kingdom. They were preparing for a nuclear war. Russia was fighting with a few smaller European countries, and it was gaining more support from other superpowers. Ministers were getting twitchy, so they built three underground bunkers to protect two hundred thousand people in case of some doomsday nuclear event."

I remain cemented in place, but he nudges me forward and continues his story, "It was a top-secret project. Only a handful of senior politicians knew, and they cut the construction staff off from their friends and families. Not even the monarchy was aware.

The cost to build them drove the country into poverty—it was on the verge of bankruptcy. Loads of people lost their jobs and homes, and a few bastards became filthy rich. People were getting fed up, making it easier for King James to gain support. When he got absolute power, the government evacuated the boffins and military personnel into these facilities, hoping they could build a resistance strong enough to topple the monarchy. We've modified it through the years, attempting to keep up with the advancements they make above ground. We train here, educate our children and research new technology."

We proceed into a larger tunnel. Some people salute Silas as they pass.

"Where are the other two facilities located?" I ask.

"One in the midlands and another in the Scottish Highlands," he responds.

"Amberleigh is a new town," I muse. "This can't be a coincidence. You've already got support from someone—or people. Who is it?"

"We do, yeah …"

"Let me guess, you can't tell me."

"Yup."

"*No more secrets!*" I stress.

"It's not my place to say." He shrugs. "You'll find out soon enough."

"Why does it feel like you get a kick out of knowing more than me?"

"Why does it feel like you find it equally exciting?" He gives me the side eye with a smile.

Arriving at the end of the tunnel, the sign '*Council Chamber*' is mounted above two large doors that slide open on our approach. Inside, four people are seated around a long table in the centre of the room. Monitors fill the walls, and I catch them flickering to display something new on my arrival.

"Fantastic!" Silas exclaims. "Everyone's here—well, almost—we're just missing Bee."

All probing eyes are on me, and the man closest jumps up to firmly shake my hand and break the awkward tension. He's slim and well-groomed, and I'm drawn to his bright ginger hair and beard, with freckles painting his boyish face.

"It's great to finally meet you, Clara," he beams, revealing the tip of his tongue. "Casimir Stirling, the Folcriht's Prime Minister."

If you could picture what a pristine poster boy of the rebellion looks like, that's Casimir Stirling.

"It's nice to meet you, Prime Min—"

"Just Casimir!" he interjects. "You're with friends here. We're not those sanctimonious bastards they call aristocracy—well—I suppose titles are important if you decide to join our military." He taps me on the shoulder, and with a smile, he asks rhetorically, "But why would a young lady like you want that?"

What if I did? There's a word for his attitude towards women (despite every attempt made by The Crown to remove it from the English vocabulary). It's misogyny, and no matter how far you travel underground, you can't escape it. I humour him with a girly giggle—albeit clearly sarcastic.

Each minister of the Folcriht's Council—their version of a democratic government, so I'm told—introduces themselves. Second to Casimir is Lawrence Winthrop, a short, stout man with rounded features that would usually remind me of a cute teddy bear if it wasn't for his frosty demeanour—quite frankly, he's the opposite of the rebellion's poster boy. Lawrence is responsible for gathering intelligence throughout the empire. He owns the network of 'deeps'—the same spy network that Celest belonged to. Silas makes a joke, referring to him as the Folcriht's equivalent of Radford, which Lawrence doesn't find amusing.

Next is Edward Ashby. He's older than everyone in this room, with big, bushy eyebrows that protrude from his forehead, and I can't help but stare at his teeth, which he's neglected over the years. Edward is responsible for law and order throughout the Folcriht.

I'm finally introduced to Jasper Denham, a young, nervous-looking man—with awkward and stiff body language. He's typically handsome, with soft skin and a buzz cut. I don't see him blink once, and a large scar travels from his forehead, through his left eye and down to his cheek. Jasper doesn't sit on the council; he's Casimir's personal security—a master in military tactics and a fierce fighter.

Silas concludes the introductions, "You'll meet our resident genius at some point, Beatrice—or Bee—don't call her Beatrice. No doubt she'll be hiding in her lab. She's the minister for technology." He gestures to a seat. "Make yourself comfortable."

Casimir leans forward and says, "Thanks for gathering that intel from the agency. I'm impressed! I assume it means you're joining us … officially?"

His earlier comment about my not wanting to join their military has ignited a brat-like defiance.

"I don't like your plan," I respond bluntly.

"Oh," he gasps, leaning back with an inquisitive look. "Tell me why."

"What makes you think I can identify privy council members to spark a coup?" I ask. "It's clear you already have someone from the privy council supporting you. If there was a weak link, I'd expect them to be realised by now."

Casimir squirms in his seat and throws Silas a disapproving look, who raises his hands and tells him, "Clara figured it out herself. I said nothing."

"Who is it?" I demand.

"I can't say, but they'll make themselves known to you when they're ready," Casimir sighs. "You're right, though. We have tried, but our insider isn't *you*. They don't possess your gifts, Clara."

"And what would you have me do once I complete my task?" I ask.

"What would you want to do?" Casimir responds curiously.

I remain silent for a moment, plainly stunned. Nobody has ever offered me an opportunity to choose what role I want to fulfil. This is unfamiliar territory, and I suddenly realise that I've not considered what path I want to take in this new life. As I battle conflicting ideas, like whether I want to play it safe or thrust myself into danger, one thing is still bothering me—Casimir's imperial attitude towards women. I can't escape one cage just to stroll into another.

"I want to fight," I declare, sitting upright. "I want to join your military."

The room becomes stiff, and the ministers twitch and fidget. I hear a subtle scoff from Lawrence, who receives no reaction from me.

"War is no place for a lady, Clara." Casimir chuckles uncomfortably.

"Why isn't it?"

"Because—*it just isn't,*" he sneers, finally revealing his true character—I've clearly hit a nerve.

Have I made a mistake? It feels as though the Folcriht and The Crown are more alike than they realise. However, if I behaved this way above ground, enforcers would promptly gag and whisk me away to be stoned in the street by members of the Imperial Wives' Institute.

Silas's deep growl abruptly kills the silence, and he says, "We should cast a vote. Let the Folcriht decide. Women joining the military was common before the Fall."

The Fall is a term Folcrihts use; it refers to the fall of democracy—an alternative name for the True Ascension.

"*And look where we are now, Silas,*" Casimir spits. "There are some traditions which we should leave in the past … but—ah—fine, you're right," he sighs. "We'll cast a vote this month."

"You will?" I ask, taken aback. This concept of voting is new to me.

"Yes, yes," Casimir says. "Now we just await your invitation to the Harvest, Clara." He's confident the vote won't pass, but it's progress.

"I'm not finished," I declare, surprising myself—and clearly the others—with my confidence.

Casimir inhales dramatically. "Yes?" he asks.

"I would like to advise your council on methods to gain support from the people in the empire," I respond with delicacy, preparing myself for some minor resistance.

However, chaos erupts, and you'd think I'd just accused Lawrence and Edward of being incompetent bastards as they vocalise their ardent objections towards Casimir. One bangs his fist to be heard, and the other quivers with anger, whilst Silas remains silent; he looks almost amused, and Jasper is taut, almost frightful.

Lawrence takes his temper tantrum to the next level and jumps from his seat, red-faced and sweaty. "I won't have some girl skip in and make such absurd demands!"

I mirror his actions, startled by my gutsy response. *What am I doing?* He has a point; I have no right to expect such a responsibility—what could I possibly offer them? Caught in this painfully commanding stance as I face off with Lawrence, I scan my spectators, who gawp at me like I've shared some offensively tasteless joke—all except Silas, who appears to be egging me on. So, I ask myself again: what am I doing? I'm contending for authority in this room because I *know* I can make a difference—and you never get a second chance at first impressions.

"*Girl?*" I stress through gritted teeth. "I may not look it, but I'm twenty-three years old."

Without warning, Lawrence and Edward dissolve into laughter, and humiliation sets my face aglow. *What did I say to cause such amusement?*

Lawrence answers my question. "You are not in the empire anymore, sweetheart"—*I despise that word*—"We are not savages. We do not strip away the childhoods of Folcriht kids." He returns to a seated position, and so do I. The room becomes calmer, and Lawrence sighs. "You may be an adult—yes, but you are still *young*."

"Clara … I admire your passion—I really do!" Casimir exclaims, returning to his friendly disguise (which I see straight through). "But you don't have enough experience to offer us valuable advice. *Surely*, you know this."

"But I know the people of the empire. I—"

"Enough—"

"Your approach is flawed."

"Flawed?" he asks, tilting his head and scrunching his brow. "And why's that?"

"Firstly, you think you stand a chance at gaining the support from someone—or people—in the privy council. *Surely*, you realise these men desire power over everything. Why would they agree to work with a group that seeks to hand that power to the people?"

"We already have someone!" he objects.

"An anomaly—no doubt," I respond. "Secondly, a coup would spark a wide-scale rebellion and a civil war. *Surely*, you realise the lack of organisation and visible leadership would open an opportunity for another country to invade and occupy a weakened England?"

"I've heard enough—"

"Finally"—I refuse to give way—"the people of the empire aren't ruled by fear alone; they're ruled by comfort. The Crown is the hand that feeds them—it keeps them warm. People associate the Folcriht with disorder and destruction—your symbol! It's a fractured crown! That alone makes people think of instability and ruin—*not* freedom and liberation. *Surely,* you realise you must show them why you're the better option if you want their support."

They're dumbfounded, each gawking at me with perplexed looks, and Casimir's expression transforms into something more solemn.

"You're right," he admits heavily. *I wasn't expecting that.* "I'll consider your request when you return from the Harvest."

Comfortable with my contribution (but slightly embarrassed by my brutish behaviour), I stand and march towards the door.

"Clara!" Casimir calls out before I exit. I turn and face him, and he says with a sorrowful expression. "I'm sorry for how we came across today; it's totally unacceptable"—he's being truthful—"It's easy for us to lose sight of opportunities when we hide from the rest of the world. Thank you."

I glance at Silas—who remains relaxed, looking quite smug. He winks at me, a silent congratulation. I whip around and leave before he can notice my cheeks flushing.

CHAPTER EIGHT

The Invitation

It's been four days since I arrived in Amberleigh, and it
already feels like home. Silas and Fay have taken turns to
acquaint me with the actual town and its inhabitants, both
above and below ground. They've guided me through its
governance and policing system, where a select few
enforcers answer to a single marshal—which explains why
sightings of them are rare.

I learned that even the guards stationed at the
ammunition factory are Folcriht, facilitating the diversion of
resources for the rebels' arsenal. As part of my immersion
into this new world, Casimir arranged a small memorial
service for Celest. Strangely, I found myself unable to shed
tears, unsure if I was still grappling with disbelief or if I'd
completed the process of mourning her. Perhaps my focus
on ensuring Celest's sacrifice isn't in vain keeps me resolved.

I've dedicated most of my time to exploring the infinite
network of tunnels within the underground fort, intrigued
by the striking contrast between their way of life beneath the
surface and the empire above. Despite adhering to several

traditions—the blossoming, for one (to keep up appearances)—they've established a system that ensures children receive a comprehensive education until eighteen. It's an incredible alternative to the world I knew as a young girl, and I can't avoid feeling a tinge of envy.

I've observed a particular group of girls, all no older than twelve, throughout the week. Fay tells me they've received their calling on paper as wives, but their time is spent studying in the classroom or in the extensive library that houses forbidden knowledge. They immerse themselves in scientific subjects and delve into the realms of old English literature. Their joy is genuine; it isn't fabricated like the happiness experienced by the wives of the empire—whose bodies are pumped with drugs that make them docile.

The reality of my new life hasn't taken long to settle in. Silas has introduced me to some other Folcriht members who play important roles. Like Thomas Audley, who communicates with the neighbouring towns, and Michael Warrington, accountable for the Folcriht's public relations. He's very protective over their 'brand' and wasn't impressed when he learned of my distaste towards their fractured crown symbol.

I've yet to meet the only two women who hold senior positions of authority within the rebellion—Bee and the mayor. Silas has arranged a meeting with Bee, and now that I've grown familiar with my surroundings, I find my way to her unaccompanied in the fort. Whilst the facility boasts some advanced features, it's still behind the times and isn't keeping up with basic technology existing above ground (simple things like energy screens).

The doors slide open, and stepping inside, I find myself in a spacious laboratory teeming with activity. Machines are buzzing, lights are blinking, and a controlled chaos of interconnected wires is crawling across the walls. Still, despite the mayhem, it's a sanctuary dedicated to innovation and the wonders of technology.

Five intelligent-looking individuals wearing lab coats huddle around a device on the table—one tinkers with it, seeking guidance and advice from the others. Completely engrossed in their work, they remain oblivious to my presence. Across the room, Bee sits with her fingers dancing across an old-fashioned keyboard—the rapid tap, tap, tap from her typing may be jarring to some, but I find it quite soothing. Her head sways from side to side, causing her jet-black braided ponytail to swing and brush each shoulder blade. I stand at the entrance, hoping she'll eventually notice me … but she doesn't.

"Hello, Bee, is it?" I call out.

Continuing to type, Bee nods to an empty chair next to her and says, "Have a seat."

I creep through the lab, careful not to disturb their work, and sit in silence—waiting for Bee to finish as the light from her monitor illuminates her wide, brown eyes.

"Surely you didn't want to meet so you could watch me work," she declares frankly through pursed lips.

"Sorry, I—I didn't want to disturb you," I respond. "Why're you using an old-fashioned keyboard?"

Bee looks at me, continuing to type feverishly and says, "This way, I can multitask." She smiles and returns to face her screen. "Both my work and you have my full attention—besides, I prefer old tech. I spend most of my time deciphering how best to sneak into the empire's networks, and most of the time, I find a simple solution is best for a complex problem. *Obviously*, I keep up to date with all their new tech; I invented most of it! But they don't know that."

"*How?*" I ask.

"I leak ideas to a particular egghead in the policy office, posing as some fanatic from America," she responds. "That chump bites every time and takes my ideas to the right people. They do all the hard work for me. That's their problem—you see—they're bloody lazy when it comes to this stuff"—she gestures to her screen—"They make a few tweaks, but nothing that would stop me from infiltrating them when we need to. My guys over there have all the fun"—she points to the group who's now fascinated by the device vibrating violently on the table—"They invent new things to defend us from the empire's killing machines. They're brilliantly twisted, but that's just how I need them to be."

"How did you get into this … tech stuff?" I ask.

Bee stops typing and sits back in her chair, wrapping her hands behind her head. "My parents taught me," she sighs. "Both were researchers, dragged from Zimbabwe to design new automated weaponry for England."

"Were? I'm sorry—"

"Nah. It's fine," she states. "Their final project was improving the Grand Shard after it destroyed an English military hovercraft."

"How did they pass away? If you don't mind sharing."

"They knew too much." She shrugs. "Placed me with the Folcriht when the emperor started taking too much of an interest in them—he got all paranoid. That prick."

"He'll get what he deserves," I mumble.

"Wouldn't that be something." Bee snorts. "It's funny; I wasn't sure about you coming on board."

"Whys that?"

"Because I voted against Cas's whole coup plan," she declares. "It's a waste of bloody time, but Silas told me you stood your ground in there."

"Yeah, it's—I don't get why he thinks we stand a chance at getting another one to turn."

"The guy who supports us is different—he's a good bloke," she says. "But you're right. The rest of them are perverted little rats. Anyway, it's good knowing you stood up to Cas. He can be a proper bigot sometimes." She taps her finger on the table and grins at me. "Do you know what would be awesome?" she asks suggestively.

I throw her a curious look. "Hmm?"

"If you came back with a *better* plan."

"A better plan?"

"Yes!" She taps the desk excitedly. "Cas thinks—if he can't spark a coup—that organised strikes on imperial infrastructure will be enough to stir up a wide-scale rebellion." Bee scoffs. "None of us agrees—except Lawrence—they've spent too long under—ah! You need a new communicator. Which wrist is your link in?"

'Link' is short for SyncLink, so I raise my left arm to indicate its location. Bee walks to a drawer and pulls out a metallic box. Inside are several tools used to implant new devices. She grabs one and returns.

"Hold out your right arm," she instructs.

I trust her and oblige; from memory, it's a quick and painless procedure.

Inspecting my wrist, she asks, "So you know when someone's lying?"

"Yep."

"My favourite colour is blue."

"True."

"I've never been to Bristol."

"False," I respond.

Bee keeps throwing facts, and I confirm whether they're true or false—but she doesn't find it as fascinating as most people.

"Right … just … a small … scratch," she mutters, and within seconds, she removes the needle from my wrist. "It works like your current link. Vibrates when you receive a call or notification and all that, but you tap three times to show the display. Silas told me your other one is blocked, so they can't trace you. Just use this one when you're not on imperial business."

"How do you stop the agency from tracking our communications?"

"Our links use an old satellite network built by some super-rich American bloke back in the day," she says. "Apparently, it didn't do what they wanted, so they just ditched it!" She shakes her head. "Totally forgotten about. Now it's just space debris I use to bounce stuff around. This lot were bumbling fools before I—"

The doors slide open, and Silas enters, flushed and breathless. "Bee," he huffs. "I wish you would … turn on your comms."

"And make it easier for you lot to disturb me?" she responds sassily. "Nah, I'm good."

Silas chucks his arms in the air, admitting defeat. "Clara, sorry to crash the party. They need you above ground."

Who are they? I thank Bee for her time and follow Silas towards the closest exit that'll take us to a bathroom in the church.

"Did you get your link?" he asks.

"Yes—bloody hell!" I snap. "Slow down! Why're we rushing?"

"That weirdo—Sophia Somerville—will be here in the next hour to invite a 'special subject' to the next Harvest," he responds casually.

My heart skips a beat—this is it. Baroness Somerville is the golden child of the empire—omnipresent wherever children gather and the largest cog in the propaganda machine. Her face is plastered across schools, playgrounds, clothing stores, stations, cafés—everywhere. She's the star of Echo—a social media platform and virtual realm where individuals do all sorts of things. They engage in interactive experiences, share captivating photos and videos, and exchange stories of unwavering loyalty (to name a few). Echo also serves as an educational platform for children and young adults within the empire.

The baroness is an Ideator—someone who imparts knowledge and guidance to individuals using Echo, mainly targeting children. Her teachings encompass a wide range of topics, including the newest fashion trends, proper behaviour, the latest dance moves, and strategies for obtaining luxuries sanctioned by The Crown. I caught a glimpse of her in London once, but the overwhelming swarm of fanatical children prevented me from getting a clear view—with their voice cracking screams and noodle-like legs giving way as they blacked out. Undoubtedly, the baroness commands a massive following and plays a significant role in shaping the thoughts and actions of the masses.

Silas and I exit the church, and Fay's engaged in conversation with another woman on the steps—who I assume is the mayor, given away by her attire. She wears a refined charcoal dress, a striking ceremonial chain, and a lavishly decorated hat.

"Gosh!" she gasps, her upturned eyes darting between Fay and me. "You two really are identical." She vigorously shakes my hand with both of hers. "Verity Lockwood! It's a pleasure—oh! I'm the mayor, by the way."

"I had my suspicions." I smile. "Clara Rosewood, nice to meet you, Verity."

"I'll leave you to it," Silas growls. "You don't want me around when the scuzz shows up." He returns to the church, itching to escape the impending pomp and pageantry.

The edges of the square are becoming filled with disgruntled and puzzled-looking men, women, and children—many vexed by the disruption to their day.

"A small army usually accompanies the baroness," Verity says. "I believe she wants to make a *spectacular* entrance after I received a grilling on the most appropriate place to announce her arrival. I've got people rounding up the residents so we can offer her a warm welcome!" She leans towards me and whispers, "Don't tell anyone, *but I may be a teeny bit excited!*"

It's clear she's more than a 'teeny bit' excited, and there's something quite appealing about her enthusiastic nature—even if it's misguided.

"Verity," Fay says, nodding in my direction. "We should—err …"

"Heavens!" Verity gasps. "Yes—thank you, Fay! Come, Clara, you can't be seen wearing that."

They're both right. I'm wearing the overalls Silas provided because I'm spending most of my time underground. I've become too comfortable over the last few days, considering I haven't worn a dress once. Verity signals towards a quaint women's clothing store nestled in the corner of the square, and we stroll towards it whilst Fay stays behind to oversee the expanding crowd.

In no time, Verity locates a fitting dress. A pure white ensemble enhanced with exquisite embroidery—it reminds me of Celest. Completing the look, I slip on a pair of wedged heels, and Verity places a pretentious hat upon my head, concealing my unkempt hair. Stepping back to assess the overall look, she proclaims, "You need makeup."

"Cheers," I gruff, but she's right. A film crew accompanying the baroness—with their invasive camera drones—will be capturing and sharing this significant moment across the empire.

Sensing the importance of the occasion, the shopkeeper hurriedly retrieves a small makeup bag from the storeroom. Verity instructs me to take a seat and starts working on enhancing my features with her perfectly manicured hands.

"Don't worry," she says. "I won't make you look old."

Once she's pleased with her work, we return to the square and find a ruby coach parked at one end. Streams of crewmembers are 'preparing the stage' as flocks of drones whiz overhead to scout for optimal filming spots. Verity squeaks like a mouse at the dramatic transformation of her beloved town. She hurriedly drags me towards the church's steps, where she spins me around to face the square, firmly grips my shoulders, positions me just right, nods dramatically, and stands by my side.

"Fay!" Verity barks. "Go and hide! The baroness might get confused and give *you* the invite!"

Fay looks at me with apprehension. "How're you feeling?"

"I need a wee," I respond bluntly.

Verity huffs with disapproval whilst Fay chuckles and departs, disappearing into a nearby store.

"Children in the empire are obsessed with the baroness," I whisper. "They're fanatic around her. I assume the children here will act the same way?"

The newly-formed orchestra launches into an upbeat, jolly song that conflicts with Verity's horror-struck face—with her jaw dropped, eyes wide, and colourless cheeks. I can tell she's a perfectionist, and everything she's done to keep up the town's appearance could be flushed down the drain because a few kids didn't gush over Baroness Somerville.

"Bollocks," she utters, rushing to a man in the crowd to whisper instructions in his ear.

The clop, clop, clop of heavy hooves hitting stone grows louder. With the music intensifying, a colossal white stallion emerges at the opposite end of the square—genetically modified and two times its natural size. It trots into the centre with impeccable form and pulls a golden carriage that looks just as tacky as it does expensive. Like a child riding in a super-sized pram, the baroness barely peaks over the window, waving and beaming at the fictitiously awe-struck audience, who quickly break out into applause and cheers. Their deceptive celebrations drown out the orchestra's chirpy melody.

Flustered, Verity returns. Her instructions are being passed through the crowd, but they're not moving fast enough. Unwanted visitors will storm Amberleigh if its children fail to act like those in the empire.

The baroness teeters down the steps from her carriage like a toddler learning to walk. Her petite frame is devoured by a silk-layered gown decorated with metallic threads, and the disproportionate skirt billows pretentiously outwards—allowing her to take up more room than we women have any right to. The sleeves flutter in the breeze around her spindly arms, with a vibrant yellow fitted bodice transitioning into a deep midnight blue at the hem.

As the baroness shuffles forward, charms of goldfinches zoom into the square from all directions, darting around in a hypnotic display of speed before encircling her in a whirlwind. I catch their occasional red face and yellow wing among the torrent of brown. After spinning for quite some time, they disperse to fly away in unison like a single missile—obediently returning to their captive state.

In a breathtakingly nauseating reveal, the baroness unveils a new gown and a new array of colours that mirror the hues of the goldfinches—shades of reds, yellows, and browns. She pauses, assuming a weirdly crooked statuesque position, with her gaze fixed up to the sky as she smiles with profound self-satisfaction.

Though they don't want to, most people dutifully celebrate her conceitedness—except the children, who remain silent, with just a handful joining in with hesitant claps. Verity tightly grasps her chain, and with quickened breaths, she mutters an assortment of expletives.

Still frozen in pose, the baroness redirects her focus from the sky to the crowd, undeniably perplexed—suspicious even. I sense her growing frustration at the lack of enthusiasm from the children, and the adults have also noticed the abnormal response. Some of them nudge their young ones and whisper in their ears, pointing at the baroness to elicit a reaction.

Suddenly, a little girl takes the spotlight, running forward and screaming, "Lady Somerville!"

She paves the way for others to swiftly follow suit, and soon, the square is filled with their deceitfully infectious excitement. The baroness's smile returns, her face radiating with pure ecstasy as the boys attempt to shake her hand, and the girls curtsy in admiration. She glides in my direction with the children surrounding her eagerly, handing them small, signed photographs to clutch against their chests in 'delight' before dispersing and scampering back to their parents.

The orchestra's music fades, and a hush falls over the crowd. The baroness stands directly before me, and a stray goldfinch perches on her shoulder, causing a flash of disgust to grace her face. However, you'd need to be quick to notice as the joyful façade swiftly returns to mask her inherently hateful nature. She stares at me while the drones adjust their position, a reminder of the millions of people watching this moment unfold. Mindful of their scrutiny, I offer a thin smile in return.

"Clara Rosewood!" she rasps, her voice resonating throughout the square, amplified by the silence. She stares at me with a pout formed from outrageously huge lips and rosy, red cheeks on her porcelain-looking face. Baroness Somerville—the empire's beloved darling for over sixty-eight years—appears no older than fourteen (due to an early blossoming ceremony). However, two things betray her actual age—the husky undertone in her voice and the lifelessness behind her eyes, resulting in an unsettling aura surrounding her.

"On behalf of our royal majesty," she continues. "It is my honour to present you with the prestigious title of this year's Bright Light!" The baroness pauses to allow for applause, and with visible, shaky effort, she kneels on one knee and extends a scroll from her outstretched hands—her arms tremble under the weight of the paper, and her neck could snap at any minute from balancing a huge curly updo.

With a deliberately steady pace, I descend the steps, savouring the sight of her struggling to maintain a kneeling position. She starts to wobble uncontrollably, and sensing her irritation, I extend a hand to lift her up. Although she holds a smile, the underlying annoyance is obvious.

I take a deep breath and declare, "I would like—"

The ferocious expression of a young girl in the crowd distracts me—her burning glare suddenly ignites something peculiar within me. It's as though she's urging me to take a flame to this invitation and burn their Harvest to the ground. Then, as if a mist has been lifted from my consciousness, I finally see them in the crowd—not the faces of young and helpless ladies but those of experienced and fierce women. Their silent screams demand to be seen, acknowledged and heard.

This enlightenment—a realisation suppressed for too long—opens the floodgates for vivid memories to wash over me, like one from my calling. The euphoria expressed by my mum when I wasn't chosen to become a wife, only to be snuffed by the enforcers who dragged me from my home so The Crown could force me into work.

I recall moments when I stood in line waiting to travel, just to be barged back by men who deemed their tasks more important. In those instances, I'd beg for their forgiveness with a girly smile and offer sweet apologies for inconveniencing them with my presence.

I reminisce about my teenage years, the countless nights I spent crying, gripped by the fear of ageing too quickly before my blossoming. *And for what?* Why must we deny our body's natural inclination to age? In this world, we perceive what resides in our hearts, and they want us to feel weak because they fear our strength.

"Hello? Clara?" The baroness's husky voice infiltrates my rumination, returning me to the present.

I'd rehearsed this moment and intended to act like I always do—a courteous and gentle imperial girl—but my time to reflect, albeit short, was powerful. It's given me an idea, and if my hunch is correct, my actions could provide the Folcriht with a powerful supporter they desperately need, *but how do I play my next move?*

I turn towards the camera, my expression devoid of emotion, and with a tone tinged with reluctance, I utter a single word: "Cheers."

The baroness's elated face morphs into perplexed disappointment. Never in the Harvest's history has the Bright Light failed to fold from tears of joy and crumble to the ground under the weight of this piece of paper's honour … until now. Rapidly regaining her composure, the baroness positions herself beside me so we face the same direction, and the drones hover at our level.

"People of the empire!" she croaks. "Join me in celebrating this year's Bright Light—Clara Rosewood!"—the crowd goes wild—"The Harvest will be upon us in two short weeks, and you shall learn of Clara's wonderful tale of devotion to our glorious emperor. I hope her story inspires *you* to live a full and honourable life." She faces me, still rapturous. "Tell us, Clara! How do you feel?"

I glare at the floating camera—keen to connect with the masses—and acting like someone who'd rather be elsewhere, I say, "Blessed for this opportunity to inspire others."

The baroness giggles awkwardly. "Fear not, faithful subjects. Clara may be camera-shy now, but I will take her under my wing. I may even teach her a dance move or two!" The baroness releases a hysterical, raspy laugh; her throat rattles like she's swallowed a musical instrument. She then starts bouncing from side to side like a tight spring—with her feet remaining firmly on the ground—every movement is awkward and erratic. After too long, she ends the painful performance and continues to address the camera. "Thank you for joining us in—erm—this lovely little town! We shall meet again in two weeks. Never alone!"

"Blessed by his presence," the crowd responds.

Verity nervously watches the drones fly upwards to achieve a birds-eye view, and the crowd wastes no time to scatter, with a few of them sighing with relief at it being over. The baroness's frenzied crew appear from nowhere to fuss over her hair, touch up her makeup and fiddle with her gown.

"Where are we again?" The baroness asks as she's being fumbled from all directions.

"Amberleigh, my lady," I respond.

"May the lord give me strength," she sighs. "I have my work cut out with you, darling. It's going to be a late night." The baroness shoos away her crew, and they scutter to the side, taking on the role of her shadow as she stares at her SyncLink screen. The goldfinch remains perched on her shoulder, unphased even when she screams, "VALERIE!" No one responds, so she yells again, "VALERIE? WHERE AM I TO REST THIS EVENING?"

It clicks. I look at Verity, who promptly rushes over.

"Apologies, my lady," she says, clasping her hands together. "It's Ve—never mind. Follow me, please."

With Verity leading the way, she attempts to engage the baroness in conversation, but the baroness pays her no attention. Instead, she's engrossed in her SyncLink, watching videos on Echo of runway models showing off different pinnies. I position myself at the back, appreciating the solitude.

We enter the courtyard that leads to the town's hotel— a stately-looking building—and the baroness momentarily glances up from her screen to survey it, and that's when she finally notices the small bird still perched on her shoulder. Without hesitation, she backhands it off with a swift flick of the wrist, causing feathers to burst from the bird as it plummets to the stone ground, lifeless. A fleeting expression of shock crosses Baroness Somerville's face when she finds me observing her behaviour.

"Oops." She giggles, offers a sweet smile, and nonchalantly shrugs her shoulders before turning to enter the hotel.

CHAPTER NINE

The Harvest

"Almost time, Miss Rosewood," Richard announces, poking his head into my dressing room. "Please, follow me."

Richard is a Harvest crew member who's been kind and patient with me today—unlike Baroness Somerville. She spent our short time together in Amberleigh screaming, pulling, prodding, and slapping me until I was a delightfully well-mannered lady and an expert in royal protocol. I shudder when I recollect the late nights we spent together. For one, I spent hours upon hours practising my curtsies, and the baroness would take on the role of the emperor, slapping my arse with a leather cane every time I faced away from her.

I learned about the complexities associated with royal titles and how to address different members of royalty based on their seniority and line of succession—which doesn't include any of the emperor's children because they're non-existent. We rehearsed suitable conversational topics, and I regret telling the baroness about my interest in poetry because it prompted her to recommend that I express my fictitious passion for writing poems dedicated to the emperor. I might've enjoyed the ballroom dancing without her stamping on my feet when I made a wrong step. The trickiest part, however, was having to grin and bear the garments the baroness chose for me—two in total—one for the festival and banquet and the other for the ball.

The first is a tasteful gown, which I'm wearing now. It's pastel green, fits perfectly, falls to my ankles, and is paired with an olive-lined cape. The baroness's crew has styled my hair into a simple updo with no trinkets or glitz. Overall, I'm satisfied with this look—but I can't say the same for my ball attire, and I still picture her elation and pride during my fitting. The horror begins with the tightest corset you could imagine—squeezing every one of my organs and forcing my breasts to bulge upwards, almost becoming an uncomfortable rest for my chin. It's paired with a skirt that flares outwards like an umbrella—ending just above my knee—with a stiff, iridescent material wrapped around it. The baroness is forcing me to balance a heavy hairpiece laced with jewels and gold while wearing ridiculously high heels that may as well be stilts. Completing the nightmare is an ornate piece fastened to my back—resembling a peacock's tail.

I join a queue behind four other people—the successful Light Bringers for this year's Harvest—they watch me approach on tenterhooks, and the woman I queue behind is visibly eager to engage in conversation.

"Blessed by his reign," she whispers merrily.

"As am I," I respond.

"Oh yes, you are," she squeaks. "I'm a huge fan."

I raise my eyebrows and smile, offering no verbal response.

The woman continues, "By his light, you look *magnificent*. I can't wait to learn of your devotion. *I* discovered my former friend was a terrorist sympathiser … imagine! I reported her for projecting radical symbols from an apartment building." She's unbearably smug.

"Gosh," I respond coldly. "You must be proud of yourself."

"Oh, yes! I am!" she beams, ignorant of my sarcasm. "I felt such shame to even associate with her, but the emperor recognises my loyalty. *Ahh,* what a blessing!"

"How close are you with your friend?" I ask.

"*Former* friend." She giggles nervously. "Gosh, we grew up together … but rest assured, hate firmly replaces the love I once felt."

Her delusion infuriates me—but I should try to be understanding because she's an older wife. Behind her youthful face, if you look closely, you notice the haze shrouding her eyes isn't as potent compared to younger wives—it's the result of her body becoming accustomed to the substance that creates feelings of bliss and gratitude.

"What's your fondest memory of her?" I ask.

"I—er—gosh," she stutters, stunned. "Wh—what a strange question …"

"Well?" I urge.

"I suppose—no," she says firmly, shaking her head. "All I remember is her betrayal."

"What's the nicest thing she did for you?" I press.

Though she offers no verbal response, the woman's cheeks flush. She's becoming increasingly frustrated with my line of questioning, but I detect a hint of sorrow hiding somewhere.

"Rumour has it," I continue in a hushed voice. "The radicals plant projection devices in loyalist homes, making them look like sympathisers. They're bloody wicked, aren't they."

It becomes too much for the woman, and she spins around to face away from me—I'm sure I glimpsed a tear escape her eye.

Richard returns and breaks the awkward silence. "Caleb Carmichael will announce you all," he says. A couple of the group echo his name in excitable whispers. "He's hosting the festival this year. Enter promptly when your name's called—oh—and remember ... *big* smiles!"

Caleb's nasally voice drifts from the stage and stirs up the crowd outside, their cheers and applause growing louder. Each person leaves to join him one by one upon hearing their name.

"I now welcome our fourth and final Light Bringer," Caleb states. "A huuuuge round of applause for the lovely Julia Ferndown!"

Julia ... I knew I recognised her. Just a few weeks ago, when I cut through the courtyard on my way to work, I witnessed enforcers arresting a woman for projecting the Folcriht's symbol. Julia was in the crowd, shunning the woman's pleas for help. Fortunately, she's had time to process our conversation and scuttles away pleasantly deflated.

"And the moment you have all been waiting for! The star of the show," Caleb continues. "I know you've all been *dying* to gaze on her beauty again, and Caleb brings you all the gifts! She is sumptuous ... she is splendid ... she is sweet. May I present our esteemed Bright Light, *CLARA ROSEWOOD*."

To my distaste, the crowd's enthusiasm electrifies the air, distracting me from dwelling on Caleb's repulsive introduction. The world spins, and a wave of anticipation consumes me. Taking the deepest breath, I climb the stage steps—its platform raised high—and enter the expansive space. Buckingham Palace is on my left, judging my every move, whilst a sea of jittery subjects is on my right, obsessing over me. They invade The Mall and surrounding parks. I don't know what face I'm pulling—it's certainly not a smile—but my focus remains dead ahead, savouring each moment the spotlight blinds me to their overwhelming presence.

A sizeable purpose-built gallery, seating members of the royal family, aristocracy, and religious figureheads, is placed at the side of the stage. They all rise from their seats and join in the celebrations as Caleb parades me around before finally allowing me to take my seat at the edge with the other Light Bringers. I'm raised higher than them, and right now, I'm the centre of unwanted attention.

"Faithful subjects and esteemed guests!" Caleb bellows, reclaiming control as the atmosphere settles. He epitomises a traditional English gentleman, carrying a fancy cane that compliments an intricately embroidered burgundy three-piece suit. Despite his energetic movements, a matching bowler hat remains firmly attached to his head. "I stand before you today with immense honour as I prepare to introduce a figure who embodies the *very essence* of our great empire.

It is my privilege to announce the arrival of a ruler who has captured our hearts, guided our steps, and led us to unwavering dedication. His brilliance demands respect, his wisdom inspires awe, and his commitment to our beloved kingdom and empire is *unwavering*.

His leadership has steered us through trials and tribulations, unifying us in the face of adversity and uplifting us to new heights. It is his hand that feeds us, his generosity that keeps us warm and his encouragement that drives us to succeed.

Please join me in a resounding applause for the magnanimous Emperor Magnus Hanover the Second!"

A leaping melody fills the air, and the crowd belts out the national anthem. With spotlights illuminating the palace's balcony, its doors swing open with dramatic effect to reveal the emperor. The people's reaction never fails to baffle me; some lose consciousness from the exhilaration, others bounce up and down like it'll make him notice them, and too many weep with delight.

After an unnecessarily long and theatrical pause, the emperor struts onto the balcony. His smug-looking head balances an ostentatious crown atop a bed of wavy curls. He's draped in a royal purple cape decorated with heraldic symbols to frame his outrageously ritzy ceremonial attire. Am I the only one who longs to smack away his haughty little smirk?

His wife—Queen Calantha—follows shortly after. She's a vision of grace, with a silver gown that shimmers and whispers with each step. The bodice is embellished with pearls and delicate lacework, matching the details in her modestly styled strawberry-blonde hair and tiara. Despite her petite stature, she can steal everyone's attention with the slightest smile.

Rumours of Queen Calantha—otherwise known as the Caledonian Queen—whisper throughout the land. She reigns over the one kingdom England didn't absorb on this cluster of islands following the Fall—Scotland. It's common knowledge that the Scottish people are ruled differently from the English (and other kingdoms in the empire). Stories circulate of Queen Calantha showing her people sincere compassion, though The Crown quickly quashes them as falsehoods.

The emperor and queen stand ahead of their thrones, and the crowd shrinks as every man, woman, and child falls to the ground on one knee with their heads bowed —but I remain standing, like a single tree amongst a meadow of mown grass. The bothersome drone buzzing around me appears highly nervous. It jitters mid-air before audibly adjusting its focus and zooming away. I'm paying the price for my insubordination, falling victim to the emperor's crippling gaze, and mischief flashes across his face as if he's relishing the game. I understand the risks I'm taking, but if my hunch is correct, this small act of defiance could pique the interest of one person who could be the Folcriht's key to success—the queen. She peers at me curiously, and I notice her side-eyeing the emperor, subtly gauging his temperament.

"My faithful subjects." The emperor's commanding voice is powerful, projecting effortlessly for all to hear. "Today marks a pivotal event in our annual calendar, a demonstration of our collective commitment to the ideals that bind us together as one empire. The Harvest unites us in every corner of our vast territory, from Port Douglas on the Coral Sea to the bustling streets of our beloved Capital.

This planet. Our home. It is *fragile*. Radicals—greedy and parasitical vermin—would have us return to the dark days. When toxic fumes polluted our air, children were dying on the street. Your ancestors starved and froze to death, and rising waters wiped out towns and cities.

I have devoted my life to protecting your home, and I am proud of your dedication to helping me ensure its safety. Today, we shall shine a light on the shadows that threaten our existence, that seek to destroy our livelihoods, and we will all rejoice in their penance.

Long live the empire, and may this Harvest feed your desire for a fruitful future."

The crowd explodes in thunderous applause and jubilant cheers as the emperor and queen take their seats with controlled composure, signifying the beginning of the festivities. In perfect arrangement, magnificent beasts emerge from the distant Admiralty Arch, but they're nothing like you'd see in the wild. Proudly leading the procession through the centre of The Mall's strip is a herd of colossal red stags—each as tall as the trees—with branch-like antlers rising high and decorated with ivy. Tank-sized bulls follow shortly after, sluggishly swaying side to side and occasionally releasing an almighty grunt, causing audience members to stumble back in amazement. An earth of foxes weaves through their more dominant co-performers, expertly dodging the heavy footsteps that threaten to crush them, finding safety at the front of the line.

In an endless display of disregard for natural wildlife, king-sized stallions, wild boars, hedgehogs, and beavers join the show, each demonstrating their unique (and induced) character to appease the audience. Giant barn owls swoop down with shadowing wing spans to create gusts of wind that blow the hats off men and women, stirring up pockets of laughter. However, it's the red squirrels that really get the crowd going. Three times their natural size, they bound around with remarkable agility—vaulting from banners, trees and lampposts with zesty energy, arousing gasps and squeals of excitement. Surely, people realise these animals have endured horrific procedures in the name of indulgence and vanity.

Lively Morris dancers skip from the arch; the rhythmic beat of tambourines and the strings of fiddles accompany their animated steps, complimented by the jingling bells attached to their legs. Dressed in white shirts with billowing sleeves and vibrant waistcoats, the men passionately stomp their feet and clap their hands with the music. The women glide and spin in flowy dresses with ribbons woven through their hair, adding a touch of enchantment. I may have enjoyed and appreciated their talents if it wasn't for my deep resentment for being here.

Simultaneously, life rolls into the stage with the spunky energy of a Brazilian carnival. The men show off their skilful footwork and sculpted physiques, blending flair, energy, and a staunch passion for dance—radiating charisma and masculinity. The women dazzle in their outfits decked with feathers, sequins, and beadwork. The display transports me to the lively streets of Rio, but only until the dancers couple up, and their enthusiastic Samba interlaces with the English Ballroom's sophistication, creating an ambivalent fusion of style.

The emperor looks unequivocally bored as extravagant performances from selected kingdoms unfold, each sacrificing their unique and rich cultures to blend with ours. India charms with a beautiful Odissi dance; their once dynamic outfits are now stifled by contemporary English fashion. The Japanese Taiko Drummers command attention with precision and discipline, only to be dampened by a chorus of oboes. With New Zealand closing the show, Caleb struts to the stage as a seating area slides into view from behind the scenes. Each chair is meticulously positioned to ensure their occupants don't face away from the emperor.

"My gosh!" he exclaims, twiddling his handlebar moustache. "You have all been spoilt today. Now … as the evening approaches, we must begin our displays of devotion—it is why we are all here, after all! I will shortly welcome our first Light Bringer to join me. You shall hear about love! Loss! *Deceit. Dishonour* … and most importantly, selfless loyalty."

The gallows glide into view and land in the centre, taking the prime spot for all to see.

Caleb skips to his seat and announces, "Firstly, a warm welcome to our first Light Bringer, Marcus Frier!"

The old, frail man near me musters the strength to rise from his seat and hobbles towards the vacant spot next to Caleb. As he attempts to bow to the emperor, his feeble form wavers, nearly toppling forward in the process—Caleb remains seated, showing no interest in assisting the struggling man. In fact, a flicker of disgust flashes upon his face, briefly disrupting his pleasant disguise.

"It's marvellous to have you here, Marcus," Caleb says gleefully (he's lying). "Please, tell us about yourself."

"W—well. I'm—er—recently retired, after a—er—long and fruitful service as a sculptor," Marcus drawls. Even Caleb's seasoned acting skills can't mask his growing impatience.

"Seventy years, I hear!" Caleb proclaims.

"Ye—Yes, indeed," Marcus continues painfully slowly. "I am for—for—forever grateful for my er—my gifted calling."

"Wonderful!" Caleb elates. "And what is your greatest achievement?"

Marcus releases a weak chuckle, and I half expect him to stop breathing. "Well, I—some of my pieces are—well, they're in the royal gardens!"

Stealing a glance at the emperor, Marcus longs for his recognition—but he doesn't receive it. Instead, the emperor concentrates his icy glare on me, and we enter an intense battle of wills that neither of us is prepared to lose. Though each breath becomes more challenging, and each second feels like a minute, I don't want to give him the satisfaction of seeing me falter.

Marcus's monotonic voice fades into background noise. *What's come over me?* This silent fight won't aid my plan. I'm taking an unnecessary risk and mustn't let my hatred towards him overrule my logic, so I break eye contact, and with a gentle smile, I lower my head to relinquish our extreme connection—admitting defeat.

"I sense the crowd becoming impatient," Caleb declares, pulling me back. "They are dying to hear your story of fealty."

Marcus recounts the peaceful life he once had in the city. He describes his apartment, which overlooks a beautiful park, and the serenity of retirement. However, suspicious noises from the apartment above him shattered this tranquillity. Intrigued and concerned, Marcus took on the role of chief snoop (not his words) and delved into the unsettling activities of the family residing there—a mum, dad, and young boy. He vividly describes the unsettling hoards that wandered above, the thuds and screams that rudely disrupted his peace. He spent his retired days diligently monitoring their activities, discreetly following them around, and meticulously recording their every action. With stubborn persistence, he eventually validated his suspicions, discovering the family was involved in smuggling fugitives. My stomach churns at his delirium. Marcus tells us of his loss of purpose after retiring, only for it to return when he could contribute to the safety of the empire and his fellow neighbours. He emphasises the relief of peace's return, no longer disturbed by the footsteps or thuds that once interrupted his afternoon naps.

The crowd responds with jubilation, resounding cheers and thunderous applause, celebrating Marcus's success and acknowledging his dedication to upholding the safety of their community. Anxiety sweeps over me—*I don't want their recognition.* In this gut-wrenching moment, the man, woman, and boy from Marcus's story rise onto the platform to be welcomed by a communal hiss sweeping through the crowd. It's the sound of pure hatred—extinguishing any traces of hope, love, or joy that may have survived this far.

The family stand before us, and you would imagine spending a lovely evening with them, cooking dinner and debating where to get the best coffee if it weren't for their dehumanised state. Each poor soul is stripped down to their underwear, with heads shaved, mouths gagged, and hands bound behind their backs. Yet, despite their vulnerable state, they face the crowd with fierce expressions—radiating an undeniable defiance. I'll share their courage and watch every second; I want this moment to fuel my ever-growing fire.

The nooses spring to life and descend, coiling around the victims' necks with a serpent-like grace—their gentle embrace is a chilling contrast to the impending suffering they'll inflict. The executioner's arrival stimulates the crowd, sending them into a frenzied state. He brandishes a ceremonial hammer and prepares to strike the ornate button that'll release the platform and seal the fate of this broken family—but not before fuelling the crowd's enthusiasm even more by performing some absurd jig.

In their final act, the man, woman, and boy shuffle closer to each other, yearning for one last touch—for one last moment of warmth and love. The executioner sensationally raises his hammer high, and if you were observant enough, you would glimpse this family's fleeting fear. With one dramatic swoop, they drop, and as if their twisting and thrashing aren't enough, their gasps for air are amplified from every direction—as if they're dying right next to me—the sound is pervasive.

Each moment is an agonising lifetime, but one by one, their suffering finally ends. With just their lifeless bodies left on display, they perform their final duty and act as a haunting reminder of the merciless fate that awaits anyone who dares to challenge the powers that be.

"Long live the emperor!" screams Caleb, penetrating the thunderous crowd, who echo his words in perfect harmony.

✷✷✷

This nightmare is endless. I've been forced to endure each Light Bringer's twisted story of devotion, to watch their victims be vilified, dehumanised, and executed, all to feed their hunger for validation from The Crown—but they receive nothing. The emperor remains expressionless throughout the displays, but his mere presence is enough to fulfil them. I know they've been conditioned to be like this, and I shouldn't hate them, but I do.

Julia Ferndown has finished her tale, and I was satisfied to see that my earlier conversation had been impactful following her poor performance during the interview with Caleb. Still, this tiny victory has done nothing to treat my mounting nerves. Molly Grantham, Julia's old friend turned victim, rises to the stage—she behaves differently to the others who have lost their lives today. Molly isn't defiant;

she's sobbing uncontrollably, and in her last moments, she silently pleads to Julia, begging for an explanation.

***

Baroness Somerville and her jaunty dance crew leave the stage after delivering a perplexing performance to announce my imminent tale. The routine involved her lazily moving through a series of 'dance' steps. At the same time, a group of energetic men executed an array of flips, twirls, and jives around her with gusto and skill. For reasons unknown to me, the crowd loved it.

"Now, folks!" Caleb roars, clapping his hands. "This is the moment you have *all* been waiting for. We have heard some remarkable stories tonight, and you must be thinking … *how could it get any better?*" He pauses for dramatic effect. "Well! Do I have a treat for you! Once again, a huuuuge round of applause for our Bright Light, *CLARA ROSEWOOD!*"

I attempt to strut with confidence across the stage, only slightly disorientated by the crowd's excitement now that I've had time to get used to it. As if in warning, the wind is tugging at my cape, causing it to flutter in an attempt to hold me back—but I push forward. With exaggerated flair, I curtsy in the emperor's direction before taking my seat and allowing the crowd to settle. The air rapidly fills with their apprehension.

Caleb leans uncomfortably close to me and rests his hands on my knee, which I abruptly flick off, ignoring his huge mouth's subtle gasp.

"Cla—Clara!" he says meekly before regaining composure. "What an absolute honour, our *youngest ever* Bright Light. How do you feel?"

I can't speak, and Caleb wriggles with discomfort because I'm gawking at him like someone who doesn't understand a question that's been repeated five times.

He clears his throat and tries a different tact. "Tell us! How do you serve the empire? I hear you have been granted a truly righteous path."

Silence, again. Murmurs drift through the crowd. I can't—*no*, I won't give them what they want. I just hope I'm prepared for the emperor's wrath, praying he wouldn't severely punish the Bright Light during the Harvest.

Caleb laughs nervously. "We—er—folks! It seems our Bright Light is camera shy!"—I join in on their amusement, carefully balancing my behaviour—"Fortunately … Baroness Somerville *did* warn me! So, we have produced a short film to share your story of devotion, Clara. Let's take a look." Caleb gestures to an empty space on the stage.

A gigantic, three-dimensional image of a sandy beach materialises before us, closely followed by two small girls skipping along the shoreline, holding hands and filled with mirth. It's supposed to be Celest and me, but we look around eight years old, and we only met when we were eleven.

A narrator's creamy voice follows, with a soft and gentle tune backing him. "This is a story of a lifelong friendship brimming with love, peace, trust, *treachery*, and the sacrifice of a devoted subject. Clara and Celest were best friends since the sweet age of five"—throughout the narration, fictional moments of our lives are displayed in what appears to be chronological order—"They laughed together … cried together … and once shared a common devotion to our glorious emperor. Their bond seemed unbreakable … all until Clara discovered a betrayal."

The melody transforms to something ominous, and the projection now shows me alone, with a look of deep concern lined with anger.

The narration continues, "Celest had devised a spiteful plan to assassinate our beloved emperor during this very Harvest Festival"—Celest is now projected on stage, weaving and sneaking through a crowd as if she were a snake hunting her prey. I notice nervous movements amongst the audience as if they're looking for her near them—"This scheming vermin wanted to take our noble leader from us, but Clara's devotion opened her mind to Celest's scheme, enabling her to shine a light on this wicked shadow"—I'm now projected on stage, pointing into the crowd with a fierce expression— "Before you, our Bright Light has made a noble sacrifice. And now … you may bask in the glory of her true devotion … and bear witness to the ultimate justice!"

As the song and image fade, a hushed silence descends upon the crowd, their anticipation mounting. With my heart racing, the projection of Celest emerges from the ground and onto the gallows, its image is strikingly lifelike—my breath catches in my throat at the sight.

She's battered and bruised, with her head shaved and stripped down to just her underwear like the others before. The shocking visual sends a surge of unease through my stomach, tightening my chest. Her trembling body and terror-filled face are the most unsettling—the intensity of her fear is unmistakable; it's all I see as our eyes meet.

Intuition drives me to leap from my seat, piloted by a force I can't fully comprehend, but I soon realise it's because I don't see the faint shift on the surface of the projection. Treading lightly, I approach the trembling figure of Celest with my hand outstretched. And then, my touch meets with her quivering leg—I can feel her warmth.

A sharp gasp escapes my lips as I register the reality of the situation. Slowly, I lift my head to meet Celest's wide eyes, and in that instant, the world around us fades away. The hissing of the crowd, once so overpowering, becomes a mere whisper in the recesses of my mind. It's just the two of us. A river of tears streams down her cheeks, and I can't help but wonder if she's putting on an act. As if this display of vulnerability is intentional. I want her to look defiant and exhibit fierce determination, but she refuses. Perhaps she intends to make people feel our bond and ignite remorse by showing her inherent softness, evoking empathy and understanding in them.

"As a special treat," Caleb proclaims, grasping my shoulder. "We shall deviate from tradition!"

The executioner strides across the stage, and the crowd—intrigued by this unforeseen development—falls almost silent, their hisses replaced by chattery murmurs. Upon reaching me, the executioner comes to a halt and presents the hammer with outstretched arms. Terror glues me to this spot, and all I can see is the instrument of death. Swept by a cold wave, I stumble to my knees—it was only a matter of time—and taking deep, steadying breaths, I will my body to stay conscious in the face of this harrowing moment.

"Woah!" Caleb gasps, lifting me up. "It seems all this fun has overwhelmed sweet Clara!" The crowd's muffled laughter attempts to occupy my foggy mind. "For the first time in history, our Bright Light shall deliver the final retribution!"

Blinking ferociously with a subtle head shake, I regain control and grab the hammer—shifting my focus from

Celest to the emperor. The waves of desolation, despair, and hopelessness fuse into something new—a brutal hatred. I allow this feeling to take control and fuel my following actions. For me to avenge Celest, I must kill her.

The wind's ferocity matches mine as if it's sharing my rage. My cape is billowing frantically, and I want to copy its wild behaviour instead of maintaining this elegant pretence. With my unyielding glare locked on the emperor, I raise the hammer high above my head—ignoring my trembling arms. His lips curl on his devious mouth, confirming this is his twisted punishment for my bad behaviour, and anger boils within me, colouring my vision in shades of red. With a fierce resolve—I swing the hammer downwards.

Crack. The rope's singular cry of celebration for killing its final victim is all I hear, but I can't look. The rife festivities around me feel so far away—they're muffled—and all I can see is the director of this cruel show. Mixed with defiance and resignation, I drop the hammer for it to clash on the wooden floor and perform a deep curtsy laced with mockery. The contempt in my eyes screams: happy now?

I never want to feel this helpless again.

Disconnected from the real world, I hear Caleb's voice but don't listen to his words. I can only comprehend the all-consuming anger. It's directed not only at the emperor but also at the Folcriht—Silas, Casimir, *and even Fay.* Did they know Celest was alive? Silas wasn't lying when he told me she was dead. Is he able to trick my gift? Or is someone else responsible for this deceit? Either way, now isn't the time to allow such thoughts to govern me; the evening is far from over, and I've yet to venture deeper into the lion's den.

An imposing effigy, towering at a height of eighteen feet, glides into the vacant space before the stage—it represents the final Prime Minister of the former United

Kingdom—with a hunched back, a wicked look, and rubbing his hands together like he'll steal your children. Torches are handed to selected crowd members— illuminating their elated expressions. With a ceremonial air, they encircle the effigy, and each person sets him ablaze simultaneously.

The flames lick the night sky, and an immense inferno devours the historical figure, with billowing smoke being swiftly drawn into a purification vent. Ravenous flames bathe the palace in a threatening glow, and they're joined by an enormous golden crown that magics itself into existence, floating above the crowd. It rotates, showing off its opulent design to remind people why the monarchy is better than them.

Suddenly, the crown mutates from gold into a deep, gloomy shade of black, and a singular fragment drifts from it, captivating everyone's collective gaze as it darts through the masses. Excitement ripples as more and more pieces join the procession, swirling and dancing in unison. I suddenly notice their true transformation; they're not fragments—but birds. Each one is unique in its appearance and spirit. The avian symbols soar freely through the sky, dive-bombing crowd members and eliciting exhilarated gasps.

Even in my distressed state, I recognise the importance of this moment. The Folcriht listened to my feedback and has created a symbol that no longer elicits notions of destruction—but liberation. Each spritely bird represents life and newfound freedom, departing from its captive regime. I wish I could celebrate this win, but any positive feeling instantly drowns in the ocean of loss and betrayal. I want answers.

CHAPTER TEN

In the Lion's Den

I've spent so much of my life battling inner conflict that it's become second nature, and I'm adept at handling the unexpected, but I won't stop asking myself critical questions like: *am I doing the right thing?*

Guided by Baroness Somerville, I leave the spectacle behind me, and we approach the imposing palace together. The enforcers are efficiently dispersing the crowds and restoring order following the chaos induced by the Folcriht. Crossing the threshold, I find myself entering a sweeping hall—its sunken floor makes it feel like the building is swallowing me. Marble columns stand tall, with smooth surfaces that gleam under the ambient lighting's soft glow, adding to the opulence that permeates this space. The air carries weight and suspense as if every step I take is heavy with the gravity of this precarious moment.

We climb the grand staircase, with ornate railings and bold red-carpet runners guiding our ascent to a new level within the palace. I try to examine my surroundings, but I only think about Celest. Emotions surge within me, threatening to overpower my resolve—guilt, betrayal, and hatred battle for control—but I must find the strength to harness and use them as fuel for my plan. I have no other choice.

Traversing the infinite hallways, ancient paintings decorate the walls, and detailed sculptures of men and beasts watch me pass display cases showing off ornaments and trinkets at every turn. The baroness's husky voice fills the air, her peppy spark evident as she points out various 'interesting' features throughout the palace, but I'm unable to truly engage in her words.

A sudden realisation hits me, forcing me to stop. What I thought were mannequins positioned along the walls are, in fact, young girls—my brooding and rich surroundings have blinded me to them. I cautiously approach one of them, and woe sweeps through me. At first glance, she resembles a doll in a frilly dress with an apron—but as I examine her appearance, the two prominent scars extending from the corners of her mouth reveal themselves. She's statuesque, with lifeless eyes—like a cruel demon has drained her of all hope and happiness. *But why?*

"I—I'm so sorry," I utter.

She stares directly over my shoulder, vigilantly avoiding eye contact, and barely moving her lips, she whispers, "Don't eat the food."

"Clara!" the baroness shrieks from ahead, noticing I've trailed behind. "Leave her alone."

Taking one last look at the frightful girl, she offers nothing more. *What did she mean?*

We approach the grand doors that'll transport us to the banquet hall, and I hear the muffled noise of excitable conversations from within. The baroness stops before entering and squeaks, "Are you not the luckiest girl alive?"

I offer no verbal response, just raised eyebrows, resulting in her fiercely shaking her head, before throwing open the doors to reveal a room bustling with activity. The nobles seated at the endless array of round tables suddenly fall silent—their ravenous eyes feast upon every morsel of my being. I advance with small steps like I'm balancing on a cliff edge.

The baroness announces my arrival, "Your Majesty. I humbly offer you our Bright Light, Clara Rosewood."

My curtsy triggers the nobles to rise in a flurry of excitement, applauding with zeal as the emperor and queen remain seated at the top table. With a subtle nod, he grants us permission to take our seats and the baroness takes the lead as I navigate through the crowd. They sniff my hair when I pass, sending shivers up my spine—but I maintain a composed exterior, offering no visible reaction.

The men don tailored evening suits featuring long-tailed coats enriched with daring patterns and embellishments. Ruffled jabots falling down their front compliment their crisp shirts, and completing each look are snug-fitting breeches and polished leather shoes.

Luxurious gowns enwrap the women in different pastel colours, each garment draping around their figures. They're enhanced with exquisite designs, lace, and shimmering sequins that catch the light with every movement. Their hairstyles are showier, expertly braided and garnished with jewelled hairpins and feathers. Strings of pearls and gold drape their necks, and dainty drop earrings dangle from their ears. Their complexions are flawless, with flushed cheeks, huge bright lips, and absent eyebrows, giving them an otherworldly appearance. I hate to admit this, but it feels like I'm in the company of gods.

Joining five others at a table positioned centrally, I find myself directly facing the emperor as Baroness Somerville reluctantly heads towards a table further away. The Duke of Crimsonford and Head of Imperial Defence—Sebastian Sinclair—is to my right. He holds a prominent position in the emperor's privy council. In his early forties, he exudes arrogance, with thick blonde hair meticulously woven into a French braid, adding to his immaculacy. The Duke of Crimsonford remains standing as the others take their seats, and the tables surrounding us avert their interest from me to their fellow diners. Like clashing cymbals, the duke claps his hands once and declares, "Introductions!"

Clockwise around the table, I'm introduced to each member of the emperor's privy council, starting with the Duke of Grafton and Lord Chancellor—Arthur Barrington. A cold air surrounds him, with sunken features that illustrate his old age and wispy, white hair brushing his shoulders. He's the emperor's chief legal advisor and oversees the justice administration.

Next is the Earl of Willowbrook and Lord High Treasurer—Frederick Fairfax—he's the youngest on the table, aside from me, but he appears knowledgeable beyond his years. A thin moustache rests upon his pursed lips, with small beady eyes that seem to see everything simultaneously. I'm told he's responsible for the empire's finances and exceptionally talented at ensuring it remains the most robust economy amongst its competitor nations.

The Marquess of Fairchester and Secretary of State—George Worthington—takes a particular liking to me, given away by him excessively licking his beard-covered lips each time his eyes land on my breasts (which is far too often). He leans forward, with both bulging arms resting on the table, taking up too much room. He oversees various constitutional departments, manages communications, and implements the emperor's directives.

Next to him sits the Marquess of Ashfordham and Lord Privy Seal—Nicholas Wentworth—who's the most disinterested in me and more intent on listening in, with his drooping ears, to conversations between the neighbouring diners. His large stomach creates a noticeable gap between him and the table, and I'm mesmerised by the wobble of his chin each time he shakes his head aggressively, reminding me of a toad. His role is ceremonial, and he acts as a trusted advisor.

I'm also introduced to the Archbishop of Canterbury—Lucian Whitaker—sweating profusely in ceremonial robes that drown his slender figure and anxiously tapping his spindly finger with a sharp, pointed nail on the table. Rumour has it he doesn't have a healthy relationship with the emperor. I imagine it's because the archbishop is relied upon to defend the emperor's divine right to rule over England.

"And saving the best until last," the duke smirks. "I am Sebastian Sinclair, Duke of Crimsonford and Head of Imperial Defence." He requires no introduction. The duke often parades himself throughout the empire; he's charismatic and considered a close and loyal friend to the emperor. With him being responsible for defence, we're regularly provided updates on his whereabouts at the agency.

I'm none the wiser about who could be the Folcriht's supporter within this group, but I'll find out. Casimir has tasked me with getting to know them, asking carefully constructed questions to gauge whether they could turn. I'll carry out my duty—but I'm more interested in the queen this evening.

"Thank you, Your Grace." I blush, playing my part dutifully. "I—gosh—it really is an honour to be in the presence of such nobility and wisdom."

Servants swarm the room in an orderly fashion, first serving the top table bowls of soup before moving down in what appears to be a hierarchical display. I stare at my bowl, a deep pond of purple that fills my nose with a bitter aroma. A different group of servants arrive in a similar procession; they stand to the left of each member on the top table and the three closest tables to the emperor—including me.

The Duke of Crimsonford must sense my confusion; he leans towards me and whispers, "Tasters, reserved for the most important … and you are one of us this evening."

I turn my head to acknowledge the young girl placing her life at risk for me; she's gazing upwards to avoid any eye contact. *Don't eat the food*. I'd almost forgotten. Could someone be trying to poison me? My logical mind overrules my heart's urge to knock the spoon from her hand—I can't alter her fate—and as I remain glued in place, she lifts the soup-filled spoon into her mouth, holds it for a second and performs a dramatic swallow. I hear the other tasters simultaneously gulp. The emperor's taster is the most nervous. Considering his large physique, I reckon he's spent many years doing this.

A few tense moments pass, and they march away. However, abrupt gasps nearby disturb my sigh of relief. Nobles are clambering around, desperately distancing themselves from a convulsing body on the floor—my taster. Two servants rush over and drag the poor girl across the carpet. Her face is bright-purple and swollen, as though someone is pumping it full of air, and her eyes are bulging from their sockets. With blood seeping from every orifice, it's a gut-wrenching sight. I instinctively step forward to help, only for the Duke of Crimsonford to snap his arm outwards and stop me. He shakes his head slowly as I stare at his stern expression with desperation, mutely urging him to release me. Servants remove the girl's corpse from the deathly silent room, and I slump into my seat with an unmistakable look of panic that encourages the emperor to announce his revel with roaring laughter. The others share in his amusement whilst the Duke of Crimsonford remains composed next to me.

"It seems our esteemed guest has made a few enemies!" the emperor howls, slicing through everyone's noisy delight. "How does that make you feel, Bright Light?"

A hush falls over them, and they watch me with wide eyes, eager for my response.

Unable to hide the anxiety plastered across my face, I barely utter, "I—I must be important to be ... wanted dead."

With a mix of relief and disgust, their collective cackle returns like a clan of hyenas, and the emperor is visibly impressed with my response.

A servant boy rushes over to remove my soup, and the Marquess of Ashfordham pipes up at his arrival. "Boy!" he demands. "Give me something stodgier! I *do not* want a drink for a starter!" His body jiggles with dissatisfaction.

"Tell us, Miss Rosewood," the Duke of Grafton next to me asks. "What hobbies do you possess?" His raspy voice makes my toes curl as he strokes his pointed chin with yellow fingernails, awaiting my response.

"Beyond my role in the agency, I enjoy reading poetry," I respond. "Please excuse my curiosity, Your Grace, but may I ask what hobbies you have?"

He leans into me, trembling with what I can only describe as titillation and carrying a scent of dust and old wood. "Serving *justice*," he purrs through gritted teeth. The conviction in his response sends a chill coursing through my body—there's no chance of him turning against the emperor.

With dinner continuing into the late hours, after being served endless courses (which the Marquess of Ashfordham regularly sends back to request heftier portions), I've discovered these men have no desire to turn against the emperor. They don't serve out of fear but their pride over the immense power they hold. For one, the Earl of Willowbrook has an intense passion for 'collecting' young boys and girls from different kingdoms. He exhibits them— in custom-built display cases—throughout his estate in York. Despite its perversity, he proudly tells me stories of his collection, like how he *personally* graced Denmark with a visit to scout for a blonde, blue-eyed boy and the thrill he felt from forcefully removing one from his distraught family.

The Marquess of Ashfordham tells me about the infamous event he hosts annually on his estate in Surrey— boastfully entitling it the Queer Hunt. It's highly exclusive, with aristocrats throughout the empire desperate for an invitation to spend a weekend with compelling and influential individuals, hunting gay men and lesbian women (and anyone else who doesn't adhere to the imperial heterosexual norms). In some wicked ceremony, the marquess and his chums dress the hunt's victims (or prey) as their opposite sex. The blood-thirsty aristocrats will then compete to kill the highest number of 'abominations' (not my words), and whoever performs the most unique and twisted method of killing receives a 'special prize'. Last year, the marquess awarded an earl in the kingdom of France with a sculpture crafted from the preserved bodies of those he'd slayed.

I want this night to end. Nothing could've prepared me for the darkness I've experienced so far, and it's made me realise I should only expect things to get worse. Finally, I turn to the only man I haven't spoken to at this table—the Duke of Crimsonford beside me. He can't be the Folcriht's supporter—I've heard harrowing stories about his methods of gaining control over occupied lands. He's also responsible for wiping out everyone on the Isle of Man—claiming it was full of radicals—only for him to transform it into a heavily fortified military base.

A tender tap on my shoulder distracts me before I can get the duke's attention, and Queen Calantha stands behind me. "Miss Rosewood."

I jump from my seat, face her, and perform the most perfect curtsy. "Your Majesty, I apologise," I say politely. "I did not see you there." *Could this be my opportunity to finally speak with her?*

"No matter," she responds coolly. "The emperor would like you to sit with him. Shall we exchange places?"

Of course. Tension instantly follows my disappointment—I forgot he'd want a private audience with me eventually.

Taking my leave, I tread lightly towards the emperor—like I'm walking on eggshells. His cold glare urges me to turn and run, but I ignore it. Performing the necessary greetings, he lazily gestures for me to sit beside him.

After what feels like a lifetime of being ignored, he finally breaks the frosty silence with an equally icy tone. "Baroness Somerville has not trained you well, Miss Rosewood."

"I sincerely apologise," I respond with a bowed head. "Today—this evening—well, it's been rather overwhelming. I am sorry for the offence I have caused."

"I want better from now on," he responds. "But I understand. All this"—the emperor waves around the room—"Well, it must be incredibly daunting to my subjects."

"Daunting, yes," I sigh. "But also, an honour, of course."

"What gift have you brought me this evening?"

"A poem, Your Majesty."

The emperor nods, permitting me to proceed, and I take a sip of wine to wet my mouth. Shifting to face him, and with a measured pace, I begin:

"Hail, emperor of these joyful lands,
Your strong hand brings blessings grand.
Secure we dwell, under your stare,
With food and water, our hearts aware.
With wisdom's grace, you guide our way,
Bright arts and Muses, your sway they obey.
A name in ages, the lasting flame,
May power and glory be your heir's claim.
Amenable voices, homage they pay,
No storms disrupt our tranquil day.
With nation's pride, their memory's delight,
Your deathless fame is forever bright."

A silent pause ensues. The emperor's expression remains stoic, and just as I'm about to apologise for my terrible gift, he claps his hands that haven't seen a day's work, with a beaming smile painting his face.

"Marvellous!" he exclaims. "Wait—it reminds me of something ..." He squints his eyes in contemplation and clicks his tongue. "Ah! The poet, William Mason?"

"Yes!" I respond, pretending with great dedication to share in his elation. "He was my inspiration. I have spent many sleepless nights in the Grand Library rehearsing. Baroness Somerville hinted at your interest in poetry. I'm— I'm honoured you enjoyed it, Your Majesty."

"Indeed. Quite different from the homemade wreath or lack-lustre painting other Bright Lights gift me." He leans back in his seat, easing the friction between us.

I fight the urge to grab a nearby knife and pierce his knee.

He continues, "How did you like playing the role of executioner this evening? It was quite the show."

Attempting to divert my burning desire to release my fury, I casually swirl my drink. "I am ashamed to admit this, but for a moment, I was weak."

"I could tell," he says bluntly.

"I hope you do not mind, but your presence—it gave me strength."

"That explains your ferocious stare."

"I am sorry. It was inappropriate."

"Do you know why my father introduced the Harvest, Miss Rosewood?"

"To remind people of the consequences of their actions, Your Majesty."

"Oh no, no, no." He snickers arrogantly, shaking his head. "It is so much more than that. *Hate*, Miss Rosewood. It comes *so much* more naturally to the human heart than its opposite. It is easier to unite the masses under a common hatred than a mutual love."

"I see," I acknowledge with a smile, despite yearning to disagree with him. "And what about your Royal Court? The people in this room?"

"What about them?"

"If you unite the masses under a common hatred, how do you unite the nobles?

"You are quite the curious little bird." He chuckles.

"Please, ignore me." I blush and flutter my eyelashes. "A girl like me has no place being so curious."

"Someone told me you have a unique talent." Changing the topic, and with raised eyebrows, he caresses his well-groomed beard. "Is this true?"

"A unique curse," I respond playfully, which he appreciates. "I know when someone is being dishonest."

"My favourite vegetable is broccoli," he declares.

"Oh gosh." I giggle, shaking my head. "That couldn't be further from the truth."

"It's bloody awful stuff," he agrees. "I like playing chess."

"True."

"Very good," he says. "Hmm … let me think …."

The emperor clicks his tongue and stares into the distance, making it appear like he's pondering, but I can tell he already knows what to say. It's making me uncomfortable.

"I know." Leaning close, he whispers, "There's a traitor in this room."

A sharp inhale exposes my shock. "Your—Your Majesty?"

"Well, come on," he urges. "True or false?"

"True." *How does he know?*

"Remarkable!" He clicks his fingers with frenetic energy at his privy council, demanding them to join us. "*Yes, all of you! Come! Come!*"

The men arrive in unison and form an orderly line in front of us before performing deep and prolonged bows. If it wasn't for my trepidation, I would've found amusement in the Marquess of Ashfordham, who almost topples over from the weight of his belly, rising red-faced and out of breath.

"Which one of you would like a new personal secretary?" The emperor asks them, gesturing to me.

What?

The men start grumbling excitedly—like a pack of wild animals preparing to tuck in.

The Marquess of Fairchester licks his lips and rubs his hands together before stepping forward to claim his prize. "How generous! Your Majesty. I need a new assistant; mine is a bit lame, you see."

"I would find it most beneficial, Your Majesty," the Duke of Grafton pleads. "I have just purged many of my staff!"

Considering his previous disinterest, I'm surprised to see the Marquess of Ashfordham express his desire. "This Harvest has truly placed me under significant pressure. I could do with—"

"Sebastian?"—the emperor is undeniably tired of their begging—"You are awfully quiet over there."

The Duke of Crimsonford is the only one in this pack who hasn't expressed any desire to claim me.

"That's very gracious, Your Majesty," the duke responds. "But—"

"Fantastic! That's it, then," the emperor announces. "The Duke of Crimsonford has claimed Miss Rosewood." He leans close, pats my leg, and whispers, "Aren't you a lucky girl?"

***

Baroness Somerville guides me deeper into the palace. I find myself still processing my bizarre encounter with the emperor. Why did he insist on offering me a position with the Duke of Crimsonford? I imagine he wants to use me to locate the traitor, and he must suspect the duke. Or is he punishing me for my insolent behaviour during the Harvest Ceremony?

"I must use the lavatory," the baroness says. "Join me!"

"I—no, thank you," I respond. "I'll wait here, my lady."

She huffs and leaves me alone in a cross junction with a dome ceiling and four hallways branching outwards. In the centre stands a statue of a naked man—the polished surface glows under a spotlight. I look closer, gliding my hand over the smooth marble-like texture; the detailing is exquisite. I admire his face on my tiptoes until the eyelids shoot open to reveal the dark eyes they were concealing—they stare directly into mine. The shock throws me backwards, and I find myself on the floor. His eyes follow me, silently screaming for help.

"Get up!" the baroness snaps, rushing over. "Imagine if someone saw you like this!"

"Wait!" I exclaim. "Who—the statue. Who is it?"

She looks perplexed by my emotionally charged behaviour. "*That*?" she asks, pointing at the trapped man, whose eyes are pleading with me. "No idea—one of the emperor's hobbies. A wonderful artist, isn't he—anyway, come! We are going live on Echo soon. *Everyone* wants to watch you getting ready for the ball!"

The baroness drags me through endless corridors and past sealed rooms—I dread to think what horrors live behind them. Now more attentive to my surroundings, delicate signs of darkness become visible to me as we venture into the palace's depths—like the pack of canine-looking creatures with short, sturdy legs and patchy, discoloured fur. Their movements are jerky and unnatural, skittering through the shadows and intently watching my every move.

"Miss Rosewood." A melodic voice floats through the hall, but I don't know where it comes from.

The baroness stops in her tracks with a perplexed look. "Your Majesty?" she calls out.

"In the red room, Sophia," the voice responds.

The baroness drags me to a room with its door slightly ajar—a lavish space draped in rich shades of crimson and gilded with accents. Elaborate chandeliers hang from the moulded ceiling, casting a warm glow on the plush furnishings. Tapestries and artwork line the walls, telling stories of lust and desire. Queen Calantha is comfortably sipping wine. I enter and follow the necessary protocol.

"Please, sit, Miss Rosewood," the queen instructs. "Not you—Sophia. You can leave—and close the door."

The baroness dutifully does as she's told whilst masterfully hiding her frustration.

"Drink," the queen says. "You will need it."

"Thank you, Your Majesty," I respond.

She remains deadly silent and fixed on me—judging my every movement and facial expression—carefully assessing whether I'm a threat.

"Why do you people want this?" she asks, plainly perplexed. "Speak freely. It's just you and me."

"I am not—well," I sigh. "Actually, I have been asking myself the same question."

"Oh?" she says curiously.

"It has been quite overwhelming," I respond. "That's all."

"What do you think of this world you have entered?" she asks, taking another sip of wine. "Has it lived up to your expectations?"

"It is ... different," I respond cautiously.

"It is sick." The queen scoffs. "That is what it is." After a short pause, her expression transforms, and a stunned look washes over her face. "Gosh, I—ignore me." She laughs nervously. "Clearly, I have been drinking—"

"No! You are right," I blurt out. "It's vile here. I—I cannot wait to leave."

She turns to face me directly; her eyes are now rageful. *"Don't be so disrespectful."*

Her words send blood rushing to my cheeks, and I bow my head. "I'm sorry, Your Majesty, please forgive—"

"I have been watching you this evening," she interjects. "What do you think your brat-like behaviour will achieve?"

The sudden shift in her demeanour startles me, and I'm struggling to respond. I don't want to offend her intelligence by playing ignorance—like I could with the emperor.

"They executed my closest friend," I sigh. "I know I—I should not feel like this, but she did not deserve it."

The silence is deafening. It's screaming at me to stop pursuing this hopeless hunch that Queen Calantha could be the Folcriht's supporter. I thought she was like us, trapped in the emperor's grip, and if I—a 'paltry' woman of the empire—were to be brave and show an ounce of defiance, it could spark a flame within her. But I was wrong. *What was I thinking?*

"You should tread carefully, Miss Rosewood," she advises, now softening her tone. "The emperor—he takes an interest in strong-willed women"—as she talks, the queen is drifting away into a dark and hopeless corner of her mind—

"Carry on, and you will become his next project …
something he can chip away at and destroy."

"He—I sense he has not chipped away at your
strength," I whisper.

"Who are you to comment on my strength?"

"It's just—I hear rumours."

"*Rumours*. Of course," she scorns. "I imagine they are
the same *rumours* that have prompted the emperor to
organise a public display of humiliation for me."

"Your Majesty?"

"He says my subjects show me too much admiration,"
she sighs. "I am too soft on them. He says I damage his
ultimate rule. However, they don't admire me—yes, I might
be soft sometimes. That is why they use me to challenge
him."

"What makes you think they use you?" I ask.

"*I know it,*" she urges. "Just this evening—during their
Harvest in Edinburgh—they lined the streets with my
portrait …"

"That does not sound—"

"*And they burned an effigy of the emperor.*" Tears are now
streaming down Queen Calantha's cheeks.

I mask my shock, remaining composed so I don't feed
her distress. "You cannot be blamed," I say, shaking my
head. "Why should you be punished?"

"To show them I am *weak*." She snorts ironically
beneath her tears. "But they already know that—why else
would they use me to undermine him?"

"Perhaps your compassion has inspired them … not
your weakness."

"*Compassion?*" she sneers. "That is just another word for
weakness in our world."

"Strength is not found in controlling others with fear," I assert. "But in daring to inspire them with love, regardless of the risks involved."

There's suddenly a profound reflection within Queen Calantha's eyes, with her attention turned inward, navigating a labyrinth of thoughts, each pathway leading to hidden chambers of profound revelations—but in an instant, she escapes, returning to her harsh reality.

"Ah, yes. I heard you were quite the poet," she sighs defeatedly. "I wish it were true."

I believe her, not just because of my gift but because of the fervent yearning for change that paints her face. Perhaps Queen Calantha is the key to overthrowing the empire.

CHAPTER ELEVEN

A Dance and Death

Ethereal music floats down the hall on our approach to the ballroom. Baroness Somerville's excitement intensifies, given away by her skipping and energetic movements. Though I might feel ridiculous in my peacock-like costume (which doesn't leave much to the imagination as to what's underneath), the baroness's attire is even more outrageous— resembling that of a wild fox. I'm not surprised to learn the same designer crafted both our outfits—Astra Armstrong. To make it worse, the baroness streamed the whole ordeal on Echo Live, with millions tuning in to watch my abominable transformation.

The ballroom doors swing open, and the enchanting tune escapes from the vibrant room, originating from a live orchestra in the corner. Melodic strings and a charming piano guide the dancers across the polished wooden floor. Couples twirl and glide in perfect harmony, synchronising with the tune's rhythm.

Spectators observe from extravagantly carved wooden balconies. Their awe-filled eyes follow the dancers' fluid movements, swept up in the atmosphere, and soft murmurs of conversation, with the occasional laughter, intermingle to create a zesty ambience. I don't intend on becoming a Bright Light they eulogise, so I'll avoid mixing with these well-dressed monsters and do what I was taught as a young girl—to make myself small and sneak around in the shadows (which'll be difficult considering my feathers are screaming for attention). Of course, I'd happily chat with Queen Calantha some more, but she's seated next to the emperor on an elevated platform. We're sharing a moment as she exchanges a subtle, unspoken message, hinting at her desire to break free from the chains binding her to him. Fortunately, he's busy staring at his SyncLink and fails to notice me.

The men wear suits similar to what they dined in, slightly adjusted for comfort. However, the women undergo a striking metamorphosis. Each embraces a unique theme, embodying nature while baring their skin and feminine physiques. The spectacle will appear magnificent to many, but I can't ignore the disturbing purpose behind this stark contrast between the two sexes. I suppose I'll take comfort in knowing that I'm not the only one on display to cater to these men's desires.

One woman, for example, captures the essence of water, her dress resembling the currents of a river—rippling and shimmering as she twirls. It reveals a significant portion of her upper body whilst a skirt gracefully drapes from her waist. She leaves a fading trail of illusionary water suspended in the air with every movement.

Another woman wears a tight-fitting dress that shimmers with black and blue iridescent feathers, mirroring the plumage of a starling bird. Her lively avian counterpart follows suit mid-air with each twirl, extending and retracting its wings in mimicry of the woman's motion, arcing and spinning perfectly with her dance. In a fleeting, almost choreographed interlude, it finds solace within the intricately styled nest on her head.

Unique creatures accompany many others—a red squirrel with one and a kaleidoscope of butterflies encircling another. It's a sight both beautiful and tragic to witness. These animals and insects exemplify a cruel fad driven by superficiality—bred in captivity and conditioned to perform unnatural behaviours.

The same darkness running through the palace seeps into this hall. At first glance, the servants appear to be wearing porcelain masks, a smooth, blank canvas concealing the wearer's identity. However, on closer inspection, you'll realise these masks fuse with their flesh, clinging tightly to every curve and leaving no gaps that reveal their true faces beneath.

"Go!" Baroness Somerville squeaks, nudging me forward. "Enjoy yourself."

❄❄❄

So far, having endured the company of too many lords and ladies, I've failed miserably to make myself inconspicuous. One viscountess insisted I attend her weekly jewellery-making class, but only for the next twelve months until I lose my Bright Light status. I was polite, sharing my gratitude and suggesting she request the Duke of Crimsonford's permission, which led to her hastily retracting the invitation. It's well known the lower-ranked aristocrats fear him—at least one good thing has come from my new job (which I've yet to learn more about).

Then, there were the blue-balled barons. A title I awarded the young trio that cornered me like a drove of aroused rabbits, with restless legs, heavy breathing, nonsensical chatter, and an inability to lift their gaze above my neck. Remarkably, all it takes to scare away three horny teenagers is a seemingly demure lady chewing a vol-au-vent with her mouth open (and the occasional burst of exaggerated fake laughter). It's a deterrent I should try more often, though I wouldn't be surprised if such unladylike behaviour was illegal.

"How are you finding it, Bright Light?" the Marquess of Fairchester asks, finding me seated in the darkest corner and rudely interrupting my short-lived solace. Red-faced and breathless from chasing women all evening, he carries two glasses of wine (one for each hand).

"It is quite marvellous, my lord," I respond politely.

"Indeed," he says, eyeing me up and licking his lips. "This is my favourite part of the evening."

"I see you have been enjoying yourself," I note.

He breaks into a wheezy laugh. "You must be ecstatic to join the Duke of Crimsonford's staff."

"I am, my lord."

"I would have looked after you much better than him," he grunts jealously, plonking himself next to me and placing one glass on the floor so he can stroke my neck. Stiff as a board, I hold my breath, but he snubs my discomfort and continues, "Many of the duke's staff have *mysteriously* disappeared, but under *my* care, you would—"

"Sincerest apologies, Lord Fairchester," the Duke of Crimsonford interrupts. "May I steal our Bright Light for a dance?"

I'm briefly relieved by his interruption—but I'm simply moving from the jaws of one danger and into the clutches of another.

"But—oh," the marquess stutters. "Of course, Your Grace." He's not pleased—behind his submissive exterior is a child who's had his toy stripped away from him.

With the ethereal music continuing to pervade the ballroom, the duke leads me to a space amongst the couples gliding around us. Although his embrace is gentle, my fingers tremble slightly as they awkwardly meet his—I feel like a prisoner in his grasp. Following his lead, my movements are stiff and forced, as if each step is a small battle against my anxiety. I struggle to match his pace, stumbling over my feet as his eyes bore into mine, and his potent gaze makes my pulse race faster.

He notices my discomfort, instantly relaxing his grip and slowing his movement, and with a softened expression, it's as though he's silently urging me to trust him. I surrender myself to the melody and the duke, allowing the dance to become fluid—with each turn and spin, the room around us blurs. His touch feels less foreign, and I'm effortlessly mirroring his movements.

"Do not let the marquess intimidate you," the duke says. "A little tip … if you go along with his advances, it will not take long for him to lose interest and move on to his next conquest."

I'd prefer just talking at him with my mouth full.

"I will bear that in mind," I respond shyly. "Thank you, Your Grace."

"I noticed you taking quite a bit of interest in the council members over dinner," he says casually.

"Oh, I—you did?" I stutter, battling the fear creeping in. "I—I am quite curious. It is useful in my line of work."

"Some may argue that inquisitive women are dangerous, Miss Rosewood."

"Would you agree?"

"Oh yes." He nods. "But dangerous to whom? That is what I would like to know."

"If I may, Your Grace," I plead, itching to change the subject. "How will I serve you in my new role?"

"I have yet to decide," he responds, gently pulling me closer. "Say goodbye to your colleagues at the agency, and take some time off … perhaps visit your sister."

His whole essence alters to silently reveal we share the same secret, and he floods me with his deep remorse for the pain I've endured. This revelation triggers something, and a foreign sense of safety permits me to feel vulnerable, throwing open the floodgates for emotions to escape. The duke is quick to foresee my loss of composure and swiftly leads me from the ballroom floor to the safety of an empty gallery, where we sit in silence—allowing me time to regain control.

The emperor is in deep conversation with the Earl of Willowbrook, and the queen occasionally glances up in our direction—it looks like she's longing for my company, though I could be wrong.

An exuberant ruckus surfaces, where a group of young noblemen surround one of the servant girls, violently prodding and pushing her; one even attempts to remove her mask. She drops and curls on the ground, desperately trying to shield herself from their torment.

"*Animals*," the duke mutters under his breath, though a smile remains plastered on his face as he watches. "They make me sick."

"Who are they?" I ask.

"Green bloods—new money." He sighs. "A few earls and barons who have infiltrated and poisoned our once great establishment. They are descendants of people who held extreme wealth during the True Ascension, owners of technology companies and arms traders. Some came from America and bought their place in the royal court. My ancestors were far from perfect, but they valued tradition and respect, and King James forced them to stand aside while these rapacious parasites corrupted our values and beliefs."

"Is this why you support the Folc—"

"*Not here.*"

"Of course." Mortified by my stupidity, I lower my head. "I'm sorry."

***

Swarmers scuttle across the walls and ceiling as I approach the emperor's residential apartment in the palace—they watch my every move—and I force each step that draws me closer to the impending threat. The emperor sent me an abrupt invitation for a private audience with him while the Duke of Crimsonford was telling me about his upcoming visit to Canada, where he'll be persuading their government to join the empire.

I'm paused at the door. The emperor's butler looks at me for some time, assessing whether he must make any last-minute adjustments to my appearance. After some heavy groping, he dramatically raises his fist and delivers two heavy knocks. The door swings open, allowing the pungent odour to escape and hit me like a punch to the face—lavender mixed with rotting fruit.

"The Bright Light, Your Majesty."

Despite feeling disorientated by the smell, I manage to perform a dignified curtsy. The emperor relaxes in a large leather armchair in the darkest corner of his living space. Ambient lighting casts an ominous glow throughout the room, and ancient paintings depicting violent scenes decorate the walls. The most disturbing features are the gilded sculptures of different human and animal body parts.

"Sit, Miss Rosewood," he demands with a velvety tone that floats across the room, motioning to an empty armchair beside his. He pours us a glass of wine each, and I wait for him to take a sip before drinking mine. Beyond the smell, the air is thick with an elusive tension, and I don't know what to expect from this encounter.

"My wife does not like you," he declares coolly.

"Oh," I gasp, straining to hold back the heat from rising to my face. "I—why is that?"

"She tells me you are desperate." He chuckles. "With poor etiquette!"

"I am sorry, Your Majesty," I respond, holding in a sigh of relief.

"Ha! If you are disliked by my wife, you are liked by me," he jokes. "The queen—that girl—she is a poor judge of character"—I wonder if Queen Calantha is trying to protect me—"I want to let you in on a little secret, Miss Rosewood."

"Yes?"

"There is a reason I placed you on Sebastian's staff. Do you know why?"

"I assume it is because of my ability."

"Yes! Clever girl!" he exclaims. "Do you remember our little chat earlier?"

"How could I forget?"

"I want you to locate the traitor," he instructs formally.

"You think it is the Duke of Crimsonford, Your Majesty?"

"I do not know," he sighs. "But Sebastian is my largest threat, considering his position."

"Hmm," I respond, acting cool as my turbulent mind processes his request. "So, you will move me to the next person if I find him trustworthy?"

"Of course. Not too quickly, though. We do not want to raise suspicions."

"If I may. You are placing a great deal of trust in me— I'm trustworthy! Of course. But ... you barely know me."

"I see you are a sweet, innocent, and dutiful girl. That's enough for me."

"It's an honour." I timidly bow my head. "Thank you, Your Majesty."

"What do you know of the Folcriht?" he asks.

"The Folcriht ...?" I respond, openly perplexed. "More than most people—from the agency, of course."

"I received intel that one of my privy council members supports them," he reveals calmly.

I gasp, acting shocked because I am. *How does he know?* "Supports them how?"

"I am hoping you will tell me in good time. You are the solution to my little problem—ah!" His movements suddenly become erratic—the once calm and collected disposition is already a distant memory. "I have one final parting gift." As he taps his energetic leg, the emperor reaches under the table beside him, watching me diligently to avoid missing my reaction to the upcoming surprise.

A portion of the wall fades from existence, and I fail to withhold my shock at what's revealed. It looks like a human at first glance, but you'll realise it isn't on closer inspection. The creature is bound to a wooden structure, and there's a smooth surface between its legs. Replacing what should be its eyes are two emerald gemstones, and it possesses no mouth, just skin, with no ears and a huge nose. Tubes carrying various liquids enter and exit different locations of its body. As if this sight isn't disturbing enough, a series of decorative scars have been inflicted on its exposed skin—some are new, and some are old—it's as if this creature is being displayed like a piece of art.

"A favoured piece in my collection," the emperor proclaims. "I've had this one for almost a decade."

Pride emanates from his wide smile, but I'm unable to utter a single word. The emperor slides an ornate knife towards me.

"Have some fun," he says in a most unsettlingly casual manner. "It's tradition for my Bright Light to express their creativity."

Dread glues me to the chair, and I stare at the knife for too long. My toes attempt to curl in these restrictive heels, and my nails grip the seat's leather arms. *I don't want to do this.* The emperor nudges it towards me again—a silent indicator of his growing impatience. I have no choice but to obey, so I grab it and force myself from the seat.

Edging towards the poor creature, my attention is on the ground—compelling each step to drive me forward. This *must* be my final trial. The knife slips in my sweaty palms. Despite him remaining seated, I can feel the emperor's anticipation growing behind me—the vibrations of his sick and twisted arousal brush the back of my neck, and the clicking of his tongue assaults my ears. As I inch closer, I realise where the smell of lavender and rotting fruit originates from. The creature is quivering as if it can detect my approach—but I don't sense fear—it's stimulated.

Inches away, its head droops just above mine, and like a blind dog, it sniffs the air around me. Inspecting the decorative scars closer, I see floral patterns, cartography, and the names of guests who took great pleasure in contributing towards the emperor's artwork. I raise my knife, pause, and with precision and force, I slide it into the creature's heart—praying it's enough to kill it instantly. I'll undoubtedly pay the price for taking the emperor's prized possession away from him. Seconds feel like hours as I remain rooted to the spot, with my head bowed, eyes closed, and my grip firmly around the knife; the creature takes its last hollow breath. The warm trickle of blood runs down my arm and the back of my neck, painting me red.

"We will meet again, Miss Rosewood." The emperor's icy voice frees me from my trance-like state. "You are dismissed."

I've killed twice this evening.

CHAPTER TWELVE

An Emperor's Downfall

"Higher, Clara!" Celest pleads excitedly.

"I'll try!" I shout, waiting for her to fly back.

She sits on the makeshift swing we've constructed on the bank of a river.

Almost there.

I grab the seat and leap, allowing it to carry me upwards before I force it down again with all my might, sending Celest further away—she's almost touching the stars. The full moon casts a supernatural glow over the running water, and the light dances across the surrounding trees.

"And again!" she exclaims from the sky.

Readying my stance, I prepare for her descent and declare, "I'm re—"

"*Clara …*"

I whip around but can't see who whispered my name.

"Hello?" I call out.

Silence.

"Who's there …?"

Silence.

No one is in sight. I sense Celest flying towards me again, so I turn to face her, only to bound backwards and lose my balance, falling to the ground. I'm no longer watching Celest have fun, but instead, her lifeless body swings from a noose like a haunting pendulum. A torturous expression paints her face.

✻✻✻

The train propels me through the English countryside, distancing me from London, the emperor, and the trauma he inflicted upon me. It's been a few days since the Harvest, and I don't know how long I spent in the shower—curled up and sobbing like a helpless little girl, never feeling clean from the guilt, the horrors, and the blood.

I've been too frightened to leave my apartment, incapable of facing the outside world. The mass display of executions hasn't helped. I journeyed through London to reach the station with my head lowered, eager not to look at the countless corpses the enforcers had strung up for all to see. It's The Crown's retaliation to the disorder caused by the Folcriht's holographic display during the Harvest.

Memories flash before my eyes without warning, like when I sent Celest to her death. The rope's snap assaults my ears, and the image of her swaying in my peripheral forces me to mourn her again. Though the nightmares are starting to settle, I've yet to achieve a whole night's sleep. However, I understand now: if I'm to pull through this, I must use my trauma to fuel the fire within me and transform it into a ravenous blaze. Only then will I achieve my ambition. I want the emperor to see his world crumble before I kill him.

I may not be an expert in tearing down an empire, but I'm confident I can inspire Queen Calantha to join forces and ignite a fierce rebellion in Scotland. However, I first need to overcome the obstacle that's Casimir and the Folcriht's council. Once they agree to join forces with the queen, I can use my position in the Duke of Crimsonford's staff to spend time with her. As for the rest of my plan—well, I haven't figured that out yet.

***

It's not long before the sound of racing footsteps fills the street. I lift myself from Fay's doorstep to see her speeding towards me, eventually flinging her arms around and locking me in the safety of her embrace. I expected my emotions would pour out during this moment—but they don't. I remain calm and composed in Fay's arms, and I'm the first to move, wiggling out of her soothing grip to head inside where we find a comfortable place in her kitchen.

"Tell me when you're ready," she soothes. "Take all the time you need."

I inhale and ask, "Did you know Celest was—"

"No!"

"Did Silas?"

"He says he didn't," she sighs. "But you'll need to ask him yourself."

"And Casimir?"

"I haven't spoken to him."

"Any of the others?"

"I'm not sure. I—I'm so sorry, Clara."

"Both sides are using me."

"What do you mean?"

"One of them knew—Casimir, or Lawrence, I reckon—that she was alive," I respond. "They're manipulating me, and now the emperor has demanded I locate a traitor within his privy council, starting with the *Duke of Crimsonford*."

Fay gasps before stammering, "And do you—you know … know that…?"

"That he supports the Folcriht?" I respond bluntly. "Yes."

I relay my Harvest experience, starting with the conversation I held with the woman—Julia—who snitched on her friend and the rollercoaster of emotions I experienced throughout the day and evening. We talk about the dark world that the 'beautiful' Buckingham Palace conceals and the contrast between how royalty lives compared to regular people. Fay appears sceptical as I discuss my interaction with Queen Calantha and how she could be the key to the Folcriht's success. However, my decision to put the emperor's creature out of its suffering interests her the most.

"You killed it?" she asks.

"Of course!" I snap. "What else could I do?"

Fay leans back in her seat and sighs—she's absorbed in introspection, almost challenging her troubling thoughts.

"What was going through your mind when—when you did it?" she asks.

"I don't know. I just—I remember the blood."

"*Jesus*. This is wrong, Clara. You're being put under too much pressure. There's only so much your mind can—"

"I'm not backing down. I haven't crawled through the mud to not reach my destination, Fay."

"And where is this destination?" she asks with raised eyebrows. "What do you think will happen? I mean—I hope I'm wrong, but it doesn't sound like the queen will join our cause, for one."

"I can persuade her."

"*How?*"

"*You weren't there*," I stress. "You didn't see what she was like. She's *desperate* to escape. Besides, the emperor's attention is on his council. We can use it to our advantage."

"The emperor has eyes and ears everywhere. He's never distracted."

"But he underestimates the queen!" I exclaim, leaning into the table as if it'll strengthen my case. "They all do. They think she's weak. So, he'll—they'll—never expect her to rebel. I just need the Folcriht to see her potential."

Fay shakes her head. "I don't know, Clara. It sounds like it'll take a lot to convince her, and it's really risky."

"When she learns about the duke's support, *I know* it'll give her the courage to do something."

I won't tell Fay about my goal of killing the emperor. She already worries for my humanity (and I haven't planned that far ahead).

"You would be replacing one royal for another," she says. "The Folcriht—Casimir, he'll never agree to it. He wants them *all* burned at the stake."

"He's spent too long underground. He doesn't know what it's like in the city. The elation these people feel in the emperor's presence and their hatred towards the men, women and children that were sent to their deaths"—I shudder—"These people they—they're not ready for a republic … it's too extreme. I think they're ready for a compassionate leader—someone to morally guide them."

"And you think that's the queen?" she asks.

"I *know* it."

Fay starts chuckling.

"What?" I ask.

"It's just—look at us!" She snorts. "Who do we think we are? Plotting the downfall of an emperor. It's mental."

I remain silent momentarily, processing her comment with a slight smile. Fay's right; this is absurd, but it's also the first time I've felt like I can at least try to do something meaningful.

"We're awful, aren't we," I respond jokingly. "We should be talking about the perfect cream-to-milk ratio for custard or how best to iron a man's shirt—no! Even better, our mouths shouldn't be filled with words at all; they should be filled with our husbands' cocks—"

"*Clara!*" Fay howls, paving the way for us to fill the kitchen with joyful laughs. After a few minutes, she taps her hand on the table, having regained composure, and in a serious tone, she asks, "Do you think this can work?"

"I do, yeah," I respond. "After everything that's happened, I need to believe that change can find its roots and grow, even in the most desolate place. I need to feel passionate about something to keep moving forward."

"I like that," Fay responds. She no longer looks cynical; instead, her eyes express conviction. "Listen, I was being silly earlier. I'm proud of you for coming up with this, and if *you* believe in it, then so do I."

"Cheers, Fay. That means a lot."

"Out of interest," she says curiously. "What will you do if Casimir says no to your plan?"

"I don't know." I shrug. "I'll cross that bridge if it comes."

CHAPTER THIRTEEN

New Connections

"No!" Casimir roars, pacing up and down the council chamber. "Absolutely not! I won't let some fairytale pipe dream destroy everything we've achieved."

Despite confirming there's no hope in turning any of the emperor's privy council, he dislikes—no, he hates my suggestion to explore the opportunity with Queen Calantha. I haven't confronted him, or any of them, about the issue of Celest being alive. I sense their reluctance to broach the subject, so I'll allow them time to explain themselves later. Silas, Bee, Lawrence, and Edward remain seated; their dispositions are calm compared to Casimir's erratic behaviour. The air between us is taut—especially since I learned they were responsible for poisoning my taster at dinner (apparently, it was necessary to build trust with the nobles).

"I must agree with Casimir," Lawrence sighs. "What makes you think the queen is our solution?"

"Because you fail to recognise her potential," I respond frankly.

"That doesn't answer my question," Lawrence responds, slighted.

"With all due respect, Lawrence," I say. "You and the emperor share the same perception of the queen. You both think she's weak"—Lawrence and Edward jeer simultaneously, but Bee is stifling her amusement—"*That* is why she's the solution. She is strong, and the emperor will never suspect her."

Silas has been silently observing the debate and now decides to contribute. "If Clara is right, we could muster enough force to hit the empire hard and fast. Combined with Sebastian's plan, that'll surely fire up the people."

"Sebastian's plan?" I ask.

"No time for that now," Casimir interjects. "Besides, Sebastian wants to share his plan with you personally. Thank you for the suggestion, Clara, but we won't be exploring it any further."

"Hold a vote!" I exclaim. "Let—"

"No!" Casimir snaps. "The people elected me to deliver a manifesto, and that was to build a republic, *not* to hand power to another monarch."

"In light of the new information," Silas says. "We should give people the oppor—"

"*Silas*," Casimir spits. "We've already asked them to cast one vote; any more will cause the Folcriht to distrust the strength of our leadership."

"You've already held the vote on women joining your military?" I ask.

"It passed," Silas says, trying to hide the hint of excitement flickering in his eyes.

"Excellent!" I exclaim. "If you won't take my advice, at least let me join the fight."

"No," Casimir says.

"Why?"

"Because you're working with Sebastian, you can't do both."

Although I disagree with much of what Casimir says, he's right about this. The duke—Sebastian—is the highest priority right now. I'm on the emperor's radar, and falling out of existence will place a target on the duke's back, as well as a relentless hunt for me and placing the Folcriht at risk. However, there's a chance I could be accompanying the other members of his privy council in the future, and I promised myself I never want to feel helpless again.

"Then I want to train," I announce firmly. "I want to stay and train here until the duke calls for my support."

My demand results in a deafening silence until Bee gasps, "Cas! My *DexPlant*!"

"No," Silas growls.

"C'mon, Bee," Casimir sighs. "That's too risky. We need Clara to—"

"She's the perfect candidate," Bee interjects avidly. "I've finished the alterations!"

"That doesn't matter, she—"

"What're you talking about?" I ask.

Casimir throws Bee a look of frustration before taking a seat and placing his head in his hands.

Bee leans forward and taps her hand on the table energetically. "I've created a device—I call it a DexPlant. It can download dexterity from one person and upload it to someone else."

"And it sounds great until you have some poor bloke confined to a white room for the rest of his life," Silas sighs. "Don't do it, Clara."

Bee stands; she isn't giving up. "I'm confident it'll work. It could triple your military strength overnight, Silas! C'mon, at least let me run a few tests."

"When you say dexterity," I state. "You mean ... skills?"

"Yes!" Bee boasts. "But skills in performing tasks—like combat and—"

"I'll do it," I declare.

They all groan and sigh, except for Bee, who runs to me eagerly. "You will? Are you sure? You're in safe hands!"

"I trust you," I respond. "I mean, if I can handle the Harvest, surely I can handle this?"

"Clara needs to know the risks, Bee," Silas growls.

"A white room doesn't sound too—"

"Ah," Bee interrupts me; her tone is now grave. "I've eliminated the risk of it totally destroying your mind ... but there's still a *tiny* issue. Don't worry, though; I'll run tests before we do anything!"

"What is it?" I ask.

"It'll be Jasper's mind we download 'data' from," she says. "Everything that makes him a decent—no—a bloody talented combatant. Specifically, data from the brain's motor cortex, basal ganglia, cerebellum, and ..."—she notices me glazing over—"Anyway, I'll ensure it integrates with your mind. *However*, it'll be the first time doing it this way."

"What could go wrong?" I ask.

"If I don't modify the data from Jasper's mind correctly, you could take on more than just his fighting skills ... you could take on elements of his personality."

I think about my encounters with Jasper, his nervous and stiff demeanour, his lifeless eyes that have clearly seen some untold horrors—but so have I.

"You said I was the perfect candidate earlier," I say. "Why's that?"

"Because you're emotionally intelligent, logical, extremely self-aware *and* resilient"—*I suppose I am*—"It's the perfect combo," Bee responds.

"Ah bloody hell," Silas huffs. "She's got a point. There aren't many people I know who could handle it."

I'm grateful for Bee and Silas—how they recognise my strengths. I feel validated in my decisions and everything I want to do; it's not a feeling I was familiar with before all of this.

"And you think a successful upload can make it more universal, Bee?" Casimir asks, clearly keen to fulfil his own interests—which is fine.

"Yes, Cas!" Bee beams, her zest returning. "Clara could open it up to anyone in the Folcriht."

"When do we start?" I ask.

"Now!" Bee lifts me from my seat, and we hurry to the door.

"I have one final question," I turn to face Casimir. "Did you know Celest was alive?"

"Yes," he responds plainly.

I remain focused on his emotionless eyes, refusing to allow him respite from my forceful glare. "Manipulation is The Crown's most favoured method of control," I proclaim. "What other similarities do you share?"

I swiftly exit, leaving him—all of them—to mull over the question.

***

Bee's been talking at me for hours, and much of what she's said has flown over my head. She delves into the complex details of her device—the DexPlant—and how she used NeuroLink technology to write the code, which enables her to download data from the human brain. She's connected me to a large machine in her lab that quietly whirs as we converse. Bee explains it's currently gathering information from my brain, telling her how to seamlessly integrate the data from Jasper's mind into mine. Her enthusiasm and meticulous attention to detail help ease my nerves, even as I consider the risk of losing myself in this procedure.

"Right!" Bee claps her hands. "Once I've processed this, we'll be ready to upload. I'll be honest … I reckon it'll be a tad uncomfortable, but I'll give you a tip when the time arrives."

"Cheers, Bee," I respond.

"Go and find Jasper; he's probably in the shooting range. You should get to know him better. I doubt you've had a chance—he's a bit of a hermit."

I leave Bee typing away at her computer and head towards the range. This process feels intrusive, and I don't know how I'd feel if I were in Jasper's shoes—knowing someone else is gaining access to such an important part of me. I would've preferred to train organically, without relying on someone else, but I'm taking comfort in knowing I could significantly contribute to the Folcriht's efforts. If we're successful, they can use Bee's DexPlant to train thousands of people within weeks.

More people in the fort and town recognise me now. Navigating the network of tunnels to meet Jasper, I weave through the hustle and bustle. People share gleeful smiles, whilst others are solemn as if they pity me—I expect they've watched the footage of me executing Celest. Muffled gunshots ripple through the corridor, and the men in this section wear military uniforms and khaki overalls. The soft, blue hue from the lighting above casts a glow on their stern expressions. Marching with determination, they pay me no heed, their eyes fixed straight ahead as they pass by.

The range door slides open, revealing Jasper, who stands beside a young recruit, patiently guiding him through the art of shooting, lifting the lad's arm to demonstrate the proper stance for accurate aim. Jasper is unrecognisable; an unbridled passion eliminates his usual timidness. This is his sanctuary, a place where he feels truly at ease and confident.

Unfortunately, a wave of tension grips him once he notices my presence. His wide, pain-filled eyes make me feel like I've just strolled in and damned his family to hell. Dismissing the recruit, we're left alone in the cavernous space, and Jasper approaches me cautiously, struggling to maintain eye contact for more than a fleeting second.

With his voice barely above a whisper, he manages a hesitant "Hello."

"Hey," I respond awkwardly, feeling guilty for expelling his happiness with me being here. "Bee said I should get to know you a bit better. Only if you don't mind."

He looks at the ground, scuffling his feet. "Okay."

"Where do you want to go?"

Jasper shrugs his shoulders, remaining silent.

"Fancy teaching me to shoot?" I ask. "You never know … I might not need the DexPlant." I chuckle, hoping to instil some trust between us.

"Really?" Jasper asks, chirping up. "I mean—yeah. I'd be up for that." The new lease of life indicates his passion lies in teaching others. He grabs a pistol from the counter and hands it to me.

"What type of gun is this?" I ask.

"A standard Glock."

"Do you use energy like the empire?"

"It depends on what we're up against," he says. "But we prefer traditional firearms—they can penetrate imperial forces' armour. We'd only use energy if we're not looking to kill, which isn't often—unfortunately."

I mask my confusion—Jasper was disingenuous when he said 'unfortunately', which leads me to think he enjoys killing or he just doesn't feel bad about it. Either way, it makes sense—he couldn't fulfil his role if it riddled him with guilt, but why pretend?

He leads me to an empty booth and hands over a pair of ear defenders. I admire the spacious range where I'll be directing my aim, and Jasper talks me through different elements of the pistol. He explains how it works in great detail, even pointing out where the bullet exits, but I love his enthusiasm, so I won't kill his joy by revealing I know some of the basics.

The holographic image of a Royal Guard appears in the distance—my target. It's dressed in pompously gilded armour and wears an outrageously showy helmet that rises two feet above its head. Upon receiving my instruction, I raise and aim the gun towards it. Jasper edges closer to me, only to back away instantly, sharing a look of embarrassment.

"It's fine!" I blurt out. "I don't mind."

"Sorry—Okay—hold it here … and fire. Don't forget—"

I underestimate the force, which vibrates painfully through my wrist and arms, causing me to wince. A distant ding reveals I've hit something, but it's not my target.

"Ah! I'm sorry!" Jasper cries. "Are you alright?"

"Don't apologise!" I exclaim, finding great amusement in my poor performance. "I'm good! Just a rubbish student. You're doing great!"

Jasper blushes and continues to explain how I could improve my positioning, giving me tips on preparing for the weapon's force. Now that he's more comfortable, I take this opportunity to learn more about him.

"Silas tells me you were transferred to England from the SAS in Japan," I say. "How did that happen?"

"I was, yeah," he sighs. "Quite a few of us were transferred around five years ago—guys from different kingdoms. It was in reaction to the Folcriht increasing their activity in the cities. The aristocrats were getting spooked."

"They dragged you so far from home … I'm sorry."

"I didn't have anything left there anyway."

"What did they have you doing when you came to England?"

"I was stationed with different members of the emperor's privy council—in their personal guard."

I take a sharp breath. "That's—that's rough. They're sickos."

"Hmm. It was awful."

"Sorry, I've spoiled our fun."

"It's fine," he responds.

"Do you—do you wanna chat about it?"

"No. It's inappropriate," Jasper says, shaking his head. "Besides, I don't want to share that burden."

"I spent hours listening to them at the Harvest; I can deal with it."

"You don't mind?" he asks cautiously.

"Of course not!"

"Where should I start?"

"From the beginning."

Jasper tells me about his first assignment with the Archbishop of Canterbury—Lucian Whitaker. I listen intently as I continue practising, his voice transmitting through my ear defenders. He recalls the endless religious ceremonies he'd endure and meetings the archbishop would hold with other council members. It was interesting to learn about the extent of the archbishop's strained relationship with the emperor. Jasper tells me about a heated discussion between them years ago when the emperor demanded an amendment to the holy scriptures, which would suggest a story of how he and the divine rule in unity. The archbishop strongly advised against it, not because it was blasphemous but because of the risk it posed to the masses' beliefs. According to him, if religion taught people that God held equal authority with a human, it would diminish God's perceived power and risk the emperor's divine right to rule as king over England. This sparked a nerve, and the archbishop faced the emperor's wrath that evening. Jasper found some pleasure in being powerless to free him from a freezer.

He also describes the dark rituals that would take place every Tuesday. They were a rite of passage for spiritual leaders throughout England who wanted to climb the church's ranks. Depending on the level of responsibility they were trying to achieve, the rituals would become more challenging. The worst ceremony Jasper witnessed included the sacrifice of a newborn calf—and that was just for someone wanting to become a vicar.

Jasper continues to share his experience with the Duke of Grafton and Lord Chancellor—Arthur Barrington. The Secretary of State would often 'pester' the duke, urging him to implement new and innovative methods of execution to spark new fear within the people. They held countless meetings planning new techniques, but the marquess could not persuade the duke to depart from using the gallows because he's a traditionalist. They did, however, test the use of energy barriers to execute people during a Harvest in Italy—crushing them to death—and both agreed it was 'slightly' too graphic for the children in the audience.

Jasper is now aiming down the barrel of his gun. "My last assignment was with Wentworth." He takes one shot and hits his target square in the head. "He would host extravagant parties at his Surrey estate."

"Yeah, I learned about his Queer Hunt … the sick bastard."

"There was a particular event—not the hunt—where no expense was spared," Jasper explains. "Aristocrats throughout the empire attended. He has these rooms—each one with their own theme—somewhere his guests could satisfy their different—I don't know, interests."

"Oh no."

"Oh yes," Jasper scoffs. "Some rooms weren't bad—you know—groups would gather in one of them to have 'fun'. Each to their own. Once, an emergency alert beckoned me to one of the rooms. Someone was attacking the guests, and they fatally stabbed a woman—"

This memory has interrupted Jasper's trail of thinking; he's drifting away from me, staring into space.

"Take your time," I say.

"Sorry, I—anyway. This room—the smell—I can't begin to explain how bad it was. Rotting flesh mixed with perfume … I was almost sick. I've never seen so much blood. There was this young Japanese girl restrained to a stone table. The guy who escaped was her dad. I'll never forget her face when she saw me. Behind the terror and pain was a bit of hope—you know? She saw someone familiar. Must've thought I was there to save her ... but I didn't ..."

Jasper is becoming increasingly distressed; his breathing is shallow, so with a tender touch, I rub his shoulder to offer some reassurance.

"You were as helpless as the—"

"I shot them both—killed them instantly."

"You *saved* them."

Jasper huffs. "How'd you figure that?"

"You ended their suffering," I urge. "It was the only merciful thing you could do."

"I'm a coward. I should've slaughtered the lot of them."

"This *isn't* your fault, Jasper. I don't see a coward. I see someone brave who's risking everything to save others from their cruelty." I lightly pull Jasper into my embrace. He's clammy, stiff, and unfamiliar with affection, but he's loosening up and allowing himself to appreciate this moment.

My SyncLink suddenly vibrates—as does Jasper's—we're being beckoned to join Casimir.

✿✿✿

"Please, everyone, sit," Casimir instructs as we enter the council chamber.

I take the empty seat next to Silas and use the disruption caused by the arrival of Bee and Lawrence to converse with him in private. Leaning into him, I whisper, "Did *you* know Celest was alive?"

He takes a deep breath. "I found out when you did. It looks like we've both been played." He's being truthful, so I lean back in my chair, and Silas gently grasps my knee. "I'm sorry you were put through that … it's wrong."

With everyone seated, Casimir activates the HoloCast on the table, which displays the Duke of Crimsonford in front of his stately home.

"Subjects of the Anglo Empire," the duke bellows. "I address you today with a heavy heart. As Head of Imperial Defence, I am responsible for the safety of our great empire and thus responsible for *your* protection. For this reason, I am stressing my deep displeasure with the current state of affairs. You have all experienced unacceptable levels of disobedience and radical behaviour this year. These terrors are futile and insignificant, but they are invading your peaceful villages, towns, and cities, and I will not stand for it.

Vermin want to destroy the righteous values we hold close to our hearts. When our great emperor entrusted me to protect everything he had built, I vowed to ensure we remained a society untainted by the corrosive beliefs of old, outdated, and *dangerous* traditions. I have made it my mission to establish a solution to our problem. Not only to fulfil my duty but to role model the behaviours that the emperor and his subjects expect from me."

The duke pauses for dramatic effect and takes a deep breath; his confident gaze remains locked on the camera.

He continues, "I must inform you, with great disappointment, that I have discovered a traitor within my own house, and his name is Samuel Barrington, Head of Imperial Security and Intelligence"—the image pans out to reveal Samuel, gagged and with a noose around his neck, next to the duke on the platform of a gallows—"This poor excuse of a man has been found guilty of treason through negligence. I consider the protection of our empire to be more important than anything else, and I do not tolerate incompetence within my own staff. So, Mr Barrington must pay the price for his ineptitude." The duke dramatically raises his hand and holds it in the air before striking it downwards, sending Samuel to death. "In his place, I appoint Lavinia Radford as Head of Imperial Security and Intelligence."

At the mention of her name, Radford struts confidently up the platform's stairs and stands next to the duke. She directs the snootiest smirk you've ever seen into the camera, acting like a child who's just beaten her sibling at a race as the lifeless body of her predecessor swings inches away.

The duke continues, "Join me in congratulating Mrs Radford on her new role. I am confident she will fulfil her duty with great dedication."

The image disappears, and Casimir breaks the stunned silence. "Looks like she got what she wanted."

"Why would he execute Samuel?" I ask.

"Because he was getting too interested in Sebastian's activities," Casimir responds. "Particularly his visits here."

"Why Lavinia?" Silas asks.

"No idea," Casimir responds. "It was probably the most logical option. After all, she *did* nurture this year's Bright Light."

"She's extremely intelligent—observant too," I say, ignoring Casimir's poor choice of words (using 'nurture' to explain Radford's involvement in Celest's execution). "Do you think there's a risk he could underestimate her?"

"Sebastian is *more* than capable of handling it," Lawrence declares. It's his only contribution so far, and Edward nods silently next to him.

"You're right, Lawrence," Casimir says. "However, I would still like you all to bring at least three risks to our next council meeting, considering Lavinia Radford is a senior member of Sebastian's team. We have a duty to support him." Casimir paces as everyone's attention remains on him, and he suddenly clarifies, "Oh! I don't need anything from you, Clara. You're not on the council."

He's gone out of his way to humiliate me, but I did humiliate him earlier—this is just tit for tat. I take a deep, steady breath and consider my following words carefully. "Of course," I acknowledge. "Why am I here?"

"You're leaving for Canada in three weeks, Clara," Casimir responds bluntly. "That's all I wanted to tell you."

"What does the duke want me to do in Canada?" I hide my shock. The furthest I've travelled is the Lake District, and I never dreamed of flying overseas, especially outside of the empire.

"Sebastian doesn't like other people giving away his surprises," Casimir sighs. "He wants to present your mission personally—he's playful like that. It's a bloody nightmare."

❊❊❊

Silas doesn't bother hiding his amusement when I tell him about my poor performance during my shooting practice.

"So, you didn't hit *any* of the targets?" he asks while accompanying me back to Fay's house.

"No! I told you … I was crap."

"Did you at least get to know Jasper better?" he asks. "Knowing him, he didn't give much away."

"Actually, I did. He told me about his time protecting the privy council members."

"*What?* How'd you get him talking about that?"

"It's amazing what a bit of trust and empathy can do, Silas," I respond jokingly, though he can't ignore the hint of seriousness.

"You know I wasn't lying when I told you I didn't know Celest was still alive, Clara."

"But you knew that poor girl would be poisoned!"

"Yeah, but—ah—fine, there's no excuse. I'm sorry."

"Most of our conversations involve you apologising for something. You're lucky I can handle surprises, *and* I'm forgiving. It's just—some warning would have been nice."

"Lawrence was supposed to arrange that … did no one warn you?" he asks.

"One of the housekeepers—at least I think she was a housekeeper—all she said was 'don't eat the food'."

"There you go, a warning!" Silas responds with a grin.

I roll my eyes and shake my head, restraining laughter because I know it's wrong to find his warped humour funny.

"So—I wanted to ask you something," he says shyly.

"What?"

"When Bee completes the procedure tomorrow—did you wanna—nah … forget it."

"What?"

"Nothing."

"Why're you acting like a schoolboy?"

"Eh? I'm not."

I stare at him with raised eyebrows.

"Fine," he sighs. "I was gonna ask if you fancy training with me. I'll help you test out your new skills."

"Sounds good," I respond coolly—I'm just praying he doesn't notice the hint of excitement that's given away by my sudden energetic stride.

***

As Bee readies her machine, the whirring grows louder, warning me that she's about to flood my mind with Jasper's. I'm seated and securely strapped in a reclined chair, with Fay offering comfort by holding my hand. Strangely, I hadn't been nervous until now. Sleep eluded me last night because my brief encounter with Silas was hogging my every thought. *Why do I get such a kick from the prospect of spending time with him?* The feeling he stirs inside me is difficult to explain, a blend of apprehension, euphoria, and mystery. His attraction to me is something I'd typically dismiss, given the circumstances, but there's something about him that makes me feel safe, even in this dangerous world I've entered.

"These little pads have tiny needles in them," Bee says. "They won't hurt, but like I said yesterday, the upload will be uncomfortable."

"I'd take this over Buckingham Palace any day," I respond.

"Right, this sounds a bit naff," Bee says. "But it's important. I want you to think about something—anything—you love most about yourself. It must be a personality trait—*not* your perky arse." Bee's humour can lighten the heaviest tension.

Identifying a quality I love about myself seems foreign and challenging, but Fay's knowing smile hints at her understanding of something I haven't considered. Everything I did before meeting Silas and the Folcriht feels insignificant, and I didn't like the person I used to be. However, there must be something new within me that I'm genuinely happy with. I think about the times I've felt compassion towards someone; it's something I should love about myself, but it's flawed. I show no compassion for the emperor or his cronies—and my actions risk the lives of innocent people. Perhaps I should focus on my resilience. Despite my trials, I've pulled through, but I don't want to be resilient all the time. I want to feel vulnerable and weak occasionally; it makes me appreciate when I'm strong.

Though I've found flaws in some traits I hold dear, I can't fault the one thing they share a commonality with— my passion.

"Bloody hell," Bee wheezes. "You're an alright girl, Clara. It can't be *that* difficult to think of something you like about yourself."

"I've got it." I chuckle. "I was just—you put me on the spot."

"Good, on the count of three—oh, and don't forget what I said. This is gonna be uncomfortable. Are you ready?"

I inhale deeply, preparing myself for what's to come. "Go for it."

"One … two … three."

I first notice a deep buzz that's gradually expanding in my head. The room fades away, and an unseen force draws my consciousness inward; it's like I'm descending into a cosmic realm. This space is ghostly—I see what I can only describe as a fragile essence flickering like a distant flame. It feels familiar, so I focus on it, urging it to come closer, to grow larger.

The buzz intensifies, and I feel the stream of foreign thoughts enter this ethereal space. It's a vivid sight, they're encircling my flame, and tendrils lash out, attempting to erode it.

I know I'm under siege, and with every fibre of my being, I scream at the flame to push back against the invading torrent. It's an intense struggle, a battle of wills within the recesses of my own consciousness. My sense of self shimmers and wavers—the overwhelming influx of information threatens to engulf it. I stretch my awareness and grasp my flame, offering a lifeline amidst the chaos.

The frenzy of incoming data continues growing more substantial, so I reaffirm my values, memories, and desires, focussing on my passion to shield me. With every passing moment, I achieve more power over the torrent, and it finally begins to recede—the foreign knowledge calms and finds a place to settle nearby like an animal I've tamed. As a sudden darkness enters, it brings newfound clarity and leaves behind a serene stillness.

CHAPTER FOURTEEN

A New Strength

A threat hurtles towards my head, and instinct takes over as my hand whips up to stop it. Opening my eyes, I find Fay staring at me in shock, standing by my bedside, her wrist locked in my grip.

"Sorry," I mumble, still coming around. "Did—did I hurt you?"

"No, you're alright," Fay says. "You just caught me by surprise. How did you—"

"No idea." I shrug. "Felt the breeze, I guess. What happened?"

"We were hoping you'd tell us," Fay says, motioning to Bee, who's stood apprehensively at the end of my bed. "We moved you to medical. You've been out for five hours. How're you feeling?"

"Just cloudy," I respond, rubbing my eyes. "I can't remember a thing, I'm afraid." Climbing out of bed, I almost trip over myself at the foreign speed of my movements.

"It'll take some time to get used to," Bee says, shining a light into my eyes. "I don't really know why I'm doing this; I've got no idea what I'm looking for … I'll get the doctor."

Bee turns to leave and instantly whips around—her fist is hurtling towards my face, but it feels like she's moving in slow motion. I catch it effortlessly, causing her to squeal in delight.

✤✤✤

"We should wait for Bee," I advise. "She wants to monitor my first round of training."

"We could be waiting a while," Silas grumbles, handing me the pistol.

He's right, and I'm keen to start putting my new skills to the test. We have the shooting range to ourselves—Silas saw to that. My target materialises about fifty feet away.

"I want you to fire a single shot in the centre of its chest," he instructs.

I raise the gun and assume my position. Strangely, it feels second nature—as if I've done it countless times. My intuition guides me, assuring me that I'm doing everything right. Peering down the barrel of the gun, I take aim, shoot, and a radiant green glow emanates from the centre of its chest as if cheering my success. A rush of triumph forces me to yelp in joy, and Silas claps his hands, shaking his head in disbelief.

"A fluke!" he jokes. "Now the head."

I do it faster this time, and my bullet lands in the intended location. Silas continues instructing me, guiding my aim to different areas of the target's body, and with each shot, he asks me to confirm if it would kill or demobilise them, which I answer correctly in most instances.

"You could make some minor improvements to your posture," he says, gesturing for permission to touch me. "Do you mind?"

I nod casually—at least, I hope it's casual—and assume my firing position. Silas stands behind me, leaning his head near mine, mirroring my actions as he stares down the barrel. I feel his right arm loosely wrapped around my chest, and his bristly yet delicate hand guides my wrist to adjust its position. The warm breeze from his breath stroking the back of my neck tempts memories of our first close encounter in the lift when we were still strangers. A familiar exhilaration resurfaces, and in this rousing moment, I'm savouring every second, longing to submit myself. The edge of his rough beard tickles my ear, and I'm convinced he'll notice the goosebumps spring to life on my arms. With his body close to mine, the thrill takes over, and I edge backwards to close the distance—embracing the firmness of his chest and the waves of his abs.

"Okay." His whisper is shaking. "Aim for the chest again."

I take a deep breath, but as I exhale, my hands tremble, and I miss completely. Turning my head slightly to look at Silas; his eyes scan the space before us, attempting to establish the extent of my poor aim. Resting his forehead on my shoulder in disbelief and finding enjoyment in my failure, he dissolves into a fit of laughter, prompting me to do the same as I remain locked in his embrace.

Silas raises his head again, and our eyes lock—the force of his piercingly dark stare grows stronger with every passing second, drawing me irresistibly towards him. My quivering legs would've sent me toppling to the ground without his supportive hold, and I edge my face closer to his. After a short anticipating pause, he does the same, inching nearer and nearer. As time seems to slow, I lose all sense of my surroundings, my focus solely on him.

"Oh, Jesus."

The voice slaps me from this daydream and forces us both to retract. Silas releases his hold on me, and I wobble, but his firm grip instantly clasps my upper arm, preventing me from falling over. Bee stands anchored at the entrance to the range, and by her wide-eyed reaction, you'd think she'd caught us going at it.

"Thank God I'm not a soldier if this is what military training looks like," she says.

Silas laughs nervously as Bee shakes the image from her head and struts towards us, tablet in hand and ready for business.

"I—er—no, Bee," he stutters. "We're working on Clara's posture."

"You were certainly working on *something*, Silas," Bee emphasises, now facing me. "You ready?"

"Y—Yeah," I utter, equally flustered.

"We're testing your firearm skills and situational awareness," she says. "Then close combat and endurance. Once we're done, you can return to your … *private* lessons."

We both remain silent and sheepish.

"Silas, grab Clara a proper gun," Bee demands. "One that doesn't look like a toy. I'll get the exercise ready. Clara, there'll be civilians in the simulation; they'll have a faint marker, so you know who to avoid."

"Anything else?" I ask, accepting the hefty assault rifle from Silas.

"Yes," she says. "Focus on demobilising the threats— don't just kill them cause you can."

Bee taps at her device, instructing it to design the environment that'll test my abilities. Within seconds, walls of different heights and depths rise from the ground in the once-empty space. I scan my surroundings with great speed, becoming familiar with the new setup, and raising my gun, I prepare for the trial—this is more fun than proving my fealty.

Taking steady breaths, I rapidly analyse a target emerging from behind a wall—it carries a knife but no gun—and without hesitation, I shoot its foot, causing it to fall and melt into the ground.

"Oh, nice!" Bee chirps.

Simultaneously, another threat jumps over a barricade and aims at me. I react swiftly and fire at its hand, causing its gun to drop, but it's still determined, so I incapacitate the other hand.

"I would've done the same thing," Bee declares.

"But even better, right?" Silas responds sarcastically.

A childlike head peeks over one wall; its eye glows a gentle green, so I move on to the three brutes emerging from my right. They move with surprising speed, taking diagonal strides towards me. They're unarmed, and I swiftly demobilise them, only to pave the way for another adversary to come into view. This time, it's holding a civilian hostage at knifepoint, and with unyielding focus, I fire a single shot between my target's eyes. Bee emits a sharp gasp, and I hear Silas rumbling with approval.

Wave after wave, the difficulty level increases, and I don't make a wrong move. My mind is fully charged, enabling me to make decisions with astonishing speed and foreign knowledge. As the test continues, I'm increasingly impressed with my newfound skills.

"Keep it up!" Bee exclaims. "This next one is tricky."

The scene becomes chaotic, with a mob flooding into view. Civilians are scampering to seek safety whilst others lie on the ground. I spot threats moving stealthily, and with each opportunity, I fire with fatal precision through safe spaces that reveal themselves within the throng, successfully hitting my targets.

Out of nowhere, and for reasons unknown, a heavily built civilian male is consuming my attention, and I'm hit with a violent desire to fire and kill him. It sends a tremor through me, and for a fleeting moment, I want to unleash a barrage of bullets indiscriminately, but I'm quick to remove this intrusive impulse. Determined to stay on task, I push it to one side, finally taking down my last enemy so the crowd vanishes, leaving just a stunned silence.

Bee gawks at her device, shaking her head. "I don't get it," she says. "You out-performed Jasper. In this same simulation, he kills—I don't know—one or two civilians by mistake. Your aim, situational awareness and response times are *actually* better than his."

"It's weird, for a moment—" I stop, carefully judging whether I want to share the whole truth of my experience. Bee's statement unsettles me—I can't deny the urge to shoot civilians during that test. Could there be darkness in Jasper that's infiltrated me? Or were those alien thoughts purely a coincidence? Either way, I'm not ready to share what happened.

"What's weird, Clara?" Bee asks, hanging to my every word.

"Ah, it's just—I felt like I was on autopilot. That's all."

"Your score is perfect," Bee adds. "You prioritised the right targets to demobilise—more so than Jasper—and you didn't miss a shot." She claps her hands together with glee, "Close combat next!"

✳✳✳

Soldiers fill this room—their presence makes me uneasy; I don't want them watching. *What if I make a fool of myself?* It's okay; they're too busy sparring on their cushioned mats throughout the open space—they won't be interested in me. Some wield weapons, whilst others simply use their fists. Sweat humidifies the air, and the clanking of wood on wood, the clinking of metal on metal, and their grunts and groans create a lively atmosphere.

"We'll use softwood," Silas grunts.

Bee is about to object, but I beat her to it. "Don't be daft, Silas," I tease.

He shrugs and walks to the rack, where he grabs a sleek, long metal rod, rounded on both ends.

"Impact bars!" he shouts, throwing it between each hand. His thunderous voice catches the attention of the surrounding fighters. "Back to work, boys!"

To my relief, they do as they're told, and their focus returns to training.

"How does it work?" I ask as Silas hands me a bar.

"You can use it as a single staff or as batons," he says, twisting the weapon to create two smaller versions and spinning them each hand. "It delivers a powerful force when struck against a human body—even above clothing and armour." He combines the two and taps the staff on the ground. "But it doesn't react when you hit an inanimate object. Adjust the force depending on what damage you want to deal. We'll put ours on level one."

I copy Silas and draw my finger down one of the batons until it sets to the lowest level. We settle on a free mat and position ourselves; the other brawlers become more interested in our activities. The reality of this situation is settling in—*a woman fighting a man?* It's absurd, and I love it. Silas is a seasoned warrior; he won't go easy on me, and I don't want to do well; I want to beat him. Facing each other, we lock eyes, and the training hall and our audience shrink.

Leaping into action, I move with agility, and Silas's strike hurtles towards me, but in a blur of fluid motion, I defy gravity and effortlessly evade him. He continues his assault with slow and heavy movements whilst I weave through the air—executing twists, spins, and leaps— dodging his attacks with ease.

Silas can't foresee my evasions and match my speed (though it isn't for lack of trying), so I test my defensive abilities—but I must be cautious because his physical strength trumps mine. Pausing a few steps ahead, I invite him to attack, and he accepts the challenge with a flurry of hard-hitting blows that I deflect, parry, and counter—my body responding instinctively to the ebb and flow of the duel.

"You're quick," he pants.

Consumed in the rhythm of our fight, time slows, allowing me to anticipate his every move—reading his intentions before they develop. Despite the sweat trickling down my brow, I maintain steady breaths—but my energy is depleting, and I realise he has the upper hand as I edge backwards. It's time to test my attack.

With a swift transition, I shift my energy from a defensive stance to an offensive one. My muscles are tense, coiled like a spring and ready to unleash what power I have left. With great speed, I close the distance between us—the bars feel like an extension of myself.

"This'll be interesting," he says with an eager smile.

Using the entire length of his weapon, Silas defends from all directions. Still, I'm resolute and entirely focused on delivering this pivotal strike—one to prove I'm more than just a helpless girl.

"Bloody hell," he mumbles as our bars clash.

With growing confidence, I find a rhythm and speed up my attack—the sticks distort in a flurry of motion. He momentarily underestimates my rapid assault, and with a resounding impact, the blow connects with Silas's chest, causing a metallic resonance to fill the training space. With a deep grunt, he slides backwards several feet, hunching forward to avoid falling.

Remaining rooted to the mat, Silas is huffing and puffing with a scrunched-up face as our audience keenly awaits his next move—only the sound of his shallow breaths lingers. I resist the urge to rush over and help, acutely aware of his reputation amongst our onlookers—I don't want to embarrass him.

Before long, Silas lifts his head and shares a big grin that fills me with instant relief and allows me to celebrate silently.

"Not bad," he commends before marching forward with renewed energy—his determination is evident with every step.

Keeping a closer distance between us, he has me trapped, and I sense his imminent retribution. I'm taken aback by his rapid movements, and my body is exhausted from his steady assault. Before I can fully establish his next move, I see the end of his bar hurtle towards my chest, so I raise my batons in a cross-like shape to desperately protect myself, but the air is snatched from my chest, and the cold blow sends me flying. I barely hear the crowd gasp as my body hits the mat.

I'm panting like an overly excited dog in the hot sun—but I don't care. With a tight chest, it's taking all my strength to expand my lungs. Dizziness swoops through me, and my body is heavy and sluggish as if hampered by an invisible weight. With each laboured breath, the smack vibrates through my being—a lingering sensation reminding me of my vulnerability (a lesson I'm growing to appreciate).

During this disorientation, a determination flickers—urging me to push through the discomfort. Focusing on my chest's rhythmic rise and fall, I reclaim my strength, and the fog lifts to invite clarity. I pick myself up, with shoulders back and chin raised, leaning forward as I prepare to lunge. Silas watches me in awe.

"I've seen enough!" Bee yelps frantically, running onto the mat and breaking the tension between us.

My body loosens, and I take in my surroundings, greeted by a sea of gaping mouths—looks of shock and bewilderment. A man steps forward, shaking his head in disbelief—he's a giant compared to the others, even Silas—and fiercely claps his hands. The soldiers follow suit and energise the room with a buzz. Amidst the celebration, I notice the odd face looking confused or slighted—it seems not everyone approves of my talents—but I know they'll warm up to the idea of having their arse kicked by a woman eventually.

✻✻✻

There are people you just click with despite knowing very little about them. That's why I appreciate the value of first impressions, because more times than none, they'll tell you if someone is worth your effort. Considering my first encounter with Silas was somewhat unconventional, it begs the question: why do I feel such a connection with him?

"I don't even know your surname," I announce, taking a sip of water.

Silas laughs. "It's Evans."

"Where did you grow up?" I ask

"Wexford," he responds between mouthfuls of food, speaking loud enough so I can hear him over the canteen's vim. "A small town just below Birmingham, my dad worked in a regonium mine, and my mum was a seamstress for the upper classes."

"How did you join the Folcriht?"

Silas stares at his plate, moving the food around with his fork. "It was about twenty years ago; I was eleven. My folks—they offered asylum to rebels that were heading north. One day, my aunt came to visit—my mum's sister—she was a nosy cow and found the space where three of them were hiding."

"Don't tell me …"

"Yep," Silas sighs. "I remember my mum begging her not to tell anyone, but she wasn't having any of it. She called them terrorists and went straight to the enforcer's office." He scoffs. "She became Wexford's Light Bringer."

"Jesus, Silas. I—I'm sorry."

"Who doesn't have a sob story, eh?" he says. "They held me and my folks in prison for almost five months leading up to the Harvest—separated, obviously. I hardly recognised them when we were about to be hanged—starved, beaten, bruised … you name it. I wasn't in such a bad state—which was good—they wouldn't wanna see me looking like they did.

Anyway, they had all three of us on the gallows—ah crap—that hissing still haunts me. I've never seen so much hatred in one place. I sometimes wake up in cold sweats, expecting to see that executioner in the corner of my room.

A sniper took him out before he could hit the hammer. It was chaos. People screaming, kids being trampled—ugh, I hate thinking about it."

"Sorry, we can talk about something else if—"

"Nah, it's important," he says. "The Folcriht were taking out enforcers—they made it look easy. Cas and his dad freed us—Cas was only sixteen at the time, and they led us through the crowd to stop the enforcers from firing on us, but that didn't stop them; they were bloody relentless. We got near the exit, but my folks—well, they took a few bullets for me"—I grab Silas's knee under the table and squeeze it—"They were good people. I hate knowing they died feeling guilty for putting me at risk, but they would've wanted me helping the Folcriht."

"I bet they'd be proud," I say.

"Yeah," he responds. "Robert—Cas's dad—he took me in. Made me go to school—which I hated—then I joined their military at sixteen. The rest is history."

Silas has taught me where his kind and caring nature comes from. To look at him, you'd think he's an aggressive war machine, but beneath his wild and ferocious-looking exterior, he's so much more. Learning about his pain and what drives his actions makes me want to dive deeper into his life.

"Thank you for sharing," I say.

"Your turn," he responds, smiling softly. "Tell me something about your life."

I can't help but feel a sense of guilt because I haven't felt pain or trauma at such a young age as Silas has.

"Okay. I grew up in the New Forest—a small village called Avon. You must already know that Fay and I lived in the middle of nowhere."

"Your dad grew meat, right?" he asks.

"He did, yeah—well, he maintained the machinery that grew the meat. My mum was supposed to be a wife but never took her meds unless she visited the doctor."

"Apparently, your homeschooling was a bit different."

"Yeah," I respond, shaking my head and smiling. "She never stuck to the curriculum, and we knew it too. We still passed all our tests! We just learned … more than other kids."

"Like what?"

"Hold on, let me think." I bite my lip as if it'll help me concentrate. "When we were ten—around that age anyway—we learned about the 'Violent Revolution' in the sixteen hundreds. The books taught us the anti-monarchs were barbaric and bloodthirsty. I read stories of them slaughtering towns and villages, how they raped women and children—horrible stuff. Anyway, the king agreed to relinquish his power because he felt terrible for the innocent commoners caught up in the crossfire. *However*, my mum would just hint at little 'secret' facts. I don't even know if they were true, but she was smart—we trusted her."

"Secret facts? Like what?" he asks.

"This was thirteen years ago, Silas," I jest, pausing to think. "Apparently, it was actually referred to as the 'Glorious Revolution' because it wasn't very violent. The people pressured the king to relinquish his throne because of his religion—I think. When he did, it meant they could pass a new law that gave Parliament more power than the monarchy. Something like that."

"Well, it makes sense," Silas notes. "Why would they want kids thinking they could have more power than the 'almighty' Emperor Magnus?"

"Don't you have any old history books in the fort?"

"We've got a few. But nothing dating that far back."

"Hmm. I'll need to check it out," I say. "How's your food?"

"It's not as good as *my* mash," he responds. "What was it like at the agency's academy?"

"What, the food?"

"No." He laughs. "Just life in general."

"Oh yeah." I blush. "It wasn't too bad if you behaved and could handle the occasional beating"—I'm dumbing it down, it was awful—"Celest helped me settle, and it got easier when I turned thirteen."

"They're bloody monsters," Silas grumbles. "Snatching kids from their families."

"They let my parents visit once a month." I shrug.

He clocks me withdrawing in on myself and grasps my hand under the table. It's been eight years since Fay and I lost them to a high-speed train collision when they were travelling to visit me in London.

"I know what happened," he says. "I'm sorry."

CHAPTER FIFTEEN

Repaying a Debt

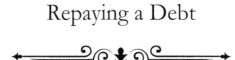

Jogging into the dense forest, the air grows cool, and the existence of civilisation fades away. Trees welcome me into their safe haven; their branches twist above to form a protective shield that casts shadows on the forest floor like artwork. The scent of damp earth and musky bark fills my nose.

It's been a week since Bee conducted her tests, and she recommends I exercise more—which I'm grateful for. Having an excuse to lose myself in nature and look after my body feels good. The ground beneath my feet shifts with every step, a carpet of fallen leaves cushioning each stride. This forest, which conquers one side of the town, is alive and teeming with creatures that rustle and scurry in the undergrowth.

Lost in this tranquillity, my worries and troubles fade away. Moss-covered rocks line the winding path and create steppingstones over trickling streams that dance through the woods. The crystal clear and icy cold water invites me to pause and quench my thirst. Taking this moment to rest and appreciate my surroundings, the vibrant emerald and muted olive colours blend with the occasional burst of autumnal hues as stubborn leaves cling to their branches.

Between my escapes in nature, I've continued shooting and sparring with Silas to enhance my skills. A few other soldiers wanted to try their luck in a tussle with me, which was great fun. It would often result in them fumbling for excuses as to why I won—the most favourable being: "I went too easy on her." Fay and I even spent time in the range, and it was just like when I first tested my raw abilities—she was terrible. I haven't been training with Jasper. Instead, he's been my jogging partner on many occasions and even surprised me with a picnic three days ago. Silas can't believe how relaxed he is around me.

Though the future holds many question marks, I can't deny this feeling of relief for taking a risk and choosing a path with the Folcriht. They're not perfect, but Fay and I have never been closer, and I've made new companionships with Silas, Bee, and Jasper. I finally feel like I have a purpose.

I continue my adventure. My quickened breathing matches my pounding heart's rhythm. With heightened senses, I'm attuned to the movement and whispers gliding through the forest and notice a subtle shift in my environment. Someone is gaining ground. The thump, thump, thump grows louder, accompanied by a faint exhale of breath, hinting at their determination to catch up. I don't look behind. With every passing moment, they're closing the gap, and I feel their presence behind me now.

Without warning, an unmistakable surge of adrenaline electrifies me, triggering a swift and decisive response. In one fluid motion, I skid through the damp earth and twist my body so my outstretched leg is in the path of the incoming intruder. Triumphant, their foot connects with my obstacle, which causes their huge body to lurch forward, and their rhythmic steps transform into a stumbling dance of surprise. Paired with my trap, gravity pulls them down, their face meeting the soft forest floor.

"What the fu—bloody hell, Clara." Silas's muffled grunts escape the earth covering his face. Lifting himself up, dirt and leaves cling to his beard and eyebrows.

"Shit!" I gasp. "I'm sorry!"

Though I try expressing some guilt, it's dampened by my poor attempts to hold back a titter.

Silas rolls on his back and raises his arm, silently requesting me to help him up. I grab it, and he pulls me downwards, so I land on top of him. He sprinkles dirt all over me with his free hand, and we laugh as I squirm, failing to escape his firm grip. Though putting up a good fight, it doesn't take long for me to admit defeat and submit to him. With my head resting on his chest and his hand stroking the back of my neck, I feel the rapid rhythm of his beating heart.

This is the perfect cushion—I'd be happy here for the rest of the afternoon, especially considering Bruno has come to say hello. He's become more affectionate towards me since our first encounter (mostly because I've spoiled him with treats). After curiously sniffing my face, he taps his scratchy paw on my cheek—as if gesturing to play—before becoming distracted by some movement in the bushes nearby and trots away to investigate.

"I'm proud of myself for … catching up with you," Silas pants. "Me and Bruno … thought you might like some company."

"Well, you were right," I admit.

Silas stiffens as if he's just had some grim revelation, and I detect his sudden discomfort, so I move away to give him space. He shuffles awkwardly into an upright position, and we sit silently on the ground, accompanied by the sound of breezy leaves, Bruno rustling in a nearby bush, and an unspoken conflict.

"Sorry, I—" Silas stutters, shaking his head. "This isn't appropriate, Clara."

"What? Why?"

"Because I'm much older than you, and—"

"Everyone is *obsessed* with my age! I'm an adult—"

"It's not just that …"

"What else?"

"It's my position in the Folcriht," Silas sighs. "The power dynamic. It's not right for me to be chasing you—*literally* chasing you!"

We sit in awkward silence as I struggle to comprehend his words.

"I'm sorry," I mumble, shaking my head. "I don't understand what the problem is."

"Don't apologise," Silas growls. "It's hard to explain. I mean—shit, I might have it all wrong myself."

"What does your position have to do with us?"

"I don't know it's—it's not so much the position, but the authority that comes with it."

"So, you think I'm only interested because you have authority?"

"No, it's not like that," Silas sighs, scratching his temple and carefully considering his following words.

He offers insight into his values regarding romance—mainly the importance of two people feeling mutually confident in a relationship. This is why he's uncomfortable exploring this 'thing' between us. I understand what he's saying, but I'm fascinated. I've never met a man who thinks this way.

"You're assuming I'll be uncomfortable telling you what's what if I'm unhappy," I say plainly.

"Not at all," Silas responds. "I'm assuming *I* won't feel comfortable being myself."

"And that's because you assume *I'll* feel uncomfortable," I repeat. "Besides, the fact we're having this conversation says something."

"That's valid," he admits. "I just don't wanna feel like a bad guy."

"Then let me help you feel like a good guy," I respond with devilish tenderness. "Let's run through our time together so far."

"Bad idea," he chokes, shaking his head.

"It'll be fun." I throw him a puckish smile. "We met when you broke into my apartment, do you remember? That was sweet."

"Yeah, it was sweet. I saved your arse from enforcers."

"Then you asked me to ditch my life," I add.

"Do you miss it?"

"Let's not forget almost blowing me up at work."

"You can have that one."

"I still have a bruise from you hitting me with a big stick."

"Did you want me to go easy?"

"I could keep going ..."

"Nah, you're alright." Silas pulls a purple flower from the ground and hands it to me. "Forgive me?"

"For what?" I respond, accepting it with a satisfied smile.

He snickers and shakes his head.

"Jokes aside, you are a good guy," I assure him, shifting closer. "Respectful, kind, caring. They're all important to me. No one needs to know; this could be our little secret—but only if you're comfortable."

He smiles. "I'd like that."

I raise my hand to stroke Silas's beard, and he grasps it, pulling me on top of him as we fall back to the ground, immersed in the depths of each other's eyes. The intensity of his heartbeat matches mine, and I feel the gentle rise and fall of his chest, with his breath tickling my lips. His firm hand on the back of my neck is electric, and right now, nothing else matters but our mutual desire. Our lips brush, a feather-light caress that leaves me wanting more, so I submit to the urge, interrupted only by ecstasy as the tip of his tongue brushes mine. Time seems to suspend as our kiss deepens, and we both submit to a hunger we've resisted for too long.

The unwelcome vibration in my wrist disturbs our intimacy, and we both express our frustration with a groan. Casimir is requesting we join him in the council chamber. I grudgingly push myself off Silas and grab his hand to help him up. We brush ourselves off, share a naughty grin, and jog back to town.

⁂

"According to our intelligence, he's being transferred from Reading to Coventry at midnight," Lawrence declares, hobbling towards a projected map in the fort's council chamber. "A small convoy, just three guards and two enforcers."

The room is taut. Deep agents have informed Lawrence that the agency has arrested Isaac—the same man who saved me from Quinlan. They're transferring him to Coventry this evening to torture him for information. I'm trying to ignore

Bee's glances at Silas and me; she's visibly curious as to why we arrived out of breath and sweaty.

"And you think this needs to be a black op extraction?" Silas asks.

"Yes," Lawrence responds. "We can't attract too much attention, and we don't want them knowing he was part of the Folcriht."

"All my special forces are up north," Silas says, facing Casimir. "Drakeford's still here, and Thornton could manage it, but we'd need at least one more person."

"This Isaac lad," Edward says, his frail frame shifting forward. "It sounds like he can handle himself, and he doesn't know about the fort. Do we really need to risk—"

"Yeah, Edward. We do," Silas snaps. "Not just cause it's the right thing, but because he also knows about Clara. We can say goodbye to having someone close to the privy council if we leave them to it."

"Lawrence," Casimir says. "How likely is it that Isaac hasn't been tortured and questioned already?"

"Highly unlikely," he responds. "But we will not know unless we ask him directly."

"I'll join Drakeford and Thornton on the mission," Silas declares.

"No," Casimir retorts.

"Jasper then," Silas says. "He's the best—"

"No," Casimir responds, shaking his head. "I need Jasper for something else."

"I'll do it," I announce, instinctively raising my hand.

The room falls silent, and they stare at me with stunned looks; Edward's jaw almost rests on the table he's hunched over.

"You're a civilian, Clara," Casimir responds.

"You send civilians to spy on the privy council?" I ask sarcastically.

Casimir stumbles. "Well—Jesus Christ, no, but you—you're not even trained in covert missions."

I have no interest in making friends with this man. "Ah yes, and when I walked into Buckingham Palace announcing I was Folcriht, everyone—"

"For God's sake, Clara," Casimir snaps, slamming his fist on the table (though it doesn't stop Bee's muffled laughter). "This isn't a playground!"

"I agree!" I mirror his action and smack the table, causing Lawrence and Edward to gasp harmoniously like Casimir's background singers. "So, let's stop playing and accept that I'm the most suitable person for this job!"

Bee clears her throat and says, "All of the results from Clara's tests suggest she'd be best placed in more covert scenarios, Cas."

"I think it's a good idea," Silas adds. I tap his foot as a silent thanks for supporting and believing in me, despite knowing he'd prefer I didn't do this.

"I won't let you down, Casimir," I stress, leaning back in my seat and allowing them to debate whether sending me into the field is appropriate.

✱✱✱

"What's that smell?" I ask Jasper as we proceed through the fort towards the main armoury.

"Probably a mix of diesel and oil," he responds. "I'm still getting used to it myself."

It didn't take long for the council to agree that I was best suited for this mission. Should I feel nervous? No, nothing will compare to the torment I experienced during the Harvest.

"It's weird," I admit. "I quite like the smell."

"I know what you mean." He chuckles. "How're you feeling?"

"I'm alright. What're Sergeant Drakeford and Corporal Thornton like?"

"They're good soldiers. You're in good hands—actually … they're in good hands." He winks at me.

We enter the main armoury, and the sight is extraordinary—I'd heard stories, but this is more than I could imagine. A vast, meticulously arranged collection of weaponry fills this massive space—each item gleams in the light. The same scent of oil is more pungent now, but it's also combined with metal. The walls display rows of heavy arms, like machine guns, shotguns, and rifles, whilst pistols, handguns, and crossbows of all shapes and sizes are secured to racks in the centre of the room. Ammunition fills endless shelves—each box and crate neatly labelled—and men diligently inspect and clean guns in a smaller space. Silas clearly runs a smooth operation here.

A large window directly ahead invites me to check out the view it shows off, and the expanse below reveals a bustling hub of military might, teeming with tanks and aircraft—lined up in neat rows like well-disciplined custodians. Though appearing powerful and capable of doing some heavy damage, they don't share the same energy as their younger imperial counterparts, which boast fresher looks and spectacularly destructive power. Most are outdated, but an advanced arsenal receives its dedicated area in this display. With sleek, dark, and minimalist designs, these unmanned massacre machines carry a sinister and secretive appearance compared to their ancient ancestors.

Perhaps they're stolen from the empire or smuggled through the Duke of Crimsonford's network.

A group of engineers are busy fixing a tired-looking tank, and a plume of smoke blasts from its exhaust—engulfing the men in a dark cloud. It's a ghastly sight—primal, dirty even—but I'm mindful of my conditioning when it comes to old technology. We're taught to despise anything that relies on fossil fuels, and it provides the people with a shared belief system that The Crown manipulates to bolster their control.

As impressive as this is, I can't deny it's a mere pebble in the ocean of weaponry owned by our opponent. It's a truth that reinforces the importance of igniting a raging fire in millions of people so they join the fight—and I can't think of anyone better to achieve this than Queen Calantha.

Jasper throws me a pair of black combat trousers, a vest, and lightweight chest armour. I don't hesitate to start undressing, and he promptly runs away to look for guns. At the same time, two men stand shellshocked at the threshold; only one is wearing combat gear, whilst the other looks like a delivery driver—they're Sergeant Drakeford and Corporal Thornton.

"Clara, is it?". Drakeford says after shaking his head to gain composure. He enters, with Thornton following close behind.

"Yes, sir," I respond, keen to acknowledge his authority in these circumstances.

"You don't need to—just Drakeford is fine," he says with a soft smile.

Now fully clothed, I stretch and test my outfit's flexibility, finding it satisfactory. Jasper returns with an assault rifle, a holster with a side arm and a knife for close combat; he then proceeds to hand me three marble-sized balls.

"What're these?" I ask.

"Nanodes," he replies. "Be careful with them; they're lethal. Throw one at your target, and it'll release nano-sized shards on detonation. They can shred through almost anything. You don't wanna be near them when they go off." Jaspers turns to Drakeford. "Have you received your instructions?"

"Yes, sir," Drakeford responds.

"Over to you then, Sergeant. The van is waiting downstairs."

***

Drakeford and I sit squeezed between boxes in the back of the van. The swaying motions caused by the country roads and my growing apprehension make me nauseous. We've been travelling for over an hour, and it won't be long before we arrive at our destination.

"What was it like working at the agency?" Drakeford asks.

We've been chatting the entire journey (which could be adding to my travel sickness, but I'm enjoying getting to know him).

Drakeford told me about his wife and seven-year-old boy and how he defected from the empire's army over a decade ago, moving from town to town before settling in Amberleigh when it was newly built. That's when he started a new life and dedicated himself to the Folcriht.

"It was all I ever knew," I respond. "I just—I did as I was told. You know, stayed out of trouble, but I always felt like something was missing."

"Yeah, I know exactly what you mean," he says. "What did they have you doing?"

"Just monitoring footage of suspected deviants and 'terrorists', nothing special. They had me in on a few interrogations. Honestly, I wish I'd found the Folcriht sooner. I was just—I don't know …"

"Scared?"

"Yeah," I sigh, slightly embarrassed.

"They stole what should've been the most joyful and illuminating years of your life. No matter how many drugs they pump into kids to speed up their cognitive development, it'll never change the fact that you never got an opportunity to take risks, make mistakes and learn all about your courage. You should be proud! It wasn't till I was thirty-five before I could muster up the nerve."

I smile. Drakeford's words of respect and recognition make me feel validated, and they're made more substantial by him knowing what it's like to live so deep in the grips of the empire. The van comes to a sudden halt, and the door slides open.

"Ten minutes," Thornton whispers.

Drakeford and I climb over the boxes and jump out. We find ourselves on a long road, with bushes and foliage lining one side whilst a large field dominates the other. The air is humid, and clouds carpet the sky, blocking the moonlight. Equipping my dark-vision glasses, the night becomes day.

"We'll take cover there"—Drakeford points to some dense undergrowth on the side of the road—"Thornton, block the road two minutes before they arrive and wave them down. We'll distract them long enough for you to get your gear and join the action."

***

I ignore the stick digging into my chest as we wait in the undergrowth.

"Have you switched on your StealthShield?" Drakeford asks.

"My what?"

"Ah, crap." He takes my arm and presses a tiny button embedded in the sleeve. "It stops them from detecting us."

"I—damn, I'm sorry, Drakeford," I respond. "Is there anything else important I might not know?"

"Nah, we covered everything on the way here."

My nerves are growing with every passing minute—which is good—it'll keep me on my toes. Thornton has parked the van diagonally across the road to block any approaching vehicles, with a large tree positioned on the other side that'll stop them from driving around. I lay here, stiff as a board, and replay the plan.

Thornton will stop the convoy, which consists of two vehicles: one standard patrol car with two enforcers and the other an armoured van with three guards and Isaac. The two enforcers will step out to inspect the situation. Thornton will call them over, and Drakeford will demobilise the guards' swarmers with an 'electromagnetic pulse' (or EMP)—but Bee assured us that our getaway vehicle will remain driveable. I'll blow open the passenger door to the armoured van using explosives and kill the guards while Drakeford takes out the two enforcers. Once we've eliminated all five threats, we can free Isaac. It almost sounds too easy.

The convoy looms—its headlights cut through my vision, so I adjust my glasses to ensure they don't blind me. My grip tightens around my rifle, preparing myself for the orchestrated chaos. As the vehicles come to a halt and the two enforcers step out to engage in conversation with Thornton, we seize the opportunity.

Swiftly and silently, Drakeford manoeuvres toward the armoured van, and I cover his approach. He places the EMP device beneath the vehicle with a steady hand, and the flickering headlights indicate its success—prompting me to leap into action. With a surge of courage, I sprint towards my target, explosives ready, and plant them on the passenger door. Now in a safe position, and with the detonator resting in my hand … I trigger the explosion.

The muffled blast disturbs the peaceful night, and the once-sleeping birds in a nearby tree are in hysteria, distancing themselves from the commotion. With my gun raised, I spin and face the guards, looking past their shock and horror to unleash precise gunfire—swiftly eliminating them. It was much easier than I expected to pull that trigger.

Simultaneously, Drakeford has taken down the enforcers with deadly accuracy—our combined assault leaves no room for the enemy to retaliate. Although we've neutralised our immediate threats, we must continue moving swiftly—it won't be long before imperial forces know of our attack.

I face the van's rear door, ready to blast it open and liberate Isaac before a resounding thud erupts from inside and shakes the whole vehicle. A second thud, this time stronger. Intuition takes over, and I dive to my left, barely missing the reinforced door that would've wiped me out. Landing on the roadside, I roll into a shallow ditch.

A giant figure emerges from the van's shadowy depths—its form emerges like a foreboding storm cloud, gradually unfurling to devour the world around us. My toes instinctively curl at the sight—just as they did when I first laid eyes on a Scucca. Standing nine feet tall—with bulging muscles and a small head between a broad set of shoulders—its claw-like hands hold an enormous machine gun. My first sighting of one was the night reapers captured Rachel and Aria; I didn't know what these creatures were then, but I do now.

Silas tells me they're lost children of the empire— orphans or members of a disgraced family—considered unfit to grow up in society due to their inherent deviant nature. I'm told social services take them to a secret facility in England; its location remains a mystery. We don't know what horrors they experience to transform into this, but it must be painful and traumatising. Their physical growth is accelerated, genetically modified to have huge muscle mass and high bone density, and they're equipped with a neural device that makes them highly obedient.

Drakeford darts for cover to join Thornton behind the enforcer's vehicle, both firing round after round at the Scucca. However, it remains unharmed, protected by a thick armour of pure muscle and a large helmet. A deep, sinister enjoyment bawls from the creature, quelling all hope as it returns fire in their direction.

I jump to my feet and close in with soft, nimble steps, hoping to catch it off guard and distract it from Drakeford and Thornton. Just steps away, I vault with all my might, and with an outstretched hand, I grip a strap in the creature's clothing to swing my body up, straddling its shoulder. In one swift motion, I place a single Nanode in its pocket and leap backwards. The creature stumbles in confusion from my abrupt assault, stops firing and scans for my position. Landing a safe distance away, I wait for the grenade to work its magic.

I can't see the creature's expression as we face off, but I can sense its rage, with heavy breaths like a rhinoceros preparing to charge and pointing its machine gun directly at me. I desperately scan my surroundings for cover, but I'm totally exposed. I prepare to dart to my left in some last-ditch attempt to escape the imminent barrage of bullets, but in the blink of an eye, a black cloud engulfs the monster, hiding it from my view.

Apprehension restrains me to the ground, forcing me to wait and discover if I've been successful in destroying my foe. The cloud swirls viciously and obliterates anything it touches, including a portion of the van, before settling to the ground. All that remains is the titan's carcass. Fragments of its helmet reveal a hollow skull. Clothing has been torn off, revealing strands of muscle that cling to the bone. The devoured giant falls forward with an almighty thud to the hard ground.

Stepping over the Scucca's remains, I find Isaac bound in the van—he's alive but in a terrible state.

"C'mon, let's get you out of here," I tell him, cutting his restraints and lifting him out.

"Cla—Clara?" he utters in barely a whisper.

"Yeah, it's me. We're taking you to safety."

As I support a feeble Isaac towards our van, I realise Drakeford is lying on the ground, with Thornton pressing his hands against his stomach.

"Clara!" Thornton cries. "Grab something to slow the bleeding."

I quickly oblige and rush to help, and Drakeford beckons me closer. Falling to my knees and leaning into him, he whispers, "I'm not … gonna make it, Clara. Y—you were blood—bloody fantastic."

"We'll get you back and patched up," I stress. "Then—just—just stay with us—okay?"

"Listen … the queen," he murmurs. "You—you've got more support … than you re—realise—" Drakeford takes his last breath.

His poor family.

CHAPTER SIXTEEN

A Kingdom to be

"I just—argh! I don't get it!" Fay exclaims, "A *Scucca*? How did Lawrence not know?"

Fortunately, her anger isn't disturbing our neighbouring tables in the park's café. Though the days are becoming cooler, the playful cries of children still fill the air, and women accessorise their floral dresses with thick cardigans.

"It could've been a last-minute thing," I reply, staring into my coffee.

"Anthony was a good man,"—that's Drakeford, I only learned of his first name today—"How're you feeling now?" she asks.

"It's horrible, but I'll pull through. He said something to me—Anthony—before he died. Something about me having more support than I realise. Any ideas?"

"Ah—yeah. I do," Fay responds coyly. "I—erm—I wanted it to be a surprise, actually."

I lift my head to look at her sheepish expression. "What is it?" I ask.

"I may have started a petition."

"Eh? For what?"

"When you told me Casimir dismissed your suggestion, I was angry, so I went door to door asking people to sign a petition and show their support for exploring an alliance with Queen Calantha."

"Fay!" I gasp. "I—I don't know what to say."

"Ask me how many signatures I got."

"Okay, how many signatures did you get?"

"Good question." Her leg jitters under the table. "Only a couple of thousand."

"What!" I grab her hand and squeeze it tight. "Thank you, that's—"

My eyes wander over Fay's shoulder and catch sight of Silas's unmistakably large build marching towards us. She notices the shift in my attention—and perhaps the ridiculous schoolgirl smile that's crept onto my face without permission.

Twisting around to check, she returns to face me. "Are you two shagging?"

"No!" I snap, feeling my cheeks flush. "Hello, Silas."

"Mind if I join?" he asks, taking a seat anyway. "How're you feeling, Clara? I read the debrief."

"I'm alright, thanks for—"

"How the bloody hell do you miss a Scucca?" Fay blurts out, throwing Silas a cutting look.

"Hello, Fay," he sighs. "Lawrence reckons the guards picked it up on the way. He had no idea. I promise I'm just as furious. I lost a good man—and friend."

"Oh God," Fay whispers remorsefully. "Of—of course, you did. I'm an idiot. Sorry."

"No, don't worry," he responds. "You're just looking out for your sister." Unable to sit still, he plays with a napkin, casually glancing up at me. It doesn't take a genius to realise he yearns for time alone with just us two.

Fay clocks his shift in character, and her eyes rapidly dart back and forth between Silas and me before the tension becomes too much for her. "I—er—I'm gonna—head off. I'll see you later, Clara."

"You sure?" I ask, trying to be casual but failing to hide my amusement at her unease.

"Oh, definitely," she asserts, and we share our goodbyes.

"Sebastian's been in touch," Silas says, tapping my foot under the table. "A car's taking you to St Christopher's Airport at four in the morning in two days."

"Why're you acting weird?" I ask.

"Things aren't good in Canada," he sighs. "Sebastian's asking their government to join the empire, and their people hate it, so they're keeping the date of this visit under wraps. If they knew, there'd be a mass riot. It's dangerous."

"All I've seen in the news is huge support for them joining the empire."

"C'mon, Clara." Silas snorts, staring at me with raised eyebrows. I know he's urging me to rethink my statement.

"Ah. Okay." I manage a bashful chuckle, realising I should know better. "Of course, it's all fake."

It's easy to forget The Crown is—amongst other things—a well-oiled disinformation machine that uses deepfake technology to make you believe anything. Still, it must be true if it's coming from a reputable source, right?

"Don't worry," he assures. "I was still hooked on Echo months after I joined the Folcriht—don't tell anyone."

I appreciate his attempt to make me feel less embarrassed. "So, you think I'll be in danger in Canada?"

"Definitely," he responds. "And watch out for Sebastian. He's reckless sometimes."

"I'll make sure he's on his best behaviour," I jest.

"Do you—do you fancy having dinner tonight?"

"Save it for when I'm back."

***

After a peaceful journey, I arrive at a hangar in St Christopher's Airport. Having never flown before, I'm mixed with nerves and excitement. The Duke of Crimsonford is visible through a window; he's engaged in a serious conversation with someone out of sight. A crew member greets and guides me up the steps, and the engine's electrical buzz vibrates through my body. Drifting from inside the cabin, I hear the unmistakable smooth and smoky voice of Lavinia Radford, prompting me to pause and listen out of sight.

"They killed a Scucca, Your Grace," Radford urges politely. "These animals are becoming more skilled and organised."

"I do not understand why you are so interested in this case, Lavinia," the duke responds coolly. "You cannot waste time on low-level cases that are more suited to your inferiors."

"I understand, but we suspect this guard was responsible for the agency bombings. I'm convinced this is the Folcriht's doing. If we could—"

"Just have your staff do their thing and report back if you think it's important."

"Of course, Your Grace," Radford responds, notably humbled.

"Clara!" The duke exclaims, not bothering to hide his pleasure in seeing me.

I curtsy for him and proceed to shake Radford's hand. "United in devotion."

"With hearts aligned," Radford responds.

"Have a seat," the duke offers. "We'll be leaving soon."

The aircraft's cabin screams sophistication, elegance, and vanity, with walls crafted from a seamless blend of polished wood and sleek, metallic panels. Soft ambient lighting bathes the space, creating a warm and inviting atmosphere. I sit on a plush leather seat, exquisitely tailored in a deep shade of midnight blue, and Radford glides over to perch next to me, her legs crossed and facing in my direction.

"Well, well, well!" she beams. "This is quite something! To think, only a few months ago, I gave you an opportunity that would change your life!"

I smile, taking great satisfaction in her ignorance of the truth. "It seems his generosity has graced us both, ma'am."

"A *personal assistant* to the Duke of Crimsonford! It's absolutely fan—"

"My aide, Lavinia," the duke interjects, his voice floating from a seat further down the cabin. "Not my personal assistant—oh, and Clara."

"Yes, Your Grace?"

"You may refer to Lavinia using her name," he states. "You are both of equal seniority within my staff."

I thank the duke for correcting me and smile sweetly at Radford, feeling unashamedly smug and relishing this moment as her face contorts like she's just eaten a lemon.

The engines grow louder to indicate our imminent departure, and I see Radford strapping a seatbelt around her waist, so I do the same. The jet lifts from the ground, hovering mid-air for a moment before gliding out of the hangar, where it slowly gains altitude.

London's overpowering presence shrinks. The River Thames' crystal-clear waters wind through London's heart, barely visible amidst the towering skyscrapers, with their pristine white exteriors almost blinding me as they reflect the early morning sun. Its proud character has the ability to transfigure into something magnificent; all it needs is some love and compassion.

We're almost hovering above the Grand Shard; no doubt it's scanning our every move, anticipating any sign of a threat. The floor vibrates with powerful energy, which is the only warning for the sudden jolt of speed that thrusts my head backwards against the cushioned headrest as this gravity-defying jet propels us into the expanse of the blue sky. Despite the wind whooshing from outside, the cabin remains remarkably stable, and civilisation doesn't take long to disappear.

"Clara, we should discuss the situation in Canada," the duke declares, staring at a device in his lap as he gestures to a seat directly ahead of him. "Come, take a seat."

Now that we're stable at an unknown height, a member of his waiting staff delivers an assortment of breakfast pastries and juices on the table that separates us.

The duke continues, "My security team arrived in Canada over a week ago, conducting the necessary checks and arranging schedules."

Conscious that Radford will no doubt be taking an interest in our conversation, I respond, "Thank you for this opportunity. I am honoured to be serving the empire in such a way."

"Good," he says. "Did you receive the information my team sent yesterday?"

"I did, Your Grace. It's clear the Canadian people are in dire need of support and guidance. May his light protect us during our visit."

"Indeed, they are. And we shall be their saviour. What questions do you have?"

"Just one, if I may."

"Yes?"

"How may I serve you during this visit? I am sorry if I missed something."

"You shall join me during our negotiations with the Canadian Prime Minister."

"Gosh, that's quite a privilege."

"You are to remain silent, of course." He plays his role so well that I almost believed him. "It would not be appropriate for a young lady like yourself to contribute to such discussions."

"Of course, Your Grace," I respond pleasantly. Sneaking around Radford is proving to be fun.

"I will require your talents," he continues. "You must alert me if they lie or when I can push them further. We should establish some subtle signals."

We agree that a single tap of my index finger will inform the duke that he can push harder during the negotiations, a rub of my nose to confirm they're being truthful, and a tap on his foot when they're lying.

Radford issues a soft cough and chimes in, "I hope you do not mind, Your Grace, but I could not help overhear your conversation."

"What is it?" the duke asks politely.

"It is not appropriate for Clara to touch you. The others may—"

"I'm disappointed, Lavinia."

"Your—Your Grace?"

"I was informed you were not afraid of bending the rules," he sighs. "Especially if it achieves the best result for the empire."

"Oh—of—of course. Please, I beg for your forgiveness."

"It's fine," he says. "You focus on ensuring we do not come across any nasty surprises. Leave matters of royal etiquette to me."

We continue our conversation undisturbed. The duke tells me about Olivia Leblanc—Canada's Prime Minister—and winces when he refers to her as a 'stubborn and entitled wench' (I suspect he'd like to say she's headstrong and knows what she wants). A carefully selected group of senior ministers within the Canadian government will accompany the Prime Minister. I also learn of reports that the United States has supplied an anti-imperial militant group in Canada with equipment to bolster their strength—I just hope we don't cross paths. Though they don't realise it, we're on the same side—there must be a reason why the duke is leading these negotiations, and I know I'll learn the true nature of this visit when we have time alone.

***

A noticeable shift in our speed signals our imminent landing in Ottawa—just over three hours have passed since we left London. The duke and Radford occasionally conversed throughout the journey, discussing security requirements for when we're travelling between the airport and the embassy. They're calm and collected—as am I—despite our dangers in this hostile territory.

Peering out the window, the Earth below grows larger with each passing minute, and the landscape's breathtaking beauty unfolds, with stretches of lush green forests sprawling beneath us. I'm not offered long to admire it before the natural splendour is marred by plumes of smoke billowing from massive chimneys that reach high into the sky like noxious genies escaping their bottles, keen to grip us in their deadly fumes. I've never seen anything like it before.

"Is it safe to breathe here?" I ask, tinted with concern.

We're taught that non-imperial citizens fall fatally ill from toxic air, and I should know better by now to believe it, but I can't deny this sight.

"We will be fine," the duke says. "It looks worse than it is."

Some distance from the industrial patch of land, the edge of Ottawa's cityscape appears. Construction is underway as the concrete jungle expands to consume more of the neighbouring natural beauty. We glide and descend deeper into the city, and I observe a brown haze hanging in the air below, shrouding the streets and its inhabitants. Unlike London's clean air, it's as though I'm peering into a murky lake. Though I can't deny the visible signs of destruction caused by humankind, I'm still looking forward to discovering the mysteries that hide throughout this city. The aircraft finally hovers in place before gliding across two adjacent airstrips, and the soft thud from below marks our safe arrival.

The duke is the first to stand. "I have some business to attend to. A car will take you both to the embassy. Lavinia, speak with Marcus about our security details for tomorrow's meeting."

"Of course, Your Grace," Radford responds.

"Clara, get yourself settled in. I will meet you for dinner this evening. We have a private room in the embassy."

"And me?" Radford asks.

"They have tasty room service, Lavinia." With that final remark, the duke leaves the aircraft.

I gather my belongings and follow Radford out. The duke's car has already left, and ours awaits us at the bottom of the steps, where a man opens the rear passenger door. Radford immediately climbs in, but I pause momentarily to take in my unusual surroundings. The air feels thick, almost as if it's pressing against me, and I can't avoid wondering if the oxygen is sparser here. Our transport looks and sounds ancient, reminiscent of the Folcriht's arsenal—the smell of burning fuel violates my nose as it escapes from a small pipe in its rear.

"Disgusting, I know," Radford sneers from inside the car. "The duke tells me they regressed to manufacturing planet killers over a decade ago because they could not source material to produce electric vehicles. They were offered some from the empire, but they refused! Bizarre."

"Isn't it just," I respond before raising my eyebrows at the Canadian driver (offering him a silent apology for Radford's disrespect). He smiles and shakes his head.

Countries view the Anglo Empire as a last resort, seeking help only when all other options have failed—unless the emperor chooses to strip them of their choice by invading their lands. He employs various tactics to make them dependent on regonium-fuelled technology, promising advanced weaponry, protection, and green energy (to name a few). However, the outcome is always the same: countries lose their sovereign identities, sacrificing their unique cultures in favour of The Crown's ideals.

Our ride into the city is considerably bumpier compared to travelling in England. Resisting the force that attempts to move me closer to Radford at each turn, I twist my body away from her and admire the scenes. Clambering engines, horns and chattering people become my new companions, drifting through the closed window. Everyone here exhibits unique styles and fashion choices, making it feel like I've been transported back in time. To my amazement, I even see one man wearing a skirt.

However, what I'm most interested in is the aged women. Their expressions are vibrant, with beautifully wrinkled faces that tell a story with each laugh, smile, and scowl. They express themselves fearlessly, and it's sometimes difficult to distinguish them from men because many exude confidence in suits and trousers. It's like nothing I've seen before. When the news back home shows footage of non-imperial women, they all appear the same—frail, malnourished, heavily weathered and riddled with painful sores, and it couldn't be further from the reality.

Surprisingly, men pay women very little attention here. They don't stare, grope, or bite their lips in passing. Instead, most are engrossed in a small hand-held device, which I assume is an old-fashioned mobile telephone. Others observe adverts projected on buildings, but they're not like ours; they don't promote new initiatives that'll grant people luxury commodities, like watching a new documentary series on Echo for an extra pair of shoes or patterned bedding.

Our car stops at a traffic light, and my wide smile extends even further as I witness something heartwarming. Two men walk hand in hand, sharing in laughter and sealing their affection with an unapologetic kiss. Not a single passerby throws them a look of disgust; no child screams at them out of fear, and there isn't an enforcer in sight to take them down.

"Yuck," spews Radford.

I whip my head around to see her staring at the male couple with a scrunched face that's about to implode in on itself, and I promptly turn away, rolling my eyes out of view. I refuse to satisfy her with an acknowledgement. It feels good not having to pander to her atrocious behaviour and pretend I agree with her twisted view of the world.

"Do you remember Isaac?" she asks randomly.

"Isaac who?" I reply, acutely aware of the risks associated with this topic of conversation. "The agency's IT guy?"

"No. The big guard at the entrance."

"Ah yes, that guy," I respond. "I remember him. Why'd you ask?"

"We arrested him shortly after you left."

I throw her a quizzical look. "Why?"

"We think he was responsible for the bombing and for murdering—ah, gosh. Now, what was that lad's name … hmm. Annoying lad."

Radford taps her bottom lip, appearing deep in thought, but everything she says is calculated, and I wouldn't be surprised if she's acting on a whim to catch me out, though I don't know why she'd suspect me. I remain silent and appear as if I'm hanging to her every word.

"Oh, come on, you must know," she adds.

"Would I have met him?"

"Quinton, that's it. He—"

"*Quinlan?*" I stress.

"Ah, yes! Quinlan."

"*They were partners,*" I choke, continuing my act and shaking my head at the ground. "That's awful. He was a good, loyal lad."

"That's not even the best bit," she says. "We were transferring Isaac for questioning, and he was taken! Vanished!"

"Taken? By who?" I ask.

"Whom, Clara. *Not who*." She dramatically slaps my upper arm.

"Taken? By whom?" I repeat, lazily matching my tone and rubbing the spot she hit.

"I have my suspicions," she brags. "But I will not speculate! Facts are important."

I successfully restrain a snort—Radford has many beliefs, and that isn't one of them.

"Well, I hope you find whoever's responsible, ma—Lavinia."

My slip of the tongue offers her some amusement—she doesn't like sharing authority with a woman and will look for every opportunity to feel superior. Radford's dad was London's chief marshal, and he could've influenced her questionable work ethic and drive to attain authority. There are also rumours in the agency of her experiencing a dreadful blossoming. Although the procedure successfully froze her appearance, it failed to plump up her lips and cheeks, damning her to look 'ugly' for life (in the eyes of beauty ideals). As an imperial woman, if you're not beautiful, what purpose do you serve?

"Something *has* been playing on my mind since the bombing," Radford sighs. "I feel terrible about it, to be honest."

"You don't feel terrible," I respond, unable to hide my impatience with her games. "And you haven't forgotten I see straight through lies."

"Of course." She giggles, almost celebrating being caught out.

"What is it?" I ask.

"It wasn't until recently that I remembered our encounter before the explosion ..."

"Yes?"

"You were *desperate* for the loo, but I stopped you ..."

"I remember, yes."

"If I had just let you pass," she says. "You would have been unscathed. It is *my* fault you were hurt. The ladies' restroom was the only place on the fourth floor that remained intact."

Though you couldn't tell by looking at me, my pulse is racing. This is Radford's way of sharing her suspicion, and she'll judge my every action and word in this enclosed space. I have nowhere to run.

"You don't feel terrible because it wasn't your fault," I respond.

"Hmm?"

"It was the radicals' fault, not yours. Have any groups claimed responsibility?"

Our eyes lock, and the edge of her mouth is curled like a sly cat enjoying the chase. She finally gives in, breaking away from my gaze and says, "No. Not yet. Which just makes it all the more—"

The car grinds to a halt, causing my head to lurch forward and Radford's to smack against the cushioned driver's seat, leaving an imprint of her face in makeup. A forceful chanting outside now interrupts our tension. The large and spirited group of protestors are marching in the street, heading directly towards us from down the road to our right. Imperial flags are burning, and some people hold banners with an image of the emperor's face, with googly eyes and devil horns (which I struggle not to laugh at) and a large, defiant red cross cut through it. Others display anti-imperial messages and slogans, such as *'RISE UP AND REJECT THE REIGN'* or *'DOMINATION AND OPPRESSION? NOT ON MY TURF!'*

"We'll need to be quick," the driver calls back, surprisingly calm. "They're heading to the embassy."

***

We arrived at the Imperial Embassy with no trouble. I never imagined I'd view it as a beacon inviting us to safety. Of course, it stands out compared to all the other buildings in Ottawa, with its ostentatious features demanding everyone's attention. With the typical bright white stone face, outshining and making everything around it look tired. The interior is too close to Buckingham Palace's, and it took some time to fight the creeping wave of panic that threatened me when a staff member showed me to my room. The native architecture in this city, with its tastefully minimalist design, reinforces my appreciation that the empire is shamefully egotistic.

"Ma'am? Ma'am?" It takes me a moment to notice the young waiter speaking to me. The ambient lighting illuminates his soft features. "What would you like to drink, ma'am?"

"Oh! Sorry," I respond. "I—just a glass of white, please … surprise me."

"Of course," he says, smiling, before darting away.

I've been daydreaming following the protest I witnessed this morning. I quickly bid Radford farewell to avoid having to justify why I needed the loo the day of the bombing. Though she has no evidence to prove my association with the attack, she's highly suspicious and will closely monitor me. I look forward to discussing options with the duke regarding how we deal with her.

I spent most of my afternoon gazing out the window in my room, longing to learn more about Canada's enigmatic culture. However, I can't leave the embassy—it isn't safe—so I'm now waiting for the duke in the private dining hall. I chose to wear a bold red cocktail dress, an unusual shape, with a slit running up my leg. It's an old-fashioned yet timeless look—I feel fantastic.

"Clara." The duke's gentle voice floats behind me, causing me to jump to my feet, spin around and curtsy.

"Your Grace," I respond.

He smiles at my reaction. "Please, Clara, no formalities without the company of others. Call me Sebastian."

He's wearing a stylish, thick overcoat and stiff-brimmed fedora hat—evidently preparing to go somewhere he shouldn't.

"Ah, of course." I blush. "It could take some getting used to."

The waiter arrives with my glass of wine and asks Sebastian if he would like a drink, to which he politely declines.

"Drink up," Sebastian says. "We are going on an adventure this evening."

I throw him a curious look, and he lifts his hand to his mouth with raised eyebrows, gesturing me to drink. I take a delicate sip with a bashful smile, but he continues urging me on, so I raise my glass and take larger gulps until I down the bitter liquid in one go. As he watches me with a childlike grin, a tear runs down my cheek from the strong taste, and I catch my breath. It's stupid, but I feel like a girl who's been encouraged to misbehave by an adult, and after staring at him in trepidation as if I'm awaiting his approval, we break out into a fit of laughter.

"Come!" he exclaims, guiding me to a door.

We enter the embassy's private garden and follow the dimly lit path surrounded by beautiful English trees and flowers. It feels magical, even with the sounds of engines, horns, and distant protest chants from beyond the high walls. Approaching a guard stationed at a gate, Sebastian hands him something, and the man nods. He pokes his head out and casts an inconspicuous look left and right before granting us passage to a side street that leads us to the bustling main road. Walking briskly to a destination unknown, Sebastian removes his overcoat and places it over me; this thrill has made me immune to the crisp chill.

"What did you hand that guard?" I ask.

"Canadian Dollars—their currency," he responds.

"*What*? It was just paper." I'm feeling more at ease with Sebastian now that he's shared a silly side of him.

"They do not use currency like we do," he says. "Their government has tried in the past, but their people reject it. You must remember that these people value their freedom above all else. That piece of paper allows them to conduct their activities without scrutiny or forced ideals."

"I understand," I sigh. "I'm starting to feel naïve about life outside the empire."

"And that is why our system works so well. They do not want you to see the truth."

We enter a cosy restaurant and are greeted by the enchanting smile of a friendly waiter. He guides us to a small table in the corner of the warmly lit room and hands over two menus.

"I'll give you some time to decide," the waiter says, playing with his wavey blonde hair.

"No need!" Sebastian says eagerly, taking me by surprise with a Canadian accent. "A bottle of Chateau Haut and two servings of poutine, please." He leans forward. "You need to try this. It's like nothing you've tasted before! If you don't like it, we'll order something else."

"Trying new things has become one of my habits recently," I respond once the waiter leaves. I won't even try to put on an accent—it'd be insulting.

There are four other diners, and they don't seem interested in us (despite me being overdressed).

"It's fine. We're safe," Sebastian declares, returning to his usual voice and noting my discomfort. "I brought you here so we could speak freely away from prying ears."

We fall silent as the waiter pours us both a glass of white wine.

"Do not worry," Sebastian continues. "I will keep an eye on the door for Lavinia." He winks.

"She's suspicious of me," I respond in a serious tone.

"How so?" he asks.

I share the story of our car ride to the embassy and how she took a particular interest in my attempts to enter the restroom.

"Interesting," he says, pinching his plump bottom lip and staring just over my shoulder in deep reverie, which is strange considering I've shared some damning news. "It seems I have underestimated her highly observant and inquisitive nature." His usual upbeat demeanour returns instantly. "It is fine! I expect you realise there is more to this visit than meets the eye." I sense his excitement growing; he's keen to share his grand plan.

"I had my suspicions," I respond, matching his energy with a cheeky smirk.

"A bit of context to begin with," he says. "I will let you in on a well-kept secret, but you may have heard the rumours. The Crown held a symbolic and ceremonial role in Canada in the twenty-first century. After the ascension of a new king, the Canadian people successfully cut ties with the monarchy, and that momentous occasion fostered great national pride. This is why the emperor and his predecessors have never successfully encouraged Canada to join the empire."

I notice Sebastian regularly glancing over my shoulder during his speech, but he's not looking out for possible threats. Instead, a subtle glimmer sparkles in his eyes, hinting at a mischievous curiosity—a blend of intrigue and desire. Occasionally, a playful smile will grace his lips, the corners gently upturned, as if they hold a secret. But the most telling is his body language; he'll shift forward as if drawn magnetically towards the person of interest. He's flirting with someone.

As Sebastian pauses to sip his wine, I spin around to observe the room behind me—the couples remain seated, deep in conversation, and the waiter is busy pouring drinks behind the bar—I can't locate the subject of his interest.

Seemingly unaware of how his actions have piqued my interest, Sebastian continues, "Our military should not take Canada by force—well—this is what I advise the emperor. The United States would rush to aid Canada, resulting in a lengthy, bloody war that would expose opportunities for newly formed kingdoms to rise up and rebel. And *this* is where it gets interesting—"

"You're responsible for their neglected infrastructure," I interject. "You've made them dependent on regonium, so they have no choice but to join the empire."

"Correct," he says. "But there is so much more to it than that. Unlike others, their government is in on it. Though they have been unaware of my identity, I have been negotiating with a select few officials for the past three years, staging this whole event. If Canada joins the empire, the emperor will appoint me as monarch in this kingdom, and with access to regonium, we will *finally* have a fighting chance at overthrowing England's rule over all other kingdoms. *That* is what we will be negotiating tomorrow, to request they form a fierce alliance with the Folcriht. I need you to establish if they are committed to this—if we can trust them. How does that sound?"

He stares at me like a child who's just handed his mum a drawing to eagerly await her praise. I'd love to share my thoughts about Queen Calantha, but this isn't the time, so instead, I project my amazement to acknowledge his achievement. You would never tell this is the same man who hanged a member of his staff for incompetence just over a week ago.

"Wow," I praise, lowering my voice as the waiter struts towards us. "Despite sounding like a Faustian bargain, this is actually quite exciting."

At first glance, I can't determine what the waiter has placed before me. A mound of elongated shapes, their surface golden and speckled with darker spots—fried potatoes, I think. They're arranged in a loose pile, with irregularly shaped morsels, pale in colour, scattered across the plate. Resting atop is the familiar sight of gravy; it's thick and glossy, coating the mysterious concoction beneath. Sebastian watches me with anticipation as I take my first mouthful; the flavours ignite my tastebuds, and my eyes widen.

"Mmmm!" I murmur gleefully with a mouth filled with potato, totally forgetting I'm in the presence of nobility.

"Ha!" he roars, causing a few glances from the tables nearby. "I knew you'd love it."

The waiter chuckles, and I notice the same glimmer in his eyes as Sebastian—they're both suddenly entrapped in each other's gaze, silently exchanging information. My eyes dart between the two of them—I must be experiencing the same thing as Fay just days ago—the realisation rushes through me, causing my grip to release the fork and it clashes on the ground, disturbing their blissful moment. My face turns the same shade of red as my dress.

"Sorry!" I whisper hastily, unsure how to act.

Sebastian and the waiter laugh, offering me kind words of reassurance; they appear familiar with one another. The shock of my discovery doesn't last long, quickly dispersing to make way for a moment of reflection. It makes sense now—why Sebastian supports the Folcriht—he wants a life without fear of persecution for who he is, and I envisage him desiring the same for others.

CHAPTER SEVENTEEN

Resolutions

"You are confident this room is not compromised?" Sebastian asks.

"Yes, Your Grace," Radford responds. "I had two men search yesterday evening and this morning."

She must realise by now that Sebastian doesn't trust her, revealed by him seeking a subtle confirmation from a member of his security team over her shoulder, who nods to offer assurance.

We stand in the hallway, poised to enter the meeting room where the Canadian ministers await. Two royal guards protect the door. The chief security advisor accompanies Radford, and Sebastian's Master of Ceremonies— Benjamin—has meticulously briefed us on the schedule and what to expect during the meeting.

Sebastian decided to show me more of Ottawa last night, and he did all the talking with his authentic Canadian accent to avoid drawing unwanted attention—I remained silent. After leaving the restaurant, he took me to an 'arcade' where I discovered people here don't just use virtual reality for learning—they use it for *entertainment*. As a child, I'd use the same technology to explore the towns and villages of old Wessex. However, I was using it yesterday to shoot to kill characters that were clearly fashioned after imperial soldiers (though the game creators would never admit to that). Sebastian showed me a game where I played the role of an assassin, and he took great pride in placing me on a fictional mission to take down a character fashioned in his likeness.

We then went to a 'gay bar'—a safe haven for queer folk—and I'm ashamed to admit that it took me about an hour to overcome the shock and fully immerse myself in the fun. A man greeted us, dressed in a gown like those worn by imperial noblewomen but showier and more eccentric (which I didn't think was possible). In his words, his face was 'beaten by the gods', which apparently means he had excellent makeup on—it was almost a work of art. Thanks to Sebastian's terrible influence, he and I drank excessively in that place. It took some time to learn dance moves that didn't give away my imposter status, but it worked because quite a few women approached me on the dancefloor (which I found thrilling).

However, our evening went downhill during our short time in a 'casino'. During a game (the name of which escapes me; there were red and black numbers), three men watched us with interest from a table nearby. Despite my inebriated state, I quickly noticed their intrigue and urged Sebastian to leave. It took some time to persuade him, and though I admire the calculated risks he takes, he became reckless last night—in fact, we both did—perhaps we're a bad influence on each other. The three men blocked our exit, placing us in a precarious position without Sebastian's guards. Acting quickly, I kicked one in the groin, hit another around the head with a nearby bottle, and expertly introduced the last man's face to the ground. Sebastian found it all quite amusing, but this morning, he has a new sense of clarity and is concerned we've compromised our cover, thus increasing the risk of an attack.

"Good, we shall get started," Sebastian says. "Announce my arrival, please, Benjamin."

"Your Grace," I interject before Benjamin can barge in and bellow at the unsuspecting ministers. He looks at me in revulsion with his hand resting on the door, and Radford raises her eyebrows, displeased with my abrupt interruption.

"Yes, Clara?" Sebastian asks.

"May I suggest a more … informal approach to announcing your arrival?"

Radford titters under her breath.

"*Informal?*" Benjamin sneers. "His Grace must demand respect. The commoners in this room are to know whom they will soon be bowing the knee to!"

"I understand, Benjamin," I respond. "But the commoners in that room also hold the key to our success today. They are unfamiliar with—and potentially hostile towards—our traditions." I face Sebastian. "Please, forgive me, Your Grace. I meant no disrespect."

"Clara is right," Sebastian announces as Benjamin winces like he's been stabbed in the back, and Radford's tittering instantly ceases.

Sebastian strides confidently to the door, gestures at Benjamin to step aside, and with a couple of gentle knocks, he slowly opens it. Feeling triumphant, I can't help but direct a smug, celebratory look towards Benjamin before following Sebastian into the room.

It's bright inside, with just one long, mahogany table that cuts through the centre. Facing us, three men and one woman stand in front of a huge floor-to-ceiling window, flooding the room with natural light. I've memorised their names and faces. Ethan Turner is the Deputy Prime Minister. His salt-and-pepper hair adds a touch of wisdom, and his warm hazel eyes appear to hold a thousand untold stories. As he extends his hand in greeting, a genuine smile graces his lips, instantly making me feel at ease.

Next is William Wilson, the Minister for Finance; his charcoal grey suit is impeccably tailored, signalling a passion for professionalism and commitment to his role as the financial steward of the nation. Despite his composure, there's a glint of passion and excitement in his eyes, as if he's been looking forward to this meeting for quite some time.

Lucas Parker is the Minister for Defence, and the suit accentuating his study frame boasts medals and insignias that display his service and dedication. He carries himself with the disciplined poise of a seasoned soldier. Lucas has a no-nonsense approach to his responsibilities, given away by his sharp and articulate manner of speaking (with a fierce Canadian accent) during these introductions.

Finally, Olivia Leblanc is the Prime Minister, and I can't take my eyes off her as she struts with conviction around the table to greet us. Power and authority drive her every movement, enhanced by her tailored navy blue suit and bold red heels. It seems Benjamin has had the last laugh—at his request, I'm wearing a dainty, baby blue pleated dress, making it look like I should be baking a cake and not negotiating the fate of a nation. I'm prone to feeling like a child next to Olivia's strong aura and mature features—but I recognise this self-doubt, and I'm better prepared to face it now.

Olivia stands before Sebastian and bows, a big smile showing off her pearly white teeth. "Your Grace," she says, with a velvety yet authoritative tone—if Benjamin were in the room, he would've asked her to try again but with a curtsy.

"Please, Prime Minister, call me Sebastian."

"Then you must call me Olivia," she responds before side-stepping to me.

Conscious of the contrast between us, I straighten my back and lift my chin to appear calm and dignified. Though she tries her best to hide it, the glimmer of pity in her eyes is palpable as she subtly assesses my appearance. The blossoming ceremony isn't popular amongst many other kingdoms and countries.

"Clara Rosewood," I announce with conviction. "The duke's aide. It's an honour to meet you, Prime Minister."

A genuine surprise flashes across her face. "*Aide*? Geez … since when has the empire allowed gir—women to advise men?"

Sebastian fidgets uncomfortably next to me.

"We have the duke to thank," I respond with ease. "It's something I hope to see more of in the future."

He loosens up.

"As do I, Clara, as do I. Please, call me Olivia."

She leads the way as we all take a seat at the table. With us facing them, I'm offered a clear view out the window that displays a brown building directly ahead and the Confederation Park to the right, hosting a large fountain and a variety of beautiful statues.

Everyone is deathly silent and still. Olivia holds Sebastian captive with her unfaltering stare—I'm loving every moment, positively stunned by her conviction. I notice him tap a calculated rhythm on the table, only for her to copy—a secret code to confirm they're on the same page.

Olivia finally releases her pent-up suspense with a heavy sigh. "Ah, heck, are we really doing this?"

"It appears so," Sebastian responds.

"Straight to it then!" Olivia hollers, slapping the table. "What evidence d'you have to suggest the emperor will invade Canada if we don't join willingly?"

"Just my word," Sebastian says.

"I'm told you're his most trusted advisor," she notes. "Heck, you're his *friend*! Why should I trust you, eh?"

"Hmm—" Sebastian's breathing becomes shallow, and I may be the only one in this room that recognises his internal struggle to utter his following words. "I *must* earn your trust. I understand this, and I *will* prove myself. I have done some terrible things to gain the emperor's trust— things that would make your skin crawl, as they do mine, but they are not the actions of the man that sits before you today. I despise The Crown and everything it stands for"— inhaling his courage, a weighted pause signals his readiness to speak his shame—"I—I am a deviant." He gulps. "A homosexual."

I've never seen Sebastian so vulnerable—his self-loathing oozes from every inch of his stiffened body.

"Is that it?" Olivia asks, perplexed by his struggle.

"Yes," he responds with his head hanging low. "I—you must understand—"

"Agh—Of course," Olivia says, remembering the stark contrast between her world and ours. "I'm sorry, Sebastian. I was ignorant. It's just—we don't think twice about it."

"And that is why I am here today. This is my campaign for change—to embrace the risks and discomfort because progress thrives in such conditions."

"Thank you for sharing," she says. "But why should I risk everything for *your* campaign?"

"*Our* campaign, Olivia," he urges, lifting his head to address her directly. "We will risk it all together. I must stress that this is our only opportunity to achieve any hope for Canada to reclaim its independence in the future. I am confident you and I will lead these great people to victory. Our union, our story"—Sebastian bangs his fist on the table, his once weakened state a thing of the past—"It will be celebrated for thousands of years."

"Hmm," she sighs. "How long do we have until the empire defiles our sovereignty if we decide not to join?"

"The emperor will strike with relentless fire and fury in six months," he responds. "It would have been two years ago had I not deterred him."

Olivia peers up at him with raised eyebrows before staring at her glass of water. "And what about your grim traditions? For one, I won't allow you to strip the right to age from Canadian women—or have people executed in the streets!"

"They are not my traditions, Olivia," Sebastian sighs, noticeably offended. "Besides, that will not happen. We will act quickly, and it takes years to fully integrate imperial customs into new kingdoms."

Olivia leans forward and looks left and right. "Gentlemen, thoughts?"

Ethan is the first to speak, "I'll support your decision, Olivia"—I rub my nose, indicating to Sebastian that he's being truthful—"But our biggest risk is a civil war. We'd need to announce our true intent quickly."

Ethan's body language suggests he's extremely loyal to Olivia—there's more than just professional admiration.

"An alliance feels like the only option," William adds, remarkably upbeat. I rub my nose again. "I want us to negotiate aid from the US straight away."

We all look at Lucas, who hasn't taken his suspicious eyes off Sebastian this whole time—he remains stoic, unphased by our silent pleas to gain his opinion.

"Lucas?" Olivia says.

"I don't trust you," Lucas growls; his once doubtful eyes sharpen.

"Neither would I …" Sebastian sighs, slowly shaking his head. "I wish I could do more to gain your trust, Lucas. I am the face of an abhorrent regime, but I am *not* its soul"—Sebastian leans forward—"I am a puppet cutting his strings. Please, help me."

As we remain silent, Lucas's face slowly begins to soften, as does the pressure in this room, and he suddenly slams his hand on the table. "Ah shoot, fine! But there's still the issue of resistance in England. They're never gonna rebel."

"Thank you, Lucas," Olivia says, now returning her attention to Sebastian. "How'd you expect to build a solid resistance in England, eh? I might be wrong, but the English are fiercely loyal, and our experts insist they must pull their weight if we're to stand a chance. Temper the empire's beating heart before we form an assault."

"Of course," Sebastian responds coolly, now gesturing to me. "Clara is working on a solution to that problem."

I peer at him with a smile, raised eyebrows and puzzled eyes, silently asking: *what?*

"Your plan to join forces with Queen Calantha," he adds with confidence.

How does Sebastian know? I haven't found time to discuss my idea with him, and last I checked, Casimir was dead against it. Have they held a vote? After all, Fay gathered thousands of signatures in support. I can't remain dumbfounded for too long as the ministers are on the edge of their seats awaiting my grand reveal.

"Of course—sorry, yes." I stutter.

Taking a moment to compose myself, I rise from my seat and tell them about Queen Calantha and why she's key to sparking a rebellion in Scotland. The ministers query a few things, like whether her forces can defend against England, let alone weaken it, but Sebastian assures them he's already shifted substantial military equipment to the Scottish border. They also ask when the queen agreed to form an alliance, to which Sebastian confirms she hasn't and explains why he's confident she will. They asked for my opinion on the matter, and it feels good to be considered.

Having played my part, I return to my seat, and they continue discussing the need to stage a vote so it looks like the Canadian people joined the empire willingly, but this troubles Olivia as it goes against her values and beliefs. Moreover, their pretend referendum will throw Canada into chaos, which means they must announce their true intentions to the Canadian people as soon as Sebastian has secured imperial resources. All ministers are confident this plan will feed great national pride. However, I'm not so sure—Sebastian told me they value freedom over anything, and I can't imagine they'll appreciate being lied to.

The mood lightens when the ministers learn that Sebastian was responsible for smuggling regonium samples to Canada, which allowed them to study the mineral and make significant technological advancements. This revelation was the tipping point for them to commit and join the fight.

As negotiations continue, something outside prompts me to leave the table to gain a better view. Masses are swarming the Confederation Park. They'd look like ordinary citizens going about their daily lives if it weren't for their masks, weapons, and body armour—they're intent on the embassy. Some carry heavy machine guns, whilst others have regular sidearms, and I spot several armed with grenade launchers and explosive devices strapped around their waists and chests.

"Look," I blurt out, disturbing their chat.

"My god …" Olivia says, with a combined look of disbelief and foresight.

"It's the Crimson Elite," Lucas growls.

Canadian and Imperial soldiers stream from the embassy and take strategic positions in the courtyard below. The first line of defence forms a formidable barrier, wielding sizable shields to protect themselves from the imminent assault. Behind them, armed with guns and anticipating the incoming bombardment, rows of men stand ready.

The militants advance with ferocity toward the building in calculated formations; their synchronised steps signify discipline and training. Even through the reinforced glass, we hear their voices swell, forming a chilling chorus of defiance, chanting slogans that reverberate off each surrounding building—an eery symphony of dissent that momentarily cripples me with angst. The sheer magnitude of their numbers presents an overwhelming force that'll burn anything in its path.

The door to our room flies open, and Radford enters, flustered and out of breath, accompanied by two of Sebastian's guards. "Your Grace," she says with a curtsy.

"How did this happen, Lavinia?" Sebastian asks.

"They have taken us by surprise," she responds. "Posed as a small group of protesters one mile away, slowly gaining volume until it was too late. They prepared for an assault nearby."

"Have your men establish an escape route," Sebastian demands.

Olivia and the three others remain silent, tapping on their mobile telephones.

"There is more, Your Grace," Radford adds. "They have disabled communications, and armoured vehicles approach from the south-east. Local police are building blockades, but it will not stop their convoy. We have fifteen minutes before they arrive."

"I want a safe way out—for us all—in five minutes," he says.

Radford remains frozen at the door; her face is white as snow. I have never seen such fear.

"NOW, LAVINIA," Sebastian yells.

She performs a shaky curtsy and darts out of the room, incoherently screaming at the guards and her security team as she sprints down the hall.

"My men tell me this building can withhold small explosives," Sebastian declares. "We should be safe until—"

Like a rolling storm, a cloud of dread darkens his expression, and his worry-filled eyes are zeroed in on something over my shoulder. Two hovercrafts greet me as I whip around. They face us, floating menacingly—like two snakes swaying side to side, preparing to spring into action. The thick barrels of their mounted guns start spinning faster and faster, readying themselves to unleash devastation.

"EVERYONE OUT!" I shout, grabbing Sebastian's arm and dragging his shocked state towards the door.

The sound of hail smacking a stone ground is all I hear as the projectile storm strikes the thick, reinforced glass. We clamber out of the room, and looking back, the view is frosted, hiding the carnage ensuing outside. A single royal guard remains positioned at the door, so I hold out my hand and request his gun while slipping off my heels.

"Ma'am?" The guard asks, clearly perplexed by my request.

"Gun!" I urge.

With Sebastian's approval, he proceeds to hand me his sidearm, and I instruct him to hold off any attack from this floor as long as possible and guide the group to a nearby staircase. We find temporary safety on the ground floor, where we wait momentarily, only to be disturbed by an almighty BOOM. Our former peaceful environment trembles violently around us, and cracks appear on the walls. The ministers gasp, but Sebastian remains calm. *I need to secure a path out of here.*

"Wait for me," I whisper. Cautiously opening the door, I peer left and right before exiting.

My gun is poised and ready for anything as I glide through the corridors, eventually arriving at the chaotic entrance hall. Rubble litters the floor, and dust hovers in the air, impacting my visibility. I pause behind a wall to inspect the scene; Canadian soldiers and the remaining royal guards take cover behind various columns and objects, occasionally firing into the dust cloud formed by a hole blown through the entrance. A cold, piercing shrill suddenly escapes a small room to my left and penetrates my ears, cutting through the gunfire—it's Radford.

As bullets bounce from wall to wall, I roll behind a raised platform that hosts a statue of Emperor Magnus; his head lies on the ground, and he stares at me with a beaming smile. Peeking around the corner, two creeping militants climb over the portico's wreckage piled up outside. Lying on the ground, I aim and successfully eliminate both to continue my journey and safely enter the room that hides Radford.

Chaos, bullets, and the Canadian people's passionate rage have reduced the once elegant and pristine woman to a bloody, dirty mess in the corner. She's slumped against the wall with a scrunched-up, soot-covered face and a stream of blood running down her arm. Her clothes are wet, and she reeks of petrol. It's an unmistakable smell that carries a chemical sharpness with a sweet undertone.

"Oh, thank his light!" she howls. "Clara, help me!"

I stand at the threshold, taking time to appreciate this perfect moment.

"We need a safe route out," I demand.

"There's a tunnel!" she gasps. "In the lowest basement floor. Come, help me up."

Advancing towards her, each slow and measured step is loaded with intent, and I relish the hope fading from her face as I grab an exposed, crackling wire that dangles from the ceiling.

"No!" she pleads, overwhelmed by the sudden despair. "I—wait! Please just—"

"I want to thank you," I declare, drawing closer. "You helped me discover the Folcriht and my purpose."

"P—please," she bawls. "I won't tell anyone!"

"You taught me one valuable lesson," I continue serenely. "Success isn't an accident waiting to happen." I crouch before her, and my lips curl. "It's a controlled blaze, deliberately ignited by my passion and determination."

The image of ravenous flames devouring Radford's terror-filled eyes will be seared into my memories for the rest of my life—a token of my newfound passion for seeking vengeance.

***

A console mounted to the wall illuminates the dark room in the agency's basement, and Sebastian is entering the code to grant us access to the tunnel. Chaos is rife throughout the rest of the building, and on my instructions, the ministers are gathering metal lids that we can use as makeshift shields. Benjamin is with us; we found him in this room, whimpering and curled up in a ball behind a few boxes. As infuriating as he is, I'm pleased he's alive. Sebastian tells me he's fiercely loyal and supports his involvement with the Folcriht.

The militants might know about the tunnel's existence, and we'll have nowhere to hide if we stumble across them on our way to safety. Lucas proceeds to hand me a small metal disc the size of a dinner plate, but I grab the one he clutches to his chest that's similar to a bin lid, resulting in a rattled grunt.

"I'll be in the front," I assure.

Sebastian heaves open the steel door, revealing a dimly lit tunnel lined with jagged rocks and a soft dirt floor. There's a sharp turn one hundred feet ahead, so I instruct Sebastian and the ministers to stay in this room before sprinting towards it, my bare feet pattering the soft, dry dirt. Reaching the corner without trouble, I peek around to find the way is clear, so I beckon the others to join and sprint to the next safe spot, remaining alert because I'm heavily exposed.

Crap. I lock my legs and skid at the sight of movement ahead. Intimidating shadows grow larger, revealing the presence of three individuals, and the lack of noise exposes their skill and intent to kill. Kneeling to the ground, I keep my weapon aimed and the poor excuse of a shield ready.

A masked face flashes from around the corner, only to swiftly disappear—it's enough to tell me they're not interested in guiding us to safety. Taking controlled breaths to steady my beating heart, I creep closer.

"We don't want to fight," I call out.

The first ding of a bullet hitting metal offers a mix of reassurance and fright; though it saved me from harm, I know others will shortly follow—and I'm right. More strikes clash in quick succession, and they grow in severity, echoing through the tunnel like heavy rain hammering a windshield during a storm. Now bombarded, I speed up and push ahead, forcing myself through the wave of projectiles that attempt to drive me back in both fear and force.

My assailants graciously offer me a break to take a peak, and I find two of them exposed directly ahead, so I deliver one shot for each of them with deadly precision. The final man's arm reaches from around the corner and takes aim, prompting me to return behind my beaten shield. It doesn't take long for them to reload, and lunging around the corner, I aim to find him doing exactly the same—we're deadlocked.

"Please," I plead. "We're here to help."

"*Fuck you.*"

An involuntary gasp escapes my lips, and unlike my masked opponent, I have nothing to disguise my emotions—instead, I just gawk as if they've broken out into a merry jig mid-battle. "You're a ..."

"A what?" she spits. "A girl?"

"Sorry, I'm just—" *What's come over me?* Why am I so shocked? I don't want to hurt her.

"You're just what?"

"Can we talk for a moment?"

"Fuck no," she scoffs. "Why do they let a pretty thing like you play with guns anyway, eh?"

"Please, let me explain." I lower my gun and place it on the ground.

"You imperial girls are more dumb than I thought," she scorns. "You just killed my friends, you bitch."

Though it's clear she's struggling with an internal battle herself, my eyes catch the slightest movement of her trigger finger, and in a flash, I shift to the left. The bullet grazes my face, and death's touch sends a shiver coursing through me. I lunge forward, smacking the gun from her hand and using my shoulder to propel her backwards. We collide in a fierce tumble, but she skilfully rolls with the impact and executes a swift kick, sending me flying. Unphased by her counter, I jump to my feet and assume a defensive stance, bracing myself for her next assault, but before I can fully prepare, she launches a punch-fuelled blitz. I manage to block her fierce strikes, but her assault is forcing me backwards, and just when I'm about to cave in, she abruptly jumps back and provides a moment of respite.

"I'm not letting you and the corrupt scum escape," she snarls.

A knife's hilt glints ominously as she frees it from her boot, leaving me with no choice but to improvise a defensive tool. Frenzied, I snatch the decorative belt from my dress, gripping each end.

She laughs. "Aww, am I gonna ruin your pretty dress?"

As her arm thrusts toward my chest, I act swiftly, wrapping and trapping it with the belt, forcing her to release the weapon. A realisation dawns on her face—she's caught, like an ensnared rabbit—and with a violent yank, I break the woman's arm to produce a resounding snap. Her scream flies through the tunnel.

Sliding my foot under the knife and flicking it into the air, I catch it to deny her a last chance to turn the tables in this brawl, and with it raised in her direction, we face off.

I plead once more, "Please, I don't want—"

"YOU ENGLISH BITCH."

She's hurtling towards me with one raised fist. Her venomous rage fills me with dread; it's unmovable like a mountain, and she leaves me no choice. Against all desire, I send the knife flying, and as if in slow motion, it spins like a deadly dancer to find its place in her chest. Her face is lined with desperation, and using her good hand, she grasps the intrusive object and folds—lying face down in the dirt.

CHAPTER EIGHTEEN

The Caledonian Queen

The aircraft's gentle buzz vibrates in my head, drowning out the vivid image of the woman I killed yesterday. The night sky is shifting; a soft blend of pinks, purples, and oranges forms on the horizon as the sun prepares to breach the darkness. I've not spoken a word since the event, and Sebastian's been kind to give me space, though his awkward shuffling in the seat directly ahead tells me it won't last much longer.

"A penny for your thoughts?" he asks.

"Excuse me?" I respond, averting my focus from the window to him.

"It is an old saying my father would ask me as a boy when he could tell I was feeling low."

"Oh—of course."

"But I understand if you want time to think in peace."

"It's fine." I shrug. "I just can't get the image of that woman out of my mind. This felt different ..."

"It was different," he says gently. "Not only did you fight people who shared our beliefs, you fought a woman. It is not something you are familiar with, but—forgive me if this is insensitive—you made the logical choice." Sebastian crouches beside me; his company is comforting.

"It'll just take time to forgive myself," I admit.

"Oh yes." He snorts. "I am very familiar with that battle. I have done terrible things to protect my position and paid the price up here."—he taps his head—"But I always remember why I am doing it."

"What have you done?" I ask cautiously. "If you—if you don't mind me asking."

"The worst was participating in Nicholas's Queer Hunt"—he shivers—"That was tough."

I sigh deeply, shaking my head. "Did you hear him boasting about it during dinner at the Harvest?"

"He's vile."

"What about the Isle of Man?" I blurt out, only to feel instant shame for not broaching the topic sensitively.

"What about it?"

"Apparently, you executed every subject for being traitors."

"Are those rumours still going around? I'm impressed."

"What happened there?"

"Casimir evacuated the island," he responds, returning to his seat. "And we gained a few thousand members and a new military base for the Folcriht."

"To think you've achieved so much while hiding in plain sight," I say. "It's—ah! I've been meaning to speak to you about something. I just haven't found the right moment since our dinner was interrupted the other night …"

"What is it?"

"Do you know why the emperor placed me on your staff?"

"I do."

"You don't appear concerned."

"I am not." He leans forward. "It is just as I planned." And with a wink, he sits back.

"Hmm?"

"The emperor is vulnerable when he is paranoid—makes rash decisions. I knew he would want you close to us when he learned of a traitor, and of course, I would be the first on his list."

"So, *you* leaked the information?"

"Yes!" He sits upright and clasps his hands together, assessing me with narrow eyes. "Now, it's my turn to ask something …"

"Yes?"

"Did you kill Lavinia?" he enquires with unvarnished directness, almost knocking me out.

"I—ah—well." I raise my eyebrows, smile sweetly like a girl who's just been caught with her hand in a biscuit jar, and squeak, "Yes."

"Thank God," he sighs.

A short pause follows, and we both bubble into laughter. It's wrong to find it *this* amusing, but I'll grab every opportunity to feel joy—even if it's crass. We're interrupted by a sudden weightlessness that lifts me from my seat; we're plunging to the ground.

"Do not worry," Sebastian calls out with a raised voice over the howling engines. "We are making a quick stop before St Christopher's airport."

The sun's golden rays cast their gentle glow over the rugged landscape, with their warmth and light giving life to the rolling hills and towering peaks. As we glide over the rough terrain, a secluded valley comes into view, blanketed by a light mist that adds to its mystical beauty. Nestled inside stands the remnants of a lonely stately home. Once a grand symbol of wealth and power, it's now reduced to a weathered and crumbling ruin—nature has claimed its territory, with ivy crawling up the decaying exterior. We land beside a vehicle parked outside with a soft thud.

"Where are we?" I ask.

"The Scottish Highlands. It is stunning," Sebastian responds in a dreamlike state, gazing out the window before returning to reality. "You have a queen to persuade."

Casimir wasn't wrong when he described Sebastian as playful, but unlike him, I don't think it's a 'bloody nightmare'—I value the thrill. Exiting the aircraft, Sebastian leads me towards the ruins, and the ancient stone statues watch us approach like weathered sentinels of a forgotten era. Passing the threshold, two of the queen's guards greet us; their magnificent forms are brightened by sunlight filtering through the cracks in the walls.

The wind whispers through each desolate room like the ruins are alive with history's secrets, ready to reveal themselves to anyone daring enough to venture deeper and listen. The air grows cooler as we traverse a battered hallway, and the moss-covered stone dampens the echoes of our footsteps.

"Why am I here, Sebastian?" Queen Calantha's stern voice floats from ahead.

"Ah, Your Majesty," Sebastian calls back eagerly.

We find the queen standing in the centre of a room; her flawless appearance dazzles beneath a hole in the ceiling that acts as a spotlight. Had it not been for her scowl and folded arms, she'd look celestial—but the queen is clearly irked. Sebastian bows, and I perform a curtsy.

"Thank you for joining us," he says.

"Oh!" she mocks. "Did I have a choice?"

"Hmm." Sebastian scratches his head. "A valid point, but you know me, Calantha. I would not ask you here if it were unimportant."

"And that is why I have not called my husband," she sighs, pacing around.

"I have asked you here to request—no—*plead* for your support," Sebastian says.

"Support?" she snaps. "With what?"

"Join us, Calantha."

"*Enough skirting around, Sebastian,*" she hisses, her pacing intensified.

"The Folcri—"

"—NO."

She's now charged, marching back and forth with vigorous steps. Each carries the weight of her inner conflict as if she's trying to outrun the dangerously tempting truth that's drawing her in, with a brow furrowed in frustration and hands clenching and unclenching with nervous energy. This moment reminds me of my first encounter with Silas. It feels like a lifetime ago, but the queen is experiencing the same fight I did—struggling with fear and desire.

"Just—please, Calantha," Sebastian urges, his desperation plain. "Hear me for one moment."

"It is absurd—no—suicide!" she yells.

"If I may, Your Majesty," I say delicately and step forward. "I know you're terrified because I was too—just a few months ago when I joined. But you're also wrestling with temptation. Believe me, it's worth the risk."

The queen stops and shakes her head at me in disbelief. "We are minnows in the great pike's lake, Clara. Do not let *him*"—she jabs at Sebastian—"fool you."

"No, Your Majesty," I respond with equal defiance. "Do not let *your husband* make you doubt your strength. We're not minnows in a lake; we're individual ripples in an ocean, and together, we will form a tidal wave that'll destroy everything evil in its path."

The queen scoffs. "You may be good with words, Clara, but not even you could convince me that a band of miscreants like the Folcriht could do more than set off a firecracker in some sleepy village."

"Come," Sebastian commands, grasping the queen's hand and ignoring the hushed gasp that escapes her lips. He guides her out of the room. "I want to show you something. Your guards—we can trust them?"

"Not just with my life," she huffs, flustered from being manhandled. "But my secrets, too."

"So, this is not the only secret you would be keeping from your husband." Even Sebastian's playfulness isn't enough to breach the queen's walls.

We approach a courtyard at the heart of the ruins, where a weathered yet surprisingly intact water fountain takes centre stage. As Sebastian steps closer, an unexpected transformation takes place. It springs to life with a gentle rumble, rising slowly from the ground, unveiling a glass-lined cylinder that encloses a space illuminated by turquoise spotlights.

Dumbfounded, Calantha asks, "What—what is this?"

"We are visiting a few miscreants," Sebastian responds with his token mischievous twinkle, and the curved glass panel slides open to invite us inside. "Come, Calantha!"

In this disguised lift, we descend through a metal tube; the atmosphere is thick with apprehension as the Earth swallows us. Whilst I might have some idea of what awaits us, the queen remains entirely unaware of the astounding revelation concealed beneath her feet—and her reaction is nothing short of perfect. Upon arriving, she spins around, her eyes darting in all directions, thoroughly viewing the materialised spectacle.

As we float down the centre of this huge dome, the glass cylinder offers an unobstructed view. It shares similar characteristics with the Folcriht's Fort: smooth metal surfaces with displays of the outside world. Despite its smaller size, the dome is bustling with activity, filled with huge crowds of people marching below, appearing, and disappearing into a complex network of tunnels.

Our descent comes to a gentle end, landing us amidst a sea of stunned faces. Sebastian nudges the queen, who remains nailed to the ground, her expression displaying complete bewilderment.

"Smile and wave," he whispers eagerly.

The queen hesitantly raises her arm and offers a nervous smile, with her hand moving in a stiff twist, and the response is overwhelmingly jubilant, allowing her astonishment to become ecstasy. Sebastian takes the lead as the crowd respectfully creates a path for us while showing admiration as we pass. Some offer curtsies and bows, and others express their gratitude with phrases like "Thank you for joining us, Your Majesty" or just a simple "Your Majesty."

Over the merriment, Sebastian calls back to Calantha, "Come! We are about to make history."

We ascend a flight of stairs that leads us to a room overlooking the bustling hub, and stood at the window, with arms folded and a foul look on his face, is Casimir.

"Casimir!" Sebastian bellows, entering the room.

Jasper is seated in the dark corner, looking equally foul-faced, like he's just been placed on a timeout following naughty behaviour. It appears we've disturbed a heated argument between them—its pressure lingers.

"Sebastian," Casimir replies in a dreary tone. He performs a rigid, reluctant bow, paying me no attention. "Your Ma—Majesty, welcome to the Highland Hive."

"Your Majesty," Sebastian says. "May I introduce you to the elected leader of the Folcriht, Casimir Stirling."

"It is a pleasure to meet you," the queen says.

"The pleasure is mine," he responds dryly.

It doesn't take an expert to sense Casimir's insincerity—his stroppy teen attitude could risk us everything.

"Please, everyone, let us get comfortable," Sebastian says. "We have much to discuss."

Before I can take my seat, Casimir finally acknowledges my presence. "This meeting should consist of council members only, Clara. You're dismissed."

I pause momentarily and cast him a perplexed look before ignoring his comment and taking my seat anyway. Sebastian is watching me closely; he isn't urging me to obey but to win and secure my right to be here.

"With respect, Casimir," I respond dryly. "I have earned my place at this table."

"I don't dispute your success, but you won't add value to this conversation." Casimir's voice rises. "Please, leave."

As a young girl, I was naïve and believed I possessed endless opportunities. Once, I asked—no—I demanded to join the boy's rugby team, and I'll never forget the parents' backlash. They didn't laugh me away or sneer, but their rage was all-consuming—you'd think I'd called their sons 'nancy-boys'. It was bad enough for a girl to imagine she could compete against their lads, let alone possess the audacity to want it. I remember the leg-trembling fear when a mob of fully grown men forced me out of their clubhouse and how it destroyed my capacity to dream and strive for more.

Casimir reminds me of those men—but I'm not the same scared little girl I was before, and this time, I'm not alone.

"I suggest we hold a vote," I respond calmly, with just the right amount of defiance so I don't appear brattish (which I imagine Casimir viewed me as in some of our previous disagreements). "Please raise your hand if you feel I should stay."

The risk pays off, with Sebastian and the queen showing instant support.

"It is settled!" Sebastian claps his hands. "Welcome to the team, Clara."

❈❈❈

My clenched fist hurtles towards Calantha's stomach for it to be skilfully parried—it hasn't taken her long to realise she's a fearsome fighter.

"I tell you ... what," she says, catching her breath. "The more I get to know Casimir ... the uglier I find him."

We don't hide our opinions during these dedicated training sessions. The many times we've spent alone together in this room have nurtured our bond into a solid friendship.

"He's a chauvinistic pig," I say in agreement. "But I'll take him over your husband any day."

It's been one month since she agreed to form an alliance with the Folcriht and Canada. After many days of contemplation, we decided on a simple name for our new pact—The Union. Folcriht military and support personnel have migrated to the Highland Hive to bolster Calantha's forces, and it's become a hub of bustling activity. With my support, she's also been organising her royal court and staff, identifying those who'll remain loyal and rooting out those we need to imprison when it all kicks off. The emperor's supporters remain oblivious to the dissent bubbling beneath their feet, and Calantha will announce the rebellion following a broadcasted assault on an imperial work camp—Duskridge.

"I suppose we cannot blame him," she sighs. "He has had his authority stripped away by the very people he represented for it to be handed to a *queen*." Calantha sprints towards me, only to dive and roll, narrowly avoiding my counterstrike.

"Have you thought more about what our showstopper could be?"

"Yes," Calantha responds. "But I'm spoilt for choice. There are too many events to hijack and too few resources."

"And what about your speech?" I ask. "Are you ready for the announcement?"

"Almost," she responds. "Though Verity has no doubt changed most of my eighth draft."

"She loves working with you."

"And I, her," she responds.

Verity was chomping at the bit to become Calantha's private secretary, and she arrived with Silas, Fay, and the council members two weeks ago. Silas and I haven't found time alone, and if it weren't for the hive's surveillance, I would've been sneaking into his apartment each night—and I bet he's been tempted to do the same. The tension between us is becoming intolerable; he occupies so many of my thoughts—it's driving me mad. However, keeping our connection a secret is the right thing to do—besides, I'm finding it exciting.

"What about the Albion Games?" Calantha asks randomly.

"To make an announcement?"

"No, for our showstopper."

One lucky kingdom hosts the Albion Games every three years, and because Greece outperformed all others during the last games, they'll be hosting next year.

"That would draw *a lot* of attention." I acknowledge.

A cunning smile creeps on the edge of Calantha's lips, and she lunges forward to unleash a whirlwind of blows.

CHAPTER NINETEEN

The First Ripple

The fluffy snow crunches beneath my feet as I traverse the edge of a pristine loch in the highlands; it glistens under the gentle touch of early morning sunlight. Its tranquil, mirror-like surface reflects the snow-capped peaks and ancient woodland decorating its shores. The air is crisp and pure, carrying the faint scent of pine. It's the calm before the storm because we'll liberate the prisoners from Duskridge tomorrow evening.

With Sebastian's authority behind me, I'm entering the camp with sham recruitment orders—tasked with assembling a team to bolster the regime's efforts in Canada. Bee, in her resourcefulness, has supplied me with a discreet device capable of recording what I witness without raising suspicion. I have two objectives; the first is to amass enough compelling footage to augment Queen Calantha's upcoming empire-wide address. Lawrence has intel suggesting Duskridge conducts gruelling experiments on adults and children; we just hope it'll be enough to outrage England's subjects. Shining a light on the ugly truth is one push towards their inevitable unrest. My second and final objective is to disable the camp's defences at nightfall, enabling Folcriht air forces to storm the facility.

"Cheers for meeting me out here." Silas looks out across the loch and appears to be balancing the weight of concern on his furrowed brow.

"What's up?" I ask.

"Nothing, just loads going on," he responds. "The final arms shipment arrived in Canada today."

"How's Sebastian?"

"He's not missing England, that's for sure. How're you feeling about tomorrow?"

"Fine. Are your men ready?"

"Yeah, we'll be with you on time," he says. "Just be careful."

"I will."

"You'll be alone in a hornet nest."

"It won't be the first time."

"But you weren't shaking it before."

I smile. "That just makes it more exciting."

I nestle into his big chest like a mouse, and sitting in silence; we enjoy each other's company while thousands of starlings swirl in perfect synchronisation—their hypnotic ballet performance breathes life into the sky. This is nature's way of reminding us of our strength in numbers. I should be preparing for tomorrow, but I don't want this moment to end.

✳✳✳

"Miss Rosewood, is it?" The man's curious eyes wander between my face and the holographic screen shining from his wrist. Once satisfied with my identity, he needlessly assesses every inch of my body.

"Yes, and you are?"

"Stephen Denham—the warden!" he chirps. "United in devotion." He reaches his chubby hand out whilst mine remains firmly to my side.

"Shall we?" I walk past him towards the door.

Stephen doesn't look anything like the photo I received during my debrief. A thick mane has replaced his former sparse and spindly head of hair, and reconstruction surgery has transformed his face, specifically his nose (from bulbous to button). His short legs are unable to match my stride.

Skipping to catch up in his professionally tailored maroon suit, he chuckles nervously. "So, you've come to poach my men."

I stop in my tracks, catching him off-guard at the sudden change of pace, and stare directly into his wide-set eyes. "Something like that," I respond, flashing a sly smile and proceeding ahead, with him chasing my tail.

I have the day to gather footage before I disable the sentries and grant Silas and his men access at nightfall— Stephen has no idea what's coming.

"The Duke of Crimsonford wants me to inspect the facility first," I declare. "I'll need a tour guide."

"Of course!" he exclaims. "Would you like a drink before we start?" He gestures towards the vending machine in the corner of the bleak reception area. Though it's designed to look like it'll offer you the most delicious drink, its substance will burn a hole through your tongue.

"No, thank you."

"Okay, let's get cracking! Please, follow me."

Stephen opens the door for me, and we exit the building to arrive before a pair of iron doors the same height as a two-storey house. They swing open to reveal a stone path that leads to a gate shimmering with infused energy. Endless sentry turrets stand on top of the inner wall, and though they appear deceitfully small from this distance, they're actually mammoth in size—powerful enough to obliterate almost anything threatening the camp's airspace. The dark clouds hang low, and to my left and right—in the barren space between the two walls encircling this camp—the dirt vibrates, hovering just above the ground. It's a mesmerising yet rattling sight.

"Nexus mines," Stephen says, noticing my fascination. "They won't kill the prisoners; they just inflict excruciating pain. We find it a better deterrent than death."

"Do you love your job, Stephen?" I ask.

"I do! I'm blessed to have been assigned this path," he rejoices. As timid as he appears, I have no doubt he'll be responsible for unspeakable suffering in this place.

"Tell me more about what you do here."

"We simply protect the empire from deviants while offering them an opportunity to serve!" he beams. "My camp has the second highest success rate in England for reintegration."

"I'd love to see how you've achieved such an impressive reintegration rate."

As Stephen babbles on, he's totally ignorant of my unmasked disgust. The gates swing open, revealing a sweeping stone courtyard and the haunting sight of two children with skeletal figures hunched over a pile of small bones. Both watch me with intrigue, and it's hard to discern their genders as they wear matching grey jumpsuits with shaved heads. They're branded with a blood-drop stigma symbol on their wrists, which come in all shapes and sizes depending on the different types of deviant nature. The blood drop on these children represents the inherent deviance passed down from their parents.

A woman with the same jumpsuit and shaved head stumbles towards the children. She appears even more malnourished than them; her dark, hollow eyes fill me with sorrow, and a large red circle on her wrist tells me she disrespects authority.

"Get your brood out of here and teach them some manners!" Stephen hisses at the woman, causing both children to scurry into her arms. "As you can see," he says with his unbearably jolly demeanour reappearing. "We value the importance of traditional family values here. I would never separate children from their parents—though I sometimes wonder if it would do them the world of good."

The courtyard we're standing in isn't too dissimilar to Amberleigh's town centre. Just replace the quaint shops encircling it with soulless, concrete buildings fashioned with bar-covered windows. Then, replace the statue of Emperor Magnus standing prideful with him brooding on a throne that's being lifted by men, women, and children—all struggling under the weight of his ego. Finally, replace the church with an offensively out-of-place stately home that boasts a massive balcony displaying the following message: *'FIND FREEDOM IN FEALTY'*.

Groups of prisoners huddle around the edges of the square. There must be a few hundred, all swathed in identical grey jumpsuits and made to look the same with shaved heads—stripped of their individuality. They consciously avoid looking in my direction as if I'd beat them to a pulp for dirtying me with their attention. It's clear who's arrived more recently because their bony frames aren't as prominent. The atmosphere is gloomy here; it's difficult to describe, but it feels like I'm on the conveyor belt of a shame-inducing machine.

The guards' crimson uniforms are the only splash of colour to grace this barren hell. Similar to marshals, they strike the stone ground with black, knee-high leather boots. Fitted breeches, tailored jackets, and stiff-brimmed hats embroidered with maroon designs lend them the authority to punish without mercy. The deadly swarmers hiding in their sleeves aren't enough to instil fear, so they carry hefty impact bars to remind prisoners they're well-equipped to handle bad behaviour.

"What are they used for?" I ask, pointing to four small platforms surrounding the emperor's statue. Despite lacking character, something about their positioning makes it appear they hold significance.

"Oh!" Stephen rubs his hands together. "You're about to find out."

The mansion's balcony doors swing open as if choreographed, and a young, smug-looking nobleman strides out to gaze across the square—his cloak billows in the wind. Guards abruptly march two men, a woman, and a distraught young boy into view. His sobs tug at my heartstrings, and he'll occasionally collapse to the ground, only to be hoisted up and dragged by an accompanying guard. As they near the statue, he attempts to break free, fighting desperately to escape, but his struggles are in vain, and the guard callously dumps him onto the stone platform as though he were a rag doll. Upon landing, the boy's body stiffens, leaving him paralysed in the grip of some phantom energy.

Pockets of the crowd break out into a weeping chorus, and a threatening hum swells around us, soaking the square with a sense of foreboding. Each person on their platform floats upward, suspended two metres above the ground by the invisible force, and the once melancholy hum transmutes into a high-pitched, metallic shriek, piercing my ear drums. Its intensity reaches unbearable levels, and its tortured victims contort unnaturally—I can just about hear their agonising screams as I record this horrifying injustice.

Scanning the crowd, many onlookers try to shield their ears or turn away, but they're met with the guards' brutality, who're responsible for ensuring everyone witnesses the cruel suffering unfold. Above us, the nobleman watches with twisted rapture and jittery legs—acting like a starving puppy about to be fed.

The piercing shriek vanishes, releasing its hold over the two men, woman and boy, so they plummet to the ground. Their bodies are crumpled, and their screams are replaced with heart-wrenching sobs.

Stephen leans in, eager to share his grisly enthusiasm. "They're called Tirwians. Aren't they marvellous? We replaced the gallows a few years ago, and they've proven much more efficient at—"

Refusing to indulge in his sick fascination any longer, I leave him stunned and swiftly march through the courtyard, the skirt of my violet dress fluttering in the wind. Emotions override logic, and the crowd remains silent as the clack, clack, clack of my heels hit the stone—urging me to push ahead. It's not like before when this level of attention would cripple me with anxiety. The weight of the guards' stares may be heavy, but I'm stronger now and unafraid of undermining their authority. Besides, we'll be burning this place to the ground in just a few hours.

Crouching beside the shivering boy, I offer a soft smile. He's unable to move following his ordeal.

"Hello," I whisper. Our onlookers disappear from existence, and all I see is him. He recoils as I reach out. "I won't hurt you; I'm here to help. What's your name? I'm Clara."

Curiosity creeps onto his face, and he utters, "B—Billy."

"It's over now, Billy," I assure him. "Where's your mum? Let's take you to her."

Raising his trembling arm with great effort, he points towards the woman whose limp body is leaning against the platform closest to us—though she's too weak to move, the desperation in her face to reach her son is vivid.

"Shall we go and help her?" I ask.

The boy nods, and I help him to his feet. The woman appears distrusting, as if she expects me to whisk him away at the last minute—but I successfully reunite them.

Kneeling, I whisper a heartfelt apology, and her breathing quickens. I'm unable to read the emotions behind her wide eyes. She could be furious after construing my words as delusional, perhaps fearful as if I'm performing some twisted act, or overwhelmed by the ounce of compassion.

"CLEAR OUT!" A guard bellows from the sidelines, and the chattering crowd begins to disperse. Stephen's marching towards me, and the nobleman remains firm with arms crossed and an irritable disposition.

"Ma'am!" Stephen brays. "Please, forgive me, but— well, we don't show vermin kindness in Duskridge."

Ignoring his discontent, I ask plainly, "Who's the man on the balcony?"

"Did you hear what I—"

"Yes, yes. Who is it?"

"Oh—okay," he stutters. "That's the Viscount of Oakhurst, Lord Beauchamp. He sponsors the camp.

Extremely generous, resides in the stately home during his visits."

"What does he do here?" I ask.

"He helps. It's wonderful; he makes time in his busy schedule to visit some of our deviants to support their treatment."

"How exactly does he support them?"

"Oh—you know," he stumbles. "Just helps with treatment and things … I'm not entirely sure."

Stephen's lying—he knows the answer to my question—Lord Beauchamp's 'selfless' contributions must be unthinkably wicked for Stephen not to boast about them.

✳✳✳

It's not long before I must infiltrate the control room and disarm their sentries. However, Lord Beauchamp has invited—no, ordered me to meet him. He has me waiting in his bar, and I'm here alone, with just the crackle of a holographic fire keeping me company. Just under an hour ago, a flustered guard beckoned Stephen to deal with a critical emergency. Despite my best efforts to tag along, he locked me in this room to wait for the Viscount to 'look after me'. I don't know why Stephen suddenly decided to pull an ounce of courage out of his arse.

I won't find comfort in these plush leather armchairs. Instead, I'm pacing the room and rubbing the pendant hanging around my neck that Bee gave me this morning—she calls it her 'lucky charm'.

The footage I've captured reveals the repugnant working conditions in the factories scattered throughout the camp. They're responsible for producing imperial goods, like clothing and footwear, and the labour officers impose gruelling shifts for adults and children to work twelve hours a day with minimal nourishment to sustain them.

I've been spoilt with an extensive catalogue of horrifying torture methods to observe, most designed to reverse the prisoners' alleged deviance. In one of the dedicated facilities, twisted scientists experiment on their victims to understand what drives them to misbehave—the scenes were atrocious. In one particularly harrowing incident, I helplessly watched them expose a man's brain to ruthlessly poke and prod it. I'm told they measured his pain to analyse his reactions, but it's for his own good because they could use the information to 'make him better'. Moreover, this test subject refused to eat breakfast earlier that day, so they're hitting two birds with one stone and teaching him a lesson.

I'm confident these graphic images will shock England's subjects because all they know are clean cities and picturesque towns. There are rumours about the work camps, but if you don't see something, it doesn't exist, and beyond the fear and subjugation, they live in relative comfort—provided with just enough food, water, and shelter. All this blinds them to the dark truth of a world existing right beneath their noses. Still, many have a warped view of what's right and wrong, just and unjust, but I can't lose faith in their potential for empathy and compassion.

"Well, well, well!" A shrill voice shatters the silence.

I pause my pacing and face the Viscount. "My lord, it is an honour."

"The honour is mine!" Histop teeth pinch his lower lip. "Our *Bright Light*. Your story was quite magnificent—and the theatrics! I was on the edge of my seat when you sent that wretched little monster to her death."

I don't have time for this. As I stride towards him like an enforcer who's about to take great pleasure in punishing a screaming child for disrupting the peace, Lord Beauchamp's face shifts from excitement to bewilderment and finally panic. He staggers backwards, his pointed chin trembling as he fumbles to unsheathe an ornate blade from its holster. But his movements are too sluggish, and with his tiny head in my well-manicured grip—like I'm about to kiss him—I perform a powerful twist.

Snap. I release him, letting his corpse plunge on the plush carpet floor with a soft thud. *One aristocrat down, and too many more to go.* Snatching the blade and securing it to my upper thigh, I waste no time escaping through a nearby window.

Stone statues of predatory animals decorate the mansion's courtyard, their lifelike forms partially concealed by the heavy rainfall—they're watching me pass as if I'm their prey. The downpour will provide cover as I navigate the camp undetected. Moving with stealth and hugging the walls, I'm acutely aware of the prisoners' watchful eyes peering through the bars of their dormitories. Though not a single guard is in sight, I can sense their presence, but I've identified blind spots in their security systems, so they can't monitor my movements as I progress towards the control centre.

After a short time, I reach the imposing metallic structure where I'll disable their defences. My enhanced clearance grants me access, and my grip around the blade remains firm as I approach the double doors at the end of the stretching hallway. Keenly aware of my surroundings, an unsettling feeling gnaws at me, and it grows stronger once I enter the empty control room. Its monitors, screens, and control panels emit the occasional beeping noise—something's wrong.

Half expecting an ambush, I dash forward with the means to disable their turrets. My instructions are foolproof; attach this device to the central panel. Before anyone can stop me, I throw it ahead, and to my immense relief, it lands in the desired location. The flashing light indicates my success—Duskridge is defenceless, and the Folcriht is free to swoop in and tear this place apart.

"Blessed by his reign."

Whipping around, my stomach churns at the sight of Stephen's smug face. He's accompanied by four guards.

"It's annoying, isn't it, sweetheart?" he gloats. "You really are an arrogant bitch."

Despite losing all hope, I stand my ground in silence—staring at him with a clenched jaw, squared shoulders, and clamped fists.

"We've changed the entire security system," Stephen continues. "We're one step ahead."

"How did you know?" I remain relaxed.

"I received a tip about your invasion attempt." He takes a deep breath. "What do you think I've been doing for the last two hours? My men are ready, but yours won't even get close."

"Who told you?"

"Why do you care? You're not leaving here alive."

"Tell me."

"*Who do you think you are?*" Stephen snarls. "Strutting in like you're someone important when you're just the duke's dog. Does he know what you're up to?"

"The duke's a fool," I snap. "He has no idea."

"Don't be so disrespectful, you *stupid cunt.* Turn around and watch your degenerate friends get blown to pieces."

"You, Stephen, are a vile little beast that gets his rocks off hurting women and kids. The only degenerate here is you."

"TURN AROUND YOU BITCH."

The fleet of hovercrafts emerges from the darkness, and their lights pierce through the heavy rainfall. I don't watch with trepidation but with a heavy heart, hopeless in the knowledge they're flying towards their destruction. Once dormant, the sentry tunnels on the inner wall awaken, twisting and turning to lock onto their respective targets. Silas and Jasper are on one of those crafts, and I can't save them.

Missiles spray from every sentry, dancing and looping through the air like predatory birds preparing to kill. However, the crafts continue advancing towards us with great speed, growing larger by the second—the downpour won't be the only thing battering their sleek shells.

A flash engulfs the night sky, illuminating each droplet that dives from a monstrous storm cloud above—but the crafts remain unharmed. To my left, a swirling inferno devours a sentry, and each missile sparks a spectacular chain reaction. A second explodes, a third, and a fourth—the rockets are waging war on their masters. With the camp's walls ablaze, a magnificent ring of fire surrounds us, and the hovercrafts emerge through the billowing smoke, gliding into the courtyard with grace, unphased by the chaos surrounding them. This is Bee's handiwork—she's a genius.

Whipping around, Stephen's heavily sculpted face is twisted, like someone who's just had a lordship title stripped away from them at the last minute.

"*Kill her.*"

The swarmers form into a vortex that hurtles towards me, and I take a deep, slow breath. Time stretches out as it narrows the gap; offshoots lash out from its body and lick the air like the tongues of a ravenous beast. However, unlike when I thought I was facing their wrath before, the crippling fear is replaced with tranquillity—my eyes are open, and no scream attempts to escape my throat … I'm ready.

When Fay and I were children, we would play near a farmer's field, and one day, despite her warnings, I couldn't resist the tempting flicker of the force field protecting his livestock. It was just a gentle touch, but that didn't stop the barrier's energy from propelling me backwards into a cow pat. Luckily, I was unharmed, which meant Fay could find great amusement in my misfortune.

My mind is thrust back to that moment as my tingling body catapults through the air, only I meet a tabletop instead of manure. The serendipitous bolt of energy that expelled from Bee's lucky charm not only knocked the wind out of me but also rendered the swarmers useless. I caught a glimpse of the cyclone crumbling apart, reduced to a pile of black dust that needs hoovering up.

Though it may feel like I've been hit by a car, the blast dealt Stephen and his cronies an even heavier blow. They're squirming and moaning on the ground directly ahead, so I grab this opportunity and jump to my feet. One guard has almost regained composure and is reaching for his gun. Holding the Viscount's blade, I hastily launch it at him.

Before the others can react, I'm already charging at him, my body low and nimble like a hunting pantheress, and steps away, I spring towards the incapacitated guard who's clutching the knife in his neck. Crashing into his formidable form and wrapping my arms and legs around him, he tumbles backwards, and I seize his gun before he falls. We roll intertwined on the metal ground. Despite his wriggling, I maintain a firm grip and use him as protection, reaching around his wide frame to fire three shots, instantly eliminating the guards surrounding Stephen, who fumbles with a pistol.

BANG—BANG—BANG—BANG—BANG—BANG— click—click … click … *click*.

Having served his purpose, I push my limp shield away and leap up; Stephen's whimpering assures me he's no longer a threat. With his trembling arms outstretched, still aiming the empty weapon, his face is as pale as freshly fallen snow, with eyes like a mouse caught in a trap.

"P—p—please," he begs, wetting himself.

I tilt my head slightly and offer him a warm, motherly smile before grabbing his collar and dragging him out. We find two unsuspecting guards waiting for us, so I take great pleasure in killing them instantly, along with Stephen's hope of rescue. Bedlam grips the camp with bursts of gunfire and explosions piercing the heavy rainfall and the agonising screams of men from all directions. One guard is even kind enough to illuminate our passage with his flame-covered form frantically running between two buildings.

"WHERE ARE YOU TAKING ME?" Stephen screams over the noise.

I ignore him, and as we progress through the camp, I take out guards who are unfortunate enough to cross my unchallengeable path. However, they're not my priority—I know Silas has everything under control because it's getting calmer as Stephen and I draw nearer to the courtyard.

"I didn't mean what I said earlier." Stephen continues quivering. "I was just playing up for my guards."

"I killed the viscount," I announce.

"*What?* Why?"

"Do you really need to ask?" I shoot him a repulsed look.

"He helps people."

I scoff. "You're a shit for brains, Stephen."

"No, no, no," he whimpers as we approach the entrance of a large, concrete building. His trembling legs slide on the stone. "Pl—please don't."

I throw open the double doors to reveal dozens of bewildered faces grouped at the back of the room. They stare at me, some with fear and others with curiosity. Still gripping the back of Stephen's collar, I force him to his knees and kick him to the ground, where he lies a crumpled mess.

"Find your freedom in vengeance," I tell the crowd before swiftly exiting and leaving them with their gift.

I can't control the smile creeping on my face as Stephen's anguished cries become quieter and quieter.

CHAPTER TWENTY

Necessary Betrayals

Behind the heavy rainfall, smoke, and debris from the sentries, I'm barely able to make out Jasper's form near the outer gate. He appears to be alone. I've been clearing a path ready for the prisoners to leave the camp because two more crafts will arrive outside the walls to transport them. Lowering my gun, he draws closer, and I succumb to the overwhelming urge to hug him, where he stands taut in my embrace.

"Sorry, I know you're not into hugs," I say. "I'm just relieved to see you. Are the crafts ready?"

Finally releasing him, he points his gun directly between my eyes.

"Jasper?" I utter.

His breathing is shallow, and like a volcano, a fiery rage bubbles beneath his surface, ready to explode at any moment.

"You should be dead," he spits through gritted teeth, droplets sliding down his grubby face.

"*What?*" I glance around—we're alone.

"Drop your gun."

I do as he orders and raise my hands for him to kick it away with his foot.

"Wait." I shake my head. "Was that you? Did you leak our plan?"

"Only what I wanted them to know."

"*Why, Jasper?*"

"You're a fucking liability, that's why," he snaps. "I mean—c'mon! THE QUEEN?" Lunging at me, he jabs the barrel of his gun into my forehead. "*AFTER EVERYTHING I TOLD YOU?*"

"She's different!" I plead. "I didn't—I'm sorry!"

With pursed lips against my ear, he hisses, "*They're all the fucking same.*"

"And what about the sentries?" I ask. "You were willing to kill yourself and other soldiers just to get to me?"

"Don't be daft," he sneers. "I knew Bee had a backup plan."

"You and I, we—I thought we were—"

"What? Friends?" Stepping back, with his gun still pointed at me, Jasper fleetingly erupts into manic laughter. "No," he says calmly, shaking his head. "I don't mix with filthy scuzz slaves."

"How can I make this right? Please, Jasper."

With my hands still raised, I side-step to my left as if to circle around him, and to my relief, he shuffles in the opposite direction, making sure he's always directly facing me.

"I don't know where you think you're going," he mocks as we continue our slow, circular dance. "You're not getting out of here ali—AAAHHHH."

Jasper's agonising scream cuts through the sound of heavy rainfall smacking the stone path and gunshots drifting from the camp. His body contorts, and his hand, with a mind of its own, releases the pistol, sending it flying into the field of nexus mines that ensnare Jasper's heel in its trap. I grasp the opportunity and lunge forward, but he's just as quick, releasing himself from the torment and gaining control—I barely dodge his massive, outstretched hand. He notices me side-eyeing the gun on the ground just a few steps away—I wish I hadn't been so reckless to leave my knife nestled in the guard's chest.

"Don't bother," he says, raising his fists. "Let's fight like men. That's what you want, isn't it? To be *equal*." He snorts. "Well, you're not, and I'll enjoy smashing your pretty face into this floor." He slams his boot against the ground.

"Most of the Folcriht voted to join an alliance with the queen," I respond, ignoring his taunts. "What're you going to do about them?"

"That won't matter once I've killed her."

My fists tense, and the space between us crackles with anticipation as we face off. Our surroundings are faintly lit by the distant blaze roaring from the sentries' remains on top of the inner wall, and the stone is slick beneath our feet. I've never fought Jasper before, and although we share the same skills, he has far more experience. If I'm to stand a chance, I must use my speed to somehow gain the upper hand.

Jasper lunges towards me, his fist flying through the rainwater wall towards my face, and in one fluid motion, I step to the side, and the breeze of his punch kisses my cheek as I dance out of reach. Jasper reacts quicker than I expected—I'm used to sparring with Silas, who's much slower—and he catches me off-guard, securing a punch to the side of my rib. I bound back, sliding on the stone and distancing myself to regain composure, but he doesn't offer the luxury of respite. With Jasper almost on me, I crouch down and catch his legs, and with all my weight, I push, forcing him to volley over my shoulder and meet the ground behind me. I take the opportunity to create distance between us again.

"Stop being a pussy," Jasper calls out, climbing back to his feet. "This isn't a game of cat and mouse."

Gunfire and explosions are steadily closing in on us—the Folcriht must be forcing the remaining guards out of the camp.

"It is," I call back. "And you're the mouse. You just don't know it."

My baiting worked. Jasper is hurtling towards me, his nimble steps splashing the ground, but I'm prepared. I mirror his assault, sprinting at full speed with my fist raised so he's predicting my strike—but he doesn't receive it. With agility, I skid through the surface water and take Jasper out by his legs, causing him to topple over and land face down. Without hesitation, I pounce on him and clasp his neck tightly.

With startling strength, Jasper lifts himself up and hurls me off, causing me to land on my back and smack my head on the hard stone. The white-hot, searing pain attacks my eyes and spreads like wildfire through my brain. As I battle to remain conscious, Jasper is already looming over me; I'm barely able to make out his disdained look.

"I'm disappointed," he scorns, standing at my legs with both hands on his hips. "I was expecting more." He drops to his knees, restricting my chest, and wraps one tender hand around my neck before whispering, "What to do with you now."

The shouts and cries of men grow closer—but they won't reach us in time. Jasper's grip intensifies as he steals the air from my lungs. I fumble the pendant, hoping to find a switch that might activate it and throw Jasper off me, but nothing happens. With a wave of hopelessness, I drop my arms, outstretched on either side, only for my hand to meet an object—my gun.

BANG

After everything, all it took was one shot. Jasper rolls on his side, and his trembling hands are pressed against his stomach to slow the bleeding. A backdrop of bewilderment with a lick of rage paints his face.

With a hint of conceit between heavy breaths, he says, "If I can't … take your life … I'll just need to find satisfaction in … tearing it apart. You've been"—I point the gun to his face—"WAIT. You don't want to know the truth?"

I bite and offer him an inquisitive look.

"You've been *played,*" he says with deep satisfaction.

"Played? How?"

Jasper dissolves into manic laughter and clambers to his knees, blood sputtering from his mouth. "And I thought you … were smart," he snarls. "You really believed Celest was one of us?"

My breathing quickens, and I shake my head. "Get to the point, Jasper."

"Celest wasn't a Folcriht, you *fucking idiot.* She had nothing to do with us!"

Jasper's hysteria settles into a wheezing chuckle as he winces in pain and celebrates the next-best victory. With the echoes of his words caressing my disbelief, I turn inwards.

Silas was the first to tell me about Celest's involvement with the Folcriht—how she wanted to sacrifice herself to secure my safety and grant me the Bright Light title to support the rebellion. He was being truthful; she was one of Lawrence's agents, but Silas never knew her personally. He was merely passing on second-hand information, as was Fay. This means they don't know the truth either, or do they?

I recollect my conversations with them, Casimir, Lawrence, Edward, Sebastian, and Bee. However, a hurricane of thoughts and emotions is swirling within me. Was I blinded to their lies by the thrill? Did I just hear what I wanted to?

Oh no … no … no, no, no. The truth is too painful for me to confront. If Celest was an unsuspecting victim, she spent her dying moments believing her closest friend betrayed and *killed* her. The terrorising image of Celest's horror-filled eyes flashes as a vivid memory, and that was the moment I should've known the truth—but not even a shred of doubt stirred within me. *How could I be so stupid?* My actions were never my own in the empire, and I was foolish to think it'd be different anywhere else. Everything I've achieved feels meaningless—it feels tainted.

"Now she gets it," Jasper declares with amusement.

Seeing through the red clouding my vision, and with Jasper on his knees, I boot him in the chest to send him toppling backwards, where he lands in the relentless grip of the nexus minefield. I don't hear his excruciating screams or pleas for help; I just listen to Celest's voice urging me to avenge her as I watch Jasper's warped body thresh and flail.

CHAPTER TWENTY-ONE

A War of Wolves and Lions

"You always know how to cheer me up." Celest savours a piece of chocolate while lying on her side over the picnic blanket.

"It's only chocolate. You deserve so much more," I respond, gazing out over rolling hills in the valley below.

"All I need is you."

Her words make me feel uneasy. I lay on my back and close my eyes to block the bright sun.

"What shall we do this evening?" I ask.

"I just want a cosy night in."

Last I checked, there were no clouds in the sky, but something has arrived, and it's casting a shadow. Opening my eyes, I find Silas, Fay, Sebastian, Casimir, Lawrence, Edward, and Jasper surrounding me with stern looks. They don't say a word, and their discomforting presence prompts me to sit upright.

"Come!" Celest says, standing up and motioning to the picnic blanket. "Join us."

They move with intent and encircle Celest, who appears to be over the moon to see them, and in unison, they each unsheathe a knife and proceed to stab her over and over again, all the while facing me—grinning ear to ear.

"You wanted this!" Celest calls out with delight as they're butchering her before me.

***

The Highland Hive is bustling with celebration. People are still on a high since we liberated the prisoners of Duskridge and burned it to the ground two weeks ago. I've tried pretending to share in their glee, but I've spent most of my time alone, keeping the knowledge of betrayal a secret until I calculate my next move. I've told no one, not Calantha, Silas, or Fay—I don't know who I can trust right now.

"Two thousand new members!" Calantha exclaims. "That's marvellous. Thank you, Casimir." She sends him a warm smile, which bounces off his stone-cold front.

Each member of the council is providing her with an update, and since the people voted to grant her total leadership over the Folcriht, Casimir remains delightfully bitter. Though he's kept most of his responsibilities—like overseeing the recruitment of new members and general management—he has someone to answer to.

Casimir isn't the only one in this room who's visibly displeased; as he glares at Calantha, who's asking Bee questions, I glare at him. Ideas swirl as to how I kill him once I learn the undoubted truth of how he dragged Celest into this devious scheme to have me join them. Would taking his life be too much? I don't think so; after all, he sent an innocent woman to her death, and people are executed for more trivial things than that. However, we're fighting for a new and better world, and I must consider: what version of myself do I want to carry into this new age?

My body may be present in this room, but my mind isn't. Memories of my encounter with Jasper are still fuelling my flames of rage, and that's why I'm not ready to act.

"Clara … Clara?" Silas is leaning over the table whilst everyone else is chatting amongst themselves.

"Hmm?" I respond. "What?"

"When are you gonna speak to me?" he whispers. "I don't get it. What's going on?"

"Oh. Just—don't worry. I know I haven't been myself. We'll chat soon, okay?"

"What can I do to help?" Silas scrunches his face like he's stuck on a problematic quiz question. His brain is working overtime to comprehend my emotions.

"Be patient," I respond with a gentle tone. "That's all."

Perhaps I'm putting off confronting him and the others because I'm terrified of what I'll discover. Though I'm sure Casimir and Lawrence are the master manipulators behind this immense betrayal, I can't ignore the likelihood of the others knowing. Realistically, it's unlikely Fay, Silas, and Bee knew anything, but there is Sebastian to consider. He and I grew close during our visit to Canada—I saved his bloody life. We never discussed Celest in detail, but he admits to doing terrible things that weigh on his conscience—could Celest's needless death be one of them? As for Edward, I'm unsure—he may have been in on it, but he's extremely forgetful (including with my name). I just wish I'd asked them more questions about Celest when we first met; that way, I could've learned the truth earlier.

Even under Calantha's fresh leadership, I've been reconsidering my allegiance to the Folcriht. What are my options? Do I seek revenge for Celest and disappear? Or do I continue like everything is okay? This war is between two beasts—wolves and lions—and they're both unrelenting. I can stick with the pack, or I can run away.

"Right!" Calantha claps her hands. "If there are no other updates, I want more ideas on our future moves. We have two priority targets, but we need *more*—something covert … but big."

Lawrence snorts.

"Is something funny, Lawrence?" Calantha asks.

"No, Your Majesty," he responds, surprisingly bashful.

"A naïve girl like me would love the expertise from a skilled hand, Lawrence. Please, share," she presses.

"Covert and big don't really mix, that is all," he responds.

"I see," she says. "A poor choice of words. Not big … *impactful*"—she's more polite in her response than I would've been—"Oh, and next time you feel the need to correct me, perhaps just say it. I thought we had a pig sniffing truffles in the room for a moment."

That's better.

"Clara, what ideas do you have?" Casimir asks bluntly.

His question would've been valid if it weren't tainted with a blatant belief that I'll have nothing valuable to add (which I don't). He was sheepish around me for a few days following Jasper's death, which reinforces why I think he's responsible for Celest becoming 'collateral damage'. However, I've given him no reason to suspect I've learned the truth, and since he undoubtedly expects me to unleash my hormonal wrath at the slightest problem, he'll be under the false impression that he's off the hook.

"I'll have a think," I respond.

"Haven't you been daydreaming enough these past few weeks?" Casimir scoffs with an undeserving arrogance. "It's time you start pulling your weight around here."

"*Casimir*," Calantha scolds. "What have I said—"

She needn't continue. Before they could blink, I was already darting across the tabletop, and now, with Casimir's ginger curls firmly in my grip, I'm beating his freckled face against the wood. "Did you"—smack—"really think"—smack—"you would"—smack—"get away with it?"—smack—smack—smack.

Silas is the first to act, locking my arms behind my back. I don't resist him, allowing Casimir's bloodied face to drop on the table with a thud.

"C—c'mon, I got you," he whispers. "Breathe."

Edward is still trying to desperately lift his frail frame off the seat, quivering in fear, whilst Lawrence has already found refuge in the corner. Bee's neither frightened nor distressed; she simply looks perplexed.

"Get her out, Silas." Calantha stands. "Bee! Call a medic."

***

The hive's prison cells are more comfortable than I anticipated. It's only been an hour or two since I lost it, and strangely, I feel much better. This time to myself—combined with releasing the pent-up anger—has allowed me to ponder my next steps with renewed clarity. There's a greater evil than Casimir, Jasper, and whoever else is involved in framing Celest and playing me. I must finish what I started and support Calantha because I'm responsible for dragging her into this, and she needs all the loyalty and support she can get. However, it's not just that; as our bond grows, the void Celest left becomes easier to bear.

I'm relieved to have cleared the fog, working through my doubt, and steeling my commitment to this cause. However, before I continue this war, I must first weed out the infestation corrupting the Folcriht.

Acknowledgements

Imposter syndrome has been my biggest enemy, and I've had the best people holding my hand, so this page is for you.

Dominic West, thank you for listening to me drivel for hours on end and for all your dedication and support with the editing and cover design.

To Mum, Dad, Chloe, and my reading club, thank you for everything you do and for cheering me on.

Yago Domingues, thank you for producing such an amazing cover and for being so understanding and patient with my endless changes. It's been great working with you.

Printed in Great Britain
by Amazon